DYING INSIDE

But why does David Selig want his power to come back? Why not let it fade? It's always been a curse to him, hasn't it? It's cut him off from his fellow men and doomed him to a loveless life. Leave well enough alone, Duvid. Let it fade. Let it fade. On the other hand, without the power, what are you? Without that one faltering unpredictable unsatisfactory means of contact with them, how will you be able to touch them at all? Your power joins you to mankind, for better or for worse, in the only joining you have: you can't bear to surrender it. Admit it. You love it and despise it, this gift of yours. You dread losing it despite all it's done to you. You'll fight to cling to the last shreds of it, even though you know the struggle's hopeless.

"A fascinating speculative novel on the theme of telepathy."
—*Chicago Daily News*

"A marvelously entertaining read."
—*London Evening Standard*

"The narrator is one of the most intensely *human* characters that has ever been presented in a work of imaginative fiction. A brilliant novel."
—*Speculation*

"Robert Silverberg's award-winning novel *Dying Inside* is one of the best written SF novels in many years: affected with warm insight and told with the rare virtue of human sensibility."
—Christopher Priest, *Oxford Mail*

DYING INSIDE

Robert Silverberg

BANTAM BOOKS
TORONTO · NEW YORK · LONDON · SYDNEY

DYING INSIDE
A Bantam Book published by arrangement with the Author
Bantam edition / March 1984

All rights reserved.
Copyright © 1972 by Robert Silverberg.
Cover art copyright © 1984 by Jim Burns.
This book may not be reproduced in whole or in part, by
mimeograph or any other means, without permission.
For information address: Bantam Books, Inc.

ISBN 0-553-24018-8

Published simultaneously in the United States and Canada

Bantam Books are published by Bantam Books, Inc. Its trade-
mark, consisting of the words "Bantam Books" and the por-
trayal of a rooster, is Registered in U.S. Patent and Trademark
Office and in other countries. Marca Registrada. Bantam
Books, Inc., 666 Fifth Avenue, New York, New York 10103.

PRINTED IN THE UNITED STATES OF AMERICA

H   0 9 8 7 6 5 4 3 2 1

For B and T and C and me—
we sweated it out

ONE.

So, then, I have to go downtown to the University and forage for dollars again. It doesn't take much cash to keep me going—$200 a month will do nicely—but I'm running low, and I don't dare try to borrow from my sister again. The students will shortly be needing their first term papers of the semester; that's always a steady business. The weary, eroding brain of David Selig is once more for hire. I should be able to pick up $75 worth of work on this lovely golden October morning. The air is crisp and clear. A high-pressure system covers New York City, banishing humidity and haze. In such weather my fading powers still flourish. Let us go then, you and I, when the morning is spread out against the sky. To the Broadway-IRT subway. Have your tokens ready, please.

You and I. To whom do I refer? I'm heading downtown alone, after all. *You and I*.

Why, of course I refer to myself and to that creature which lives within me, skulking in its spongy lair and spying on unsuspecting mortals. That sneaky monster within me, that ailing monster, dying even more swiftly than I. Yeats once wrote a dialogue of self and soul; why then shouldn't Selig, who is divided against himself in a way poor goofy Yeats could never have understood, speak of his unique and perishable gift as though it were some encapsulated intruder lodged in his skull? Why not? Let us go then, you and I. Down the hall. Push the button. Into the elevator. There is a stink of garlic in it. These peasants, these swarming Puerto Ricans, they leave their emphatic smells everywhere. My neighbors. I love them. Down. Down.

It is 10:43 A.M., Eastern Daylight Savings Time. The

current temperature reading in Central Park is 57°. The humidity stands at 28% and the barometer is 30.30 and falling, with the wind northeast at 11 miles per hour. The forecast is for fair skies and sunny weather today, tonight, and tomorrow, with the highs in the low to middle 60's. The chance of precipitation is zero today and 10% tomorrow. Air quality level is rated good. David Selig is 41 and counting. Slightly above medium height, he has the lean figure of a bachelor accustomed to his own meager cooking, and his customary facial expression is a mild, puzzled frown. He blinks a lot. In his faded blue denim jacket, heavy-duty boots, and 1969-vintage striped bells he presents a superficially youthful appearance, at least from the neck down; but in fact he looks like some sort of refugee from an illicit research laboratory where the balding, furrowed heads of anguished middle-aged men are grafted to the reluctant bodies of adolescent boys. How did this happen to him? At what point did his face and scalp begin to grow old? The dangling cables of the elevator hurl shrieks of mocking laughter at him as he descends from his two-room refuge on the twelfth floor. He wonders if those rusty cables might be even older than he is. He is of the 1935 vintage. This housing project, he suspects, might date from 1933 or 1934. The Hon. Fiorello H. LaGuardia, Mayor. Though perhaps it's younger—just immediately pre-war, say. (Do you remember 1940, Duvid? That was the year we took you to the World's Fair. This is the trylon, that's the perisphere.) Anyway the buildings are getting old. What isn't?

The elevator halts grindingly at the 7th floor. Even before the scarred door opens I detect a quick mental flutter of female Hispanic vitality dancing through the girders. Of course, the odds are overwhelming that the summoner of the elevator is a young Puerto Rican wife—the house is full of them, the husbands are away at work at this time of day—but all the same I'm pretty certain that I'm reading her psychic emanations and not just playing the hunches. Sure enough. She is short, swarthy, maybe about 23 years old, and very pregnant. I can pick up the double neural output clearly: the quicksilver darting of her shallow, sensual mind and the furry, blurry thumpings of the fetus, about six months old, sealed within her hard bulging body. She is flat-faced and broad-hipped, with little glossy eyes and a thin, pinched mouth. A second child, a dirty girl of about two, clutches her mother's thumb. The babe giggles up at me and the woman favors me with a brief, suspicious smile as they enter the elevator.

They stand with their backs toward me. Dense silence. *Buenos dias, señora*. Nice day, isn't it, ma'am? What a lovely little child. But I remain mute. I don't know her; she looks just like all the others who live in this project, and even her cerebral output is standard stuff, unindividuated, indistinguishable: vague thoughts of plantains and rice, this week's lottery results, and tonight's television highlights. She is a dull bitch but she is human and I love her. What's her name? Maybe it's Mrs. Altagracia Morales. Mrs. Amantina Figueroa. Mrs. Filomena Mercado. I love their names. Pure poetry. I grew up with plump clumping girls named Sondra Wiener, Beverly Schwartz, Sheila Weisbard. Ma'am, can you possibly be Mrs. Inocencia Fernandez? Mrs. Clodomira Espinosa? Mrs. Bonifacia Colon? Perhaps Mrs. Esperanza Dominguez. Esperanza. Esperanza. I love you, Esperanza. Esperanza springs eternal in the human breast. (I was there last Christmas for the bullfights. Esperanza Springs, New Mexico; I stayed at the Holiday Inn. No, I'm kidding.) Ground floor. Nimbly I step forward to hold the door open. The lovely stolid pregnant chiquita doesn't smile at me as she exits.

To the subway now, hippity-hop, one long block away. This far uptown the tracks are still elevated. I sprint up the cracking, peeling staircase and arrive at the station level hardly winded at all. The results of clean living, I guess. Simple diet, no smoking, not much drinking, no acid or mesc, no speed. The station, at this hour, is practically deserted. But in a moment I hear the wailing of onrushing wheels, metal on metal, and simultaneously I pick up the blasting impact of a sudden phalanx of minds all rushing toward me at once out of the north,

packed aboard the five or six cars of the oncoming train.
The compressed souls of those passengers form a single
inchoate mass, pressing insistently against me. They
quiver like trembling jellylike bites of plankton squeezed
brutally together in some oceanographer's net, creating
one complex organism in which the separate identities
of all are lost. As the train glides into the station I am
able to pick up isolated blurts and squeaks of discrete
selfhood: a fierce jab of desire, a squawk of hatred, a
pang of regret, a sudden purposeful inner mumbling,
rising from the confusing totality the way odd little
scraps and stabs of melody rise from the murky orches-
tral smear of a Mahler symphony. The power is decep-
tively strong in me today. I'm picking up plenty. This is
the strongest it's been in weeks. Surely the low humidity is a factor. But I'm not deceived into thinking that
the decline in my ability has been checked. When I
first began to lose my hair, there was a happy period
when the process of erosion seemed to halt and reverse
itself, when new patches of fine dark floss began to
sprout on my denuded forehead. But after an initial
freshet of hope I took a more realistic view: this was no
miraculous reforestation but only a twitch of the hor-
mones, a temporary cessation of decay, not to be relied
upon. And in time my hairline resumed its retreat. So
too in this instance. When one knows that something is
dying inside one, one learns not to put much trust in
the random vitalities of the fleeting moment. Today the
power is strong yet tomorrow I may hear nothing but
distant tantalizing murmurs.

I find a seat in the corner of the second car, open my
book, and wait out the ride downtown. I am reading
Beckett again, *Malone Dies*; it plays nicely to my pre-
vailing mood, which as you have noticed is one of
self-pity. *My time is limited. It is thence that one fine
day, when all nature smiles and shines, the rack lets
loose its black unforgettable cohorts and sweeps away
the blue for ever. My situation is truly delicate. What
fine things, what momentous things, I am going to miss
through fear, fear of falling back into the old error, fear
of not finishing in time, fear of revelling, for the last*

time, in a last outpouring of misery, impotence and hate. The forms are many in which the unchanging seeks relief from its formlessness. Ah yes, the good Samuel, always ready with a word or two of bleak comfort.

Somewhere about 180th Street I look up and see a girl sitting diagonally opposite me and apparently studying me. She is in her very early twenties, attractive in a sallow way, with long legs, decent breasts, a bush of auburn hair. She has a book too—the paperback of *Ulysses*, I recognize the cover—but it lies neglected on her lap. Is she interested in me? I am not reading her mind; when I entered the train I automatically stopped my inputs down to the minimum, a trick I learned when I was a child. If I don't insulate myself against scatter-shot crowd-noises on trains or in other enclosed public places I can't concentrate at all. Without attempting to detect her signals, I speculate on what she's thinking about me, playing a game I often play. *How intelligent he looks. . . . He must have suffered a good deal, his face is so much older than his body . . . tenderness in his eyes . . . so sad they look . . . a poet, a scholar. . . . I bet he's very passionate . . . pouring all his pent-up love into the physical act, into screwing. . . . What's he reading? Beckett? Yes, a poet, a novelist he must be . . . maybe somebody famous. . . . I mustn't be too agressive, though. He'll be turned off by pushiness. A shy smile, that'll catch him. . . . One thing leads to another. . . . I'll invite him up for lunch. . . .* Then, to check on the accuracy of my intuitive perceptions, I tune in on her mind. At first there is no signal. My damnable waning powers betraying me again! But then it comes—static, first, as I get the low-level muzzy ruminations of all the passengers around me, and then the clear sweet tone of her soul. She is thinking about a karate class she will attend later this morning on 96th Street. She is in love with her instructor, a brawny pockmarked Japanese. She will see him tonight. Dimly through her mind swims the memory of the taste of sake and the image of his powerful naked body rearing above her. There is nothing in her mind about me. I am simply part of the scenery, like the map of the subway system on the wall above my head. Selig, your egocentricity kills you every time. I note that she does indeed wear a shy smile now, but it is not for me, and when she sees me staring at her the smile vanishes abruptly. I return my attention to my book.

The train treats me to a long sweaty unscheduled halt in the tunnel between stations north of 137th Street; eventually it gets going again and deposits me at 116th Street, Columbia University. I climbed toward the sunlight. I first climbed these stairs a full quarter of a century ago, October '51, a terrified high-school senior with acne and a crew-cut, coming out of Brooklyn for my college entrance interview. Under the bright lights in University Hall. The interviewer terribly poised, mature—why, he must have been 24, 25 years old. They let me into their college, anyway. And then this was my subway station every day, beginning in September '52 and continuing until I finally got away from home and moved up close to the campus. In those days there was an old cast-iron kiosk at street level marking the entrance to the depths; it was positioned between two lanes of traffic, and students, their absent minds full of Kierkegaard and Sophocles and Fitzgerald, were forever stepping in front of cars and getting killed. Now the kiosk is gone and the subway entrances are placed more rationally, on the sidewalks.

I walk along 116th Street. To my right, the broad greensward of South Field; to my left, the shallow steps rising to Low Library. I remember South Field when it was an athletic field in the middle of the campus: brown dirt, basepaths, fence. My freshman year I played softball there. We'd go to the lockers in University Hall to change, and then, wearing sneakers, polo shirts, dingy gray shorts, feeling naked amidst the other students in business suits or ROTC uniforms, we'd sprint down the endless steps to South Field for an hour of outdoor activity. I was good at softball. Not much muscle, but quick reflexes and a good eye, and I had the advantage of knowing what was on the pitcher's mind. He'd stand there thinking, *This guy's too skinny to hit, I'll give him a high fast one,* and I'd be ready for it and bust it out into left field, circling the bases before anyone knew what was happening. Or the other side would try some clumsy bit of strategy like hit-and-run, and I'd move effortlessly over to gather up the grounder and start the double play. Of course it was only softball and my classmates were mostly pudgy dubs who couldn't even run, let alone read minds, but I enjoyed the unfamiliar sensation of being an outstanding athlete and indulged in fantasies of playing shortstop for the Dodgers. The *Brooklyn* Dodgers, remember? In my sophomore year they ripped up South Field and turned it into a fine grassy showplace divided by a paved promenade, in honor of the University's 200th birthday. Which happened in 1954. Christ, so very long ago. I grow old . . . I grow old . . . I shall wear the bottoms of my trousers rolled. The mermaids singing, each to each. I do not think that they will sing to me.

I go up the steps and take a seat about fifteen feet to the left of the bronze statue of Alma Mater. This is my office in fair weather or foul. The students know where to look for me, and when I'm there the word quickly spreads. There are five or six other people who provide the service I provide—impecunious graduate students, mostly, down on their luck—but I'm the quickest and most reliable, and I have an enthusiastic following. Today, though, business gets off to a slow start. I sit for twenty minutes, fidgeting, peering into Beckett, staring at Alma Mater. Some years ago a radical bomber blew a hole in her side, but there's no sign of the damage now. I remember being shocked at the news, and then shocked at being shocked—why should I give a damn about a dumb statue symbolic of a dumb school? That was about 1969, I guess. Back in the Neolithic.

"Mr. Selig?"

Big brawny jock looming above me. Colossal shoulders, chubby innocent face. He's deeply embarrassed. He's taking Comp Lit 18 and needs a paper fast, on the novels of Kafka, which he hasn't read. (This is the football season; he's the starting halfback and he's very very busy.) I tell him the terms and he hastily agrees. While he stands there I covertly take a reading of him, getting the measure of his intelligence, his probable vocabulary, his style. He's smarter than he appears. Most of them are. They could write their own papers well enough if they only had the time. I make notes, setting down my quick impressions of him, and he goes away happy. After that, trade is brisk: he sends a fraternity brother, the brother sends a friend, the friend sends one of *his* fraternity brothers, a different fraternity, and the daisy-chain lengthens until by early afternoon I find I've taken on all the work I can handle. I know my capacity. So all is well. I'll eat regularly for two or three weeks, without having to tap my sister's grudging generosity. Judith will be pleased not to hear from me. Home, now, to begin my ghostly tasks. I'm good—glib, earnest, profound in a convincingly sophomoric way—and I can vary my styles. I know my way around literature, psychology, anthropology, philosophy, all the soft subjects. Thank God I kept my own term papers; even after twenty-odd years they can still be mined. I charge $3.50 a typed page, sometimes more if my probing reveals that the client has money. A minimum grade of B+ guaranteed or there's no fee. I've never had to make a refund.

TWO.

When he was seven and a half years old and causing a great deal of trouble for his third-grade teacher, they sent little David to the school psychiatrist, Dr. Hittner, for an examination. The school was an expensive private one on a quiet leafy street in the Park Slope section of Brooklyn; its orientation was socialist-progressive, with a smarmy pedagogical underpinning of warmed-over Marxism and Freudianism and John Deweyism, and the psychiatrist, a specialist in the disturbances of middle-class children, paid a call every Wednesday afternoon to peer into the soul of the current problem child. Now it was David's turn. His parents gave their consent, of course. They were deeply concerned about his behavior. Everyone agreed that he was a brilliant child: he was extraordinarily precocious, with a reading-comprehension score on the twelve-year-old level, and adults found him almost frighteningly bright. But he was uncontrollable in class, raucous, disrespectful; the schoolwork, hopelessly elementary for him, bored him to desperation; his only friends were the class misfits, whom he persecuted cruelly; most of the children hated him and the teachers feared his unpredictability. One day he had up-ended a hallway fire extinguisher simply to see if it would spray foam as promised. It did. He brought garter snakes to school and let them loose in the auditorium. He mimed classmates and even teachers with vicious accuracy. "Dr. Hittner would just like to have a little chat with you," his mother told him. "He's heard you're a very special boy and he'd like to get to know you better." David resisted, kicking up a great fuss over the psychiatrist's name. "Hitler? Hitler? I don't want to talk to Hitler!" It was the fall of 1942 and the childish pun was an inevitable one, but he clung to it with irritating stubbornness. "Dr. Hitler wants to see me. Dr. Hitler wants to get to know me." And his mother said, "No, Duvid, it's *Hittner, Hittner,* with an *n.*" He went anyway. He strutted into the psychiatrist's office, and when Dr. Hittner smiled benignly and said, "Hello, there, David," David shot forth a stiff arm and snapped: *"Heil!"*

Dr. Hittner chuckled. "You've got the wrong man," he said. "I'm *Hittner,* with an *n.*" Perhaps he had heard such jokes before. He was a huge man with a long horsey face, a wide fleshy mouth, a high curving forehead. Watery blue eyes twinkled behind rimless glasses. His skin was soft and pink and he had a good tangy smell, and he was trying hard to seem friendly and amused and big-brotherly, but David couldn't help picking up the impression that Dr. Hittner's brotherliness was just an act. It was something he felt with most adults: they smiled a lot, but inside themselves they were thinking things like, *What a scary brat, what a creepy little kid.* Even his mother and father sometimes thought things like that. He didn't understand why adults said one thing with their faces and another with their minds, but he was accustomed to it. It was something he had come to expect and accept.

"Let's play some games, shall we?" Dr. Hittner said.

Out of the vest pocket of his tweed suit he produced a little plastic globe on a metal chain. He showed it to David; then he pulled on the chain and the globe came apart into eight or nine pieces of different colors. "Watch closely, now, while I put it back together," said Dr. Hittner. His thick fingers expertly reassembled the globe. Then he pulled it apart again and shoved it across the desk toward David. "Your turn. Can you put it back together too?"

David remembered that the doctor had started by taking the E-shaped white piece and fitting the D-shaped blue piece into one of its grooves. Then had come the yellow piece, but David didn't recall what to do with it; he sat there a moment, puzzled, until Dr. Hittner obligingly flashed him a mental image of the proper manipulation. David did it and the rest was easy. A couple of times he got stuck, but he was always able to pull the answer out of the doctor's mind. Why does he think he's testing me, David wondered, if he keeps giving me so many hints? What's he proving? When the globe was intact David handed it back. "Would you like to keep it?" Dr. Hittner asked.

"I don't need it," David said. But he pocketed it anyway.

They played a few more games. There was one with little cards about the size of playing cards, with drawings of animals and birds and trees and houses on them; David was supposed to arrange them so that they told a story, and then tell the doctor what the story was. He scattered them at random on the desk and made up a story as he went along. "The duck goes into the forest, you see, and he meets a wolf, so he turns into a frog and jumps over the wolf right into the elephant's mouth, only he escapes out of the elephant's tushie and falls into a lake, and when he comes out he sees the pretty princess here, who says come home and I'll give you gingerbread, but he can read her mind and he sees that she's really a wicked witch, who—" Another game involved slips of paper that had big blue ink-blots on them. "Do any of these shapes remind you of real things?" the doctor asked. "Yes," David said, "this is an elephant, see, his tail is here and here all crumpled up, and this is his tushie, and this is where he makes pee-pee." He had already discovered that Dr. Hittner became very interested when he talked about tushies or pee-pee, so he gave the doctor plenty to be interested about, finding such things in every ink-blot picture. This seemed a very silly game to David, but apparently it was important to Dr. Hittner, who scribbled notes on everything David was saying. David studied Dr. Hittner's mind while the psychiatrist wrote things down. Most of the words he picked up were incomprehensible, but he did recognize a few, the grown-up terms for the parts of the body that David's mother had taught him: *penis, vulva, buttocks, rectum,* things like that. Obviously Dr. Hittner liked those words a great deal, so David began to use them. "This is a picture of an eagle that's picking up a little sheep and flying away with it. This is the eagle's penis, down here, and over here is the sheep's rectum. And in the next one there's a man and a woman, and they're both naked, and the man is trying to put his penis inside the woman's vulva only it won't fit, and—" David watched the fountain pen flying over the paper. He grinned at Dr. Hittner and turned to the next ink-blot.

Next they played word games. The doctor spoke a word and asked David to say the first word that came into his head. David found it more amusing to say the first word that came into Dr. Hittner's head. It took only a fraction of a second to pick it up, and Dr. Hittner didn't seem to notice what was going on. The game went like this:

"Father."
"Penis."
"Mother."
"Bed."
"Baby."
"Dead."
"Water."
"Belly."

"Tunnel."

"Shovel."

"Coffin."

"Mother."

Were those the right words to say? Who was the winner in this game? Why did Dr. Hittner seem so upset?

Finally they stopped playing games and simply talked. "You're a very bright little boy," Dr. Hittner said. "I don't have to worry about spoiling you by telling you that, because you know it already. What do you want to be when you grow up?"

"Nothing."

"*Nothing?*"

"I just want to play and read a lot of books and swim."

"But how will you earn a living?"

"I'll get money from people when I need it."

"If you find out how, I hope you'll tell me the secret," the doctor said. "Are you happy here in school?"

"No."

"Why not?"

"The teachers are too strict. The work is too dumb. The children don't like me."

"Do you ever wonder why they don't like you?"

"Because I'm smarter than they are," David said. "Because I—" Ooops. Almost said it. *Because I can see what they're thinking*. Mustn't ever tell anyone that. Dr. Hittner was waiting for him to finish the sentence. "Because I make a lot of trouble in class."

"And why do you do that, David?"

"I don't know. It gives me something to do, I guess."

"Maybe if you didn't make so much trouble, people would like you more. Don't you want people to like you?"

"I don't care. I don't need it."

"Everybody needs friends, David."

"I've got friends."

"Mrs. Fleischer says you don't have very many, and that you hit them a lot and make them unhappy. Why do you hit your friends?"

"Because I don't like them. Because they're dumb."

"Then they aren't really friends, if that's how you feel about them."

Shrugging, David said, "I can get along without them. I have fun just being by myself."

"Are you happy at home?"

"I guess so."

"You love your mommy and daddy?"

A pause. A feeling of great tension coming out of the doctor's mind. This is an important question. Give the right answer, David. Give him the answer he wants.

"Yes," David said.

"Do you ever wish you had a baby brother or sister?"

No hesitation now. "No."

"Really, no? You like being all alone?"

David nodded. "The afternoons are the best time. When I'm home from school and there's nobody around. Am I going to have a baby brother or sister?"

Chuckles from the doctor. "I'm sure I don't know. That would be up to your mommy and daddy, wouldn't it?"

"You won't tell them to get one for me, will you? I mean, you might say to them that it would be good for me to have one, and then they'd go and get one, but I really don't want—" I'm in trouble, David realized suddenly.

"What makes you think I'd tell your parents it would be good for you to have a baby brother or sister?" the doctor asked quietly, not smiling now at all.

"I don't know. It was just an idea." Which I found inside your head, doctor. And now I want to get out of here. I don't want to talk to you any more. "Hey, your name isn't really Hittner, is it? With an *n*? I bet I know your real name. *Heil!*"

THREE.

I never could send my thoughts into anybody else's head. Even when the power was strongest in me, I couldn't transmit. I could only receive. Maybe there are people around who do have that power, who can transmit thoughts even to those who don't have any special receiving gift, but I wasn't ever one of them. So right there I was condemned to be society's ugliest toad, the eavesdropper, the voyeur. Old English proverb: *He who peeps through a hole may see what will vex him*. Yes. In those years when I was particularly eager to communicate with people, I'd work up fearful sweats trying to plant my thoughts in them. I'd sit in a classroom staring at the back of some girl's head, and I'd think hard at her: *Hello, Annie, this is David Selig calling, do you read me? Do you read me? I love you, Annie. Over. Over and out*. But Annie never read me, and the currents of her mind would roll on like a placid river, undisturbed by the existence of David Selig.

No way, then, for me to speak to other minds, only to spy on them. The way the power manifests itself in me has always been highly variable. I never had much conscious control over it, other than being able to stop down the intensity of input and to do a certain amount of fine tuning; basically I had to take whatever came drifting in. Most often I would pick up a person's surface thoughts, his subvocalizations of the things he's just about to say. These would come to me in a clear conversational manner, exactly as though he *had* said them, except the tone of voice was different, it was plainly not a tone produced by the vocal apparatus. I don't remember any period even in my childhood when I confused spoken communication with mental communication. This ability to read surface thoughts has been fairly consistent throughout: I still can anticipate

14

verbal statements more often than not, especially when I'm with someone who has the habit of rehearsing what he intends to say.

I could also and to some extent still can anticipate immediate intentions, such as the decision to throw a short right jab to the jaw. My way of knowing such things varies. I might pick up a coherent inner verbal statement—*I'm now going to throw a short right jab to his jaw*—or, if the power happens to be working on deeper levels that day, I may simply pick up a series of non-verbal instructions to the muscles, which add up in a fraction of a second to the process of bringing the right arm up for a short jab to the jaw. Call it body language on the telepathic wavelength.

Another thing I've been able to do, though never consistently, is tune in to the deepest layers of the mind—where the soul lives, if you will. Where the consciousness lies bathed in a murky soup of indistinct unconscious phenomena. Here lurk hopes, fears, perceptions, purposes, passions, memories, philosophical positions, moral policies, hungers, sorrows, the whole ragbag accumulation of events and attitudes that defines the private self. Ordinarily some of this bleeds through to me even when the most superficial mental contact is established: I can't help getting a certain amount of information about the coloration of the soul. But occasionally— hardly ever, now—I fasten my hooks into the real stuff, the whole person. There's ecstasy in that. There's an electrifying sense of contact. Coupled, of course, with a stabbing, numbing sense of guilt, because of the totality of my voyeurism: how much more of a peeping tom can a person be? Incidentally, the soul speaks a universal language. When I look into the mind of Mrs. Esperanza Dominguez, say, and I get a gabble of Spanish out of it, I don't really know what she's thinking, because I don't understand very much Spanish. But if I were to get into the depths of her soul I'd have complete comprehension of anything I picked up. The mind may think in Spanish or Basque or Hungarian or Finnish, but the soul thinks in a languageless language accessible to any prying sneaking freak who comes along to peer at its mysteries.

No matter. It's all going from me now.

FOUR.

Paul F. Bruno
Comp Lit 18, Prof. Schmitz
October 15, 1976

The Novels of Kafka

In the nightmare world of *The Trial* and *The Castle*, only one thing is certain: that the central figure, significantly known by the initial K, is doomed to frustration. All else is dreamlike and unsure; courtrooms spring up in tenements, mysterious warders devour one's breakfast, a man thought to be Sordini is actually Sortini. The central fact is certain, though: K will fail in his attempt to attain grace.

The two novels have the same theme and approximately the same basic structure. In both, K seeks for grace and is led to the final realization that it is to be withheld from him. (*The Castle* is unfinished, but its conclusion seems plain.) Kafka brings his heroes into involvement with their situations in opposite ways: in *The Trial*, Joseph K. is passive until he is jolted into the action of the book by the unexpected arrival of the two warders; in *The Castle*, K is first shown as an active character making efforts on his own behalf to reach the mysterious Castle. To be sure, though, he has originally been summoned by the Castle; the action did not originate in himself, and thus he began as as passive a character as Joseph K. The distinction is that *The Trial* opens at a point earlier in the time-stream of the action—at the earliest possible point, in fact. *The Castle* follows more closely the ancient rule of beginning *in medias res*, with K already summoned and trying to reach the Castle.

Both books get off to rapid starts. Joseph K. is arrested in the very first sentence of *The Trial*, and his counterpart K arrives at what he thinks is going to

16

be the last stop before the Castle on the first page of that novel. From there, both K's struggle futilely toward their goals (in *The Castle*, simply to get to the top of the hill; in *The Trial*, first to understand the nature of his guilt, and then, despairing of this, to achieve acquittal without understanding). Both actually get farther from their goals with each succeeding action. *The Trial* reaches its peak in the wonderful Cathedral scene, quite likely the most terrifying single sequence in any of Kafka's work, in which K is given to realize that he is guilty and can never be acquitted; the chapter that follows, describing K's execution, is little more than an anticlimactic appendage. *The Castle*, less complete than *The Trial*, lacks the counterpart of the Cathedral scene (perhaps Kafka was unable to devise one?) and thus is artistically less satisfying than the shorter, more intense, more tightly constructed *Trial*.

Despite their surface artlessness, both novels appear to be built on the fundamental threepart structure of the tragic rhythm, labeled by the critic Kenneth Burke as "purpose, passion, perception." *The Trial* follows this scheme with greater success than does the incomplete *Castle;* the purpose, to achieve acquittal, is demonstrated through as harrowing a passion as any fictional hero has undergone. Finally, when Joseph K. has been reduced from his original defiant, self-confident attitude to a fearful, timid state of mind, and he is obviously ready to capitulate to the forces of the Court, the time is at hand for the final moment of perception.

The agent used to bring him to the scene of the climax is a classically Kafkaesque figure—the mysterious "Italian colleague who was on his first visit to the town and had influential connexions that made him important to the Bank." The theme that runs through all of Kafka's work, the impossibility of human communication, is repeated here: though Joseph has spent half the night studying Italian in preparation for the visit, and is half asleep in consequence, the stranger speaks an unknown southern dialect which Joseph cannot understand. Then—a crowning comic touch—the stranger shifts to French, but his

French is just as difficult to follow, and his bushy mustache foils Joseph's attempts at lip-reading.

Once he reaches the Cathedral, which he has been asked to show to the Italian (who, as we are not surprised to find, never keeps the date), the tension mounts. Joseph wanders through the building, which is empty, dark, cold, lit only by candles flickering far in the distance, while night inexplicably begins fast to fall outside. Then the priest calls to him, and relates the allegory of the Doorkeeper. It is only when the story is ended that we realize we did not at all understand it; far from being the simple tale it had originally seemed to be, it reveals itself as complex and difficult. Joseph and the priest discuss the story at great length, in the manner of a pair of rabbinical scholars disputing a point in the Talmud. Slowly its implications sink in, and we and Joseph see that the light streaming from the door to the Law will not be visible for him until it is too late.

Structurally the novel is over right here. Joseph has received the final perception that acquittal is impossible; his guilt is established, and he is not yet to receive grace. His quest is ended. The final element of the tragic rhythm, the perception that ends the passion, has been reached.

We know that Kafka planned further chapters showing the progress of Joseph's trial through various later stages, ending in his execution. Kafka's biographer Max Brod says the book could have been prolonged infinitely. This is true, of course; it is inherent in the nature of Joseph K.'s guilt that he could never get to the highest Court, just as the other K could wander for all time without ever reaching the Castle. But structurally the novel ends in the Cathedral; the rest of what Kafka intended would not have added anything essential to Joseph's self-knowledge. The Cathedral scene shows us what we have known since page one: that there is no acquittal. The action concludes with that perception.

The Castle, a much longer and more loosely constructed book, lacks the power of *The Trial*. It rambles. The passion of K is much less clearly defined, and K is a less consistent character, not as interesting psychologically as he is in *The Trial*. Whereas in the earlier book he takes active charge of his case as soon as he realizes his danger, in *The Castle* he quickly becomes the victim of the bureaucracy. The transit of character in *The Trial* is from early passivity to activity back to passive resignation after the epiphany in the Cathedral. In *The Castle* K undergoes no such clearcut changes; he is an active character as the novel opens, but soon is lost in the nightmare maze of the village below the Castle, and sinks deeper and deeper into degradation. Joseph K. is almost an heroic character, while K of *The Castle* is merely a pathetic one.

The two books represent varying attempts at telling the same story, that of the existentially disengaged man who is suddenly involved in a situation from which there is no escape, and who, after making attempts to achieve the grace that will release him from his predicament, succumbs. As they exist today, *The Trial* is unquestionably the greater artistic success, firmly constructed and at all times under the author's technical control. *The Castle*, or rather the fragment of it we have, is potentially the greater novel, however. Everything that was in *The Trial* would have been in *The Castle*, and a great deal more. But, one feels, Kafka abandoned work on *The Castle* because he saw he lacked the resources to carry it through. He could not handle the world of the Castle, with its sweeping background of Brueghelesque country life, with the same assurance as he did the urban world of *The Trial*. And there is a lack of urgency in *The Castle*; we are never too concerned over K's doom because it is inevitable; Joseph K., though, is fighting more tangible forces, and until the end we have the illusion that victory is possible for him. *The Castle*, also, is too ponderous. Like a Mahler symphony, it collapses of its own weight. One wonders if Kafka had in mind some structure enabling him to end *The Castle*. Perhaps he never intended to close the novel at all, but meant to have K wander in ever-widening circles, never arriving at the tragic perception that he can never reach the Castle. Perhaps this is the reason for the comparative formlessness of the later work: Kafka's discovery that the true tragedy of K, his archetypical hero-as-victim figure, lies not in his final perception of the impossibility of attaining grace, but in the fact that he will never reach even as much as that final perception. Here we have the tragic rhythm, a structure found throughout literature, truncated to depict more pointedly the contemporary human condition—a condition so abhorrent to Kafka. Joseph K., who actually reaches a form of grace, thereby attains true tragic stature; K, who simply sinks lower and lower, might symbolize for Kafka the contemporary individual, so crushed by the general tragedy of the times that he is incapable of any tragedy on an individual level. K is a pathetic figure, Joseph K. a tragic one. Joseph K. is a more interesting character, but perhaps it was K whom Kafka understood more deeply. And for K's story no ending is possible, perhaps, save the pointless one of death.

That's not so bad. Six double-spaced typed pages. At $3.50 per, it earns me a cool $21 for less than two hours' work, and it'll earn the brawny halfback, Mr. Paul F. Bruno, a sure B+ from Prof. Schmitz. I'm confident of that because the very same paper, differing only in a few minor stylistic flourishes, got me a B from the very demanding Prof. Dupee in May, 1955. Standards are lower today, after two decades of academic inflation. Bruno may even rack up an A— for the Kafka job. It's got just the right quality of earnest intelligence, with the proper undergraduate mixture of sophisticated insight and naive dogmatism, and Dupee found the writing "clear and forceful" in '55, according to his note in the margin. All right, now. Time out for a little chow mein, with maybe a side order of eggroll. Then I'll tackle *Odysseus as a Symbol of Society* or perhaps *Aeschylus and the Aristotelian Tragedy*. I can't work from my own old term papers for those, but they shouldn't be too tough to do. Old typewriter, old humbugger, stand me now and ever in good stead.

FIVE.

Aldous Huxley thought that evolution has designed our brains to serve as filters, screening out a lot of stuff that's of no real value to us in our daily struggle for bread. Visions, mystical experiences, psi phenomena such as telepathic messages from other brains—all sorts of things along these lines would forever be flooding into us were it not for the action of what Huxley called, in a little book entitled *Heaven and Hell,* "the cerebral reducing valve." Thank God for the cerebral reducing valve! If we hadn't evolved it, we'd be distracted all the time by scenes of incredible beauty, by spiritual insights of overwhelming grandeur, and by searing, utterly honest mind-to-mind contact with our fellow human beings. Luckily, the workings of the valve protect us—most of us—from such things, and we are free to go about our daily lives, buying cheap and selling dear.

Of course, some of us seem to be born with defective valves. I mean the artists like Bosch or El Greco, whose eyes did not see the world as it appears to thee and me; I mean the visionary philosophers, the ecstatics and the nirvana-attainers; I mean the miserable freakish flukes who can read the thoughts of others. Mutants, all of us. Genetic sports.

However, Huxley believed that the efficiency of the cerebral reducing valve could be impaired by various artificial means, thus giving ordinary mortals access to the extrasensory data customarily seen only by the chosen few. The psychedelic drugs, he thought, have this effect. Mescaline, he suggested, interferes with the enzyme system that regulates cerebral function, and by so doing "lowers the efficiency of the brain as an instrument for focusing mind on the problems of life on the surface of our planet. This . . . seems to permit the entry into consciousness of certain classes of mental events, which are normally excluded, because they possess no survival value. Similar intrusions of biologically useless, but aesthetically and sometimes spiritually valuable, material may occur as the result of illness or fatigue; or they may be induced by fasting, or a period of confinement in a place of darkness and complete silence."

Speaking for himself, David Selig can say very little about the psychedelic drugs. He had only one experience with them, and it wasn't a happy one. That was in the summer of 1968, when he was living with Toni.

Though Huxley thought highly of the psychedelics, he didn't see them as the only gateway to visionary experience. Fasting and physical mortification could get you there also. He wrote of mystics who "regularly used upon themselves the whip of knotted leather or even of iron wire. These beatings were the equivalent of fairly extensive surgery without anaesthetics, and heir effects on the body chemistry of the penitent were considerable. Large quantities of histamine and adrenalin were released while the whip was actually being plied; and when the resulting wounds began to fester (as wounds practically always did before the age of soap), various toxic substances, produced by the decomposition of protein, found their way into the bloodstream. But histamine produces shock, and shock affects the the mind no less profoundly than the body. Moreover, large quantities of adrenalin may cause hallucinations, and some of the products of its decomposition are known to induce symptoms resembling those of schizophrenia. As for toxins from wounds—these upset the enzyme systems regulating the brain, and lower its efficiency as an instrument for getting on in a world where the biologically fittest survive. This may explain why the Curé d'Ars used to say that, in the days when he was free to flagellate himself without mercy, God would refuse him nothing. In other words, when remorse, self-loathing, and the fear of hell release adrenalin, when self-inflicted surgery releases adrenalin and histamine, and when infected wounds release decomposed protein into the blood, the efficiency of the cerebral reducing valve is lowered and unfamiliar aspects of Mind-at-Large (including psi phenomena, visions, and, if he is philosophically and ethically prepared for it, mystical experiences) will flow into the ascetic's consciousness."

Remorse, self-loathing, and the fear of hell. Fasting and prayer. Whips and chains. Festering wounds. Everybody to his own trip, I suppose, and welcome to it. As the power fades in me, as the sacred gift dies, I toy with the idea of trying to revive it by artificial means. Acid, mescaline, psilocybin? I don't think I'd care to go there again. Mortification of the flesh? That seems obsolete to me, like marching off to the Crusades or wearing spats: something that simply isn't appropriate for 1976. I doubt that I could get very deep into flagellation, anyway. What does that leave? Fasting and prayer? I could fast, I suppose. Prayer? To whom? To what? I'd feel like a fool. Dear God, give me my power again. Dear Moses, please help me. Crap on that. Jews don't pray for favors, because they know nobody will answer. What's left, then? Remorse, self-loathing, and the fear of hell? I have those three already, and they do me no good. We must try some other way of goading the power back to life. Invent something new. Flagellation of the mind, perhaps? Yes. I'll try that. I'll get out the metaphorical cudgels and let myself have it. Flagellation of the aching, weakening, throbbing, dissolving mind. The treacherous, hateful mind.

SIX.

But why does David Selig want his power to come back? Why not let it fade? It's always been a curse to him, hasn't it? It's cut him off from his fellow men and doomed him to a loveless life. Leave well enough alone, Duvid. Let it fade. Let it fade. On the other hand, without the power, what are you? Without that one faltering unpredictable unsatisfactory means of contact with them, how will you be able to touch them at all? Your power joins you to mankind, for better or for worse, in the only joining you have: you can't bear to surrender it. Admit it. You love it and you despise it, this gift of yours. You dread losing it despite all it's done to you. You'll fight to cling to the last shreds of it, even though you know the struggle's hopeless. Fight on, then. Read Huxley again. Try acid, if you dare. Try flagellation. Try fasting, at least. All right, fasting. I'll skip the chow mein. I'll skip the eggroll. Let's slide a fresh sheet into the typewriter and think about Odysseus as a symbol of society.

SEVEN.

Hark to the silvery jangle of the telephone. The hour is late. Who calls? Is it Aldous Huxley from beyond the grave, urging me to have courage? Dr. Hittner, with some important questions about making pee-pee? Toni, to tell me she's in the neighborhood with a thousand mikes of dynamite acid and is it okay to come up? Sure. Sure. I stare at the telephone, clueless. My power even at its height was never equal to the task of penetrating the consciousness of the American Telephone & Telegraph Company. Sighing, I pick up the receiver on the fifth ring and hear the sweet contralto voice of my sister Judith.

"Am I interrupting something?" Typical Judith opening.

"A quiet night at home. I'm ghosting a term paper on *The Odyssey*. Got any bright ideas for me, Jude?"

"You haven't called in two weeks."

"I was broke. After that scene the last time I didn't want to bring up the subject of money, and lately it's been the only subject I can think of talking about, so I didn't call."

"Shit," she says, "I wasn't angry at you."

"You sounded mad as hell."

"I didn't mean any of that stuff. Why did you think I was serious? Just because I was yelling? Do you really believe that I regard you as—as—what did I call you?"

"A shiftless sponger, I think."

"A shiftless sponger. Shit. I was tense that night, Duv; I had personal problems, and my period was coming on besides. I lost control. I was just shouting the first dumb crap that came into my head, but why did you believe I meant it? You of all people shouldn't have thought I was serious. Since when do you take what people say with their mouths at face value?"

"You were saying it with your head too, Jude."

"I was?" Her voice is suddenly small and contrite. "Are you sure?"

"It came through loud and clear."

"Oh, Jesus, Duv, have a heart! In the heat of the moment I could have been thinking anything. But underneath the anger—*underneath*, Duv—you must have seen that I didn't mean it. That I love you, that I don't want to drive you away from me. You're all I've got, Duv, you and the baby."

Her love is unpalatable to me, and her sentimentalism is even less to my taste. I say, "I don't read much of what's underneath any more, Jude. Not much comes through these days. Anyway, look, it isn't worth hassling over. I *am* a shiftless sponger, and I *have* borrowed more from you than you can afford to give. The black sheep big brother feels enough guilt as it is. I'm damned if I'm ever going to ask for money from you again."

"Guilt? You talk about guilt, when I—"

"No," I warn her, "don't you go on a guilt trip now, Jude. Not now." Her remorse for her past coldness toward me has a flavor even more stinking than her newfound love. "I don't feel up to assigning the ratio of blames and guilts tonight."

"All right. All right. Are you okay now for money, though?"

"I told you, I'm ghosting term papers. I'm getting by."

"Do you want to come over here for dinner tomorrow night?"

"I think I'd better work instead. I've got a lot of papers to write, Jude. It's the busy season."

"It would be just the two of us. And the kid, of course, but I'll put him to sleep early. Just you and me. We could talk. We've got so much to talk about. Why don't you come over, Duv? You don't need to work all day and all night. I'll cook up something you like. I'll do the spaghetti and hot sauce. Anything. You name it." She is pleading with me, this icy sister who gave me nothing but hatred for twenty-five years. Come over and I'll be a mama for you, Duv. Come let me be loving, brother.

"Maybe the night after next. I'll call you."

"No chance for tomorrow?"

"I don't think so," I say. There is silence. She doesn't want to beg me. Into the sudden screeching silence I say, "What have you been doing with yourself, Judith? Seeing anyone interesting?"

"Not seeing anyone at all." A flinty edge to her voice. She is two and a half years into her divorce; she sleeps around a good deal; juices are souring in her soul. She is 31 years old. "I'm between men right now. Maybe I'm off men altogether. I don't care if I never do any screwing again ever."

I throttle a somber laugh. "What happened to that travel agent you were seeing? Mickey?"

"Marty. That was just a gimmick. He got me all over

Europe for 10% of the fare. Otherwise I couldn't have afforded to go. I was using him."

"So?"

"I felt shitty about it. Last month I broke off. I wasn't in love with him. I don't think I even liked him."

"But you played around with him long enough to get a trip to Europe, first."

"It didn't cost *him* anything, Duv. I had to go to bed with him; all he had to do was fill out a form. What are you saying, anyway? That I'm a whore?"

"Jude—"

"Okay, I'm a whore. At least I'm trying to go straight for a while. Lots of fresh orange juice and plenty of serious reading. I'm reading Proust now, would you believe that? I just finished *Swann's Way* and tomorrow—"

"I've still got some work to do tonight, Jude."

"I'm sorry. I didn't mean to intrude. Will you come for dinner this week?"

"I'll think about it. I'll let you know."

"Why do you hate me so much, Duv?"

"I don't hate you. And we were about to get off the phone, I think."

"Don't forget to call," she says. Clutching at straws.

EIGHT.

Toni. I should tell you about Toni now.

I lived with Toni for seven weeks, one summer eight years ago. That's as long as I've ever lived with anybody, except my parents and my sister, whom I got away from as soon as I decently could, and myself, whom I can't get away from at all. Toni was one of the two great loves of my life, the other being Kitty. I'll tell you about Kitty some other time.

Can I reconstruct Toni? Let's try it in a few swift strokes. She was 24 that year. A tall coltish girl, five feet six, five feet seven. Slender. Agile and awkward, both at once. Long legs, long arms, thin wrists, thin ankles.

Glossy black hair, very straight, cascading to her shoulders. Warm, quick brown eyes, alert and quizzical. A witty, shrewd girl, not really well educated but extraordinarily wise. The face by no means conventionally pretty—too much mouth, too much nose, the cheekbones too high—but yet producing a sexy and highly attractive effect, sufficient to make a lot of heads turn when she enters a room. Full, heavy breasts. I dig busty women: I often need a soft place to rest my tired head. So often so tired. My mother was built 32-A, no cozy pillows there. She couldn't have nursed me if she'd wanted to, which she didn't. (Will I ever forgive her for letting me escape from the womb? Ah, now, Selig, show some filial piety, for God's sake!)

I never looked into Toni's mind except twice, once on the day I met her and once a couple of weeks after that, plus a third time on the day we broke up. The third time was a sheer disastrous accident. The second was more or less an accident too, not quite. Only the first was a deliberate probe. After I realized I loved her I took care never to spy on her head. *He who peeps through a hole may see what will vex him*. A lesson I learned very young. Besides, I didn't want Toni to suspect anything about my power. My curse. I was afraid it might frighten her away.

That summer I was working as an $85-a-week researcher, latest in my infinite series of odd jobs, for a well-known professional writer who was doing an immense book on the political machinations involved in the founding of the State of Israel. Eight hours a day I went through old newspaper files for him in the bowels of the Columbia library. Toni was a junior editor for the publishing house that was bringing out his book. I met her one afternoon in late spring at his posh apartment on East End Avenue. I went over there to deliver a bundle of notes on Harry Truman's 1948 campaign speeches and she happened to be there, discussing some cuts to be made in the early chapters. Her beauty stung me. I hadn't been with a woman in months. I automatically assumed she was the writer's mistress—screwing editors, I'm told, is standard practice on cer-

tain high levels of the literary profession—but my old
peeping-tom instincts quickly gave me the true scoop. I
tossed a fast probe at him and found that his mind was a
cesspool of frustrated longings for her. He ached for her
and she had no yen for him at all, evidently. Next I
poked into *her* mind. I sank in, deep, finding myself in
warm, rich loam. Quickly got oriented. Stray fragments
of autobiography bombarded me, incoherent, non-linear:
a divorce, some good sex and some bad sex, college
days, a trip to the Caribbean, all swimming around in
the usual chaotic way. I got past that fast and checked
out what I was after. No, she wasn't sleeping with the
writer. Physically he registered absolute zero for her.
(Odd. To me he seemed attractive, a romantic and
appealing figure, so far as a drearily heterosexual soul
like me is able to judge such things.) She didn't even
like his writing, I learned. Then, still rummaging around,
I learned something else, much more surprising: *I*
seemed to be turning her on. Forth from her came the
explicit line: *I wonder if he's free tonight*. She looked
upon the aging researcher, a venerable 33 and already
going thin on top, and did not find him repellent. I was
so shaken by that—her dark-eyed glamour, her leggy
sexiness, aimed at *me*—that I got the hell out of her
head, fast. "Here's the Truman stuff," I said to my
employer. "There's more coming in from the Truman
Library in Missouri." We talked a few minutes about
the next assignment he had for me, and then I made as
though to leave. A quick guarded look at her.

"Wait," she said. "We can ride down together. I'm
just about done here."

The man of letters shot me a poisonous envious
glance. Oh, God, fired again. But he bade us both civil
goodbyes. In the elevator going down we stood apart.
Toni in this corner, I in that one, with a quivering wall
of tension and yearning separating and uniting us. I had
to struggle to keep from reading her; I was afraid,
terrified, not of getting the wrong answer but of getting
the right one. In the street we stood apart also, dithering
a moment. Finally I said I was getting a cab to take me
to the Upper West Side—me, a cab, on $85 a week!

—and could I drop her off anywhere? She said she lived on 105th and West End. Close enough. When the cab stopped outside her place she invited me up for a drink. Three rooms, indifferently furnished: mostly books, records, scatter-rugs, posters. She went to pour some wine for us and I caught her and pulled her around and kissed her. She trembled against me, or was I the one who was trembling?

Over a bowl of hot-and-sour soup at the Great Shanghai, a little later that evening, she said she'd be moving in a couple of days. The apartment belonged to her current roommate—male—with whom she'd split up just three days before. She had no place to stay. "I've got only one lousy room," I said, "but it has a double bed." Shy grins, hers, mine. So she moved in. I didn't think she was in love with me, not at all, but I wasn't going to ask. If what she felt for me wasn't love, it was good enough, the best I could hope for; and in the privacy of my own head I could feel love for her. She had needed a port in a storm. I had happened to offer one. If that was all I meant to her now, so be it. So be it. There was time for things to ripen.

We slept very little, our first two weeks. Not that we were screwing all the time, though there was a lot of that; but we *talked*. We were new to each other, which is the best time of any relationship, when there are whole pasts to share, when everything pours out and there's no need to search for things to say. (Not quite everything poured out. The only thing I concealed from her was the central fact of my life, the fact that had shaped my every aspect.) She talked of her marriage—young, at 20, and brief, and empty—and of how she had lived in the three years since its ending—a succession of men, a dip into occultism and Reichian therapy, a newfound dedication to her editing career. Giddy weeks.

* * *

Then, our third week. My second peep into her mind. A sweltering June night, with a full moon send-

ing cold illumination through the slatted blinds into our
room. She was sitting astride me—her favorite position—
and her body, very pale, wore a white glow in the eerie
darkness. Her long lean form rearing far above me. Her
face half hidden in her own dangling unruly hair. Her
eyes closed. Her lips slack. Her breasts, viewed from
below, seeming even bigger than they really were.
Cleopatra by moonlight. She was rocking and jouncing
her way to a private ecstasy, and her beauty and the
strangeness of her so overwhelmed me that I could not
resist watching her at the moment of climax, watching
on all levels, and so I opened the barrier that I had so
scrupulously erected, and, just as she was coming, my
mind touched a curious finger to her soul and received
the full uprushing volcanic intensity of her pleasure. I
found no thought of me in her mind. Only sheer animal
frenzy, bursting from every nerve. I've seen that in
other women, before and after Toni, as they come: they
are islands, alone in the void of space, aware only of
their bodies and perhaps of that intrusive rigid rod
against which they thrust. When pleasure takes them it
is a curiously impersonal phenomenon, no matter how
titanic its impact. So it was then with Toni. I didn't
object; I knew what to expect and I didn't feel cheated
or rejected. In fact my joining of souls with her at that
awesome moment served to trigger my own coming and
to treble its intensity. I lost contact with her then. The
upheavals of orgasm shatter the fragile telepathic link.
Afterwards I felt a little sleazy at having spied, but not
overly guilty about it. How magical a thing it was, after
all, to have been with her in that moment. To be aware
of her joy not just as mindless spasms of her loins but as
jolts of brilliant light flaring across the dark terrain of
her soul. An instant of beauty and wonder, an illumination never to be forgotten. But never to be repeated,
either. I resolved, once more, to keep our relationship
clean and honest. To take no unfair advantage of her. To
stay out of her head forever after.

* * *

Despite which, I found myself some weeks later entering Toni's consciousness a third time. By accident. By damnable abominable accident. Oy, that third time! That bummer—that disaster—

That catastrophe—

NINE.

In the early spring of 1945, when he was ten years old, his loving mother and father got him a little sister. That was exactly how they phrased it: his mother, smiling her warmest phony smile, hugging him, telling him in her best this-is-how-we-talk-to-bright-children tone, "Dad and I have a wonderful surprise for you, David. We're going to get a little sister for you."

It was no surprise, of course. They had been discussing it among themselves for months, maybe for years, always making the fallacious assumption that their son, clever as he was, didn't understand what they were talking about. Thinking that he was unable to associate one fragment of conversation with another, that he was incapable of putting the proper antecedents to their deliberately vague pronouns, their torrent of "it" and "him." And, naturally, he had been reading their minds. In those days the power was sharp and clear; lying in his bedroom, surrounded by his dog-eared books and his stamp albums, he could effortlessly tune in on everything that went on behind the closed door of theirs, fifty feet away. It was like an endless radio broadcast without commercials. He could listen to WJZ, WHN, WEAF, WOR, all the stations on the dial, but the one he listened to most was WPMS, Paul-and-Martha-Selig. They had no secrets from him. He had no shame about spying. Preternaturally adult, privy to all their privities, he meditated daily on the raw torrid stuff of married life: the financial anxieties, the moments of sweet undifferentiated lovingness, the moments of guiltily suppressed hatred for the wearisome eternal spouse, the copulatory joys and anguishes, the comings together and the fallings apart, the mysteries of failed orgasms and wilted erections, the intense and terrifyingly singleminded concentration on the growth and proper development of The Child. Their minds poured forth a steady stream of rich yeasty foam and he lapped it all up. Reading their souls was his game, his toy, his religion, his revenge. They never suspected he was doing it. That was one point on which he constantly sought reassurance, anxiously prying for it, and constantly he was reassured: they didn't dream his gift existed. They merely thought he was abnormally intelligent, and never questioned the means by which he learned so much about so many improbable things. Perhaps if they had realized the truth, they would have choked him in his crib. But they had no inkling. He went on comfortably spying, year after year, his perceptions deepening as he came to comprehend more and more of the material his parents unwittingly offered.

He knew that Dr. Hittner—baffled, wholly out of his depth with the strange Selig child—believed it would be better for everyone if David had a sibling. That was the word he used, *sibling*, and David had to fish the meaning out of Hittner's head as though out of a dictionary. Sibling: a brother or a sister. Oh, the treacherous horse-faced bastard! The one thing young David had asked Hittner not to suggest, and naturally he had suggested it. But what else could he have expected? The desirability of siblings had been in Hittner's mind all along, lying there like a grenade. David, picking his mother's mind one night, had found the text of a letter from Hittner. *The only child is an emotionally deprived child. Without the rough-and-tumble interplay with siblings he has no way of learning the best techniques of relating to his peers, and he develops a dangerously burdensome relation with his parents, for whom he becomes a companion instead of a dependent.* Hittner's universal panacea: lots of siblings. As though there are no neurotics in big families.

David was aware of his parents' frantic attempts at filling Hittner's prescription. No time to waste; the boy grows older all the time, siblingless, lacking each day the means of learning the best techniques of relating to his peers. And so, night after night, the poor aging bodies of Paul and Martha Selig grapple with the problem. They force themselves sweatily onward to self-defeating prodigies of lustfulness, and each month the bad news comes in a rush of blood: there will be no sibling this time. But at last the seed takes root. They said nothing about that to him, ashamed, perhaps, to admit to an eight-year-old that such things as sexual intercourse occurred in their lives. But he knew. He knew why his mother's belly was beginning to bulge and why they still hesitated to explain it to him. He knew, too, that his mother's mysterious "appendicitis" attack of July, 1944, was actually a miscarriage. He knew why they both wore tragic faces for months afterward. He knew that Martha's doctor had told her that autumn that it really wasn't wise for her to be having babies at the age of 35, that if they were going to insist on a second child the best course was to adopt one. He knew his father's traumatic response to that suggestion: *What, bring into the household a bastard that some shiksa threw away?* Poor old Paul lay tossing awake every night for weeks, not even confessing to his wife why he was so upset, but unknowingly spilling the whole thing to his nosy son. The insecurities, the irrational hostilities. *Why do I have to raise a stranger's brat, just because this psychiatrist says it'll do David some good? What kind of garbage will I be taking into the house? How can I love this child that isn't mine? How can I tell it that it's a Jew when—who knows?—it may have been made by some Irish mick, some Italian bootblack, some carpenter?* All this the all-perceiving David perceives. Finally the elder Selig voices his misgivings, carefully edited, to his wife, saying, Maybe Hittner's wrong, maybe this is just a phase David's going through and another child isn't the right answer at all. Telling her to consider the expense, the changes they'd have to make in their way of life—they're not young, they've grown settled in their ways, a child at this time of their lives, the getting up at four in the morning, the crying, the diapers. And David silently cheering his father on, because who needs this intruder, this sibling, this enemy of the peace? But Martha tearfully fights back, quoting Hittner's letter, reading key passages out of her extensive library on child psychology, offering damning statistics on the incidence of neurosis, maladjustment, bed-wetting, and homosexuality among only children. The old man yields by Christmas. *Okay, okay, we'll adopt, but let's not take just anything, hear? It's got to be Jewish.* Wintry weeks of touring the adoption agencies, pretending all the while to David that these trips to Manhattan are mere innocuous shopping excursions. He wasn't fooled. How could anyone fool this omniscient child? He had only to look behind their foreheads to know that they were shopping for a sibling. His one comfort was the hope that they would fail to find one. This was still wartime: if you couldn't buy a new car, maybe you couldn't get siblings either. For many weeks that appeared to be the case. Not many babies were available, and those that were seemed to have some grave defect: insufficiently Jewish, or too fragile-looking, or too cranky, or of the wrong sex. Some boys were available but Paul and Martha had decided to get David a little sister. Already that limited things considerably, since people tended not to give girls up for adoption as readily as they did boys, but one snowy night in March David detected an ominous note of satisfaction in the mind of his mother, newly returned from yet another shopping trip, and, looking more closely, he realized that the quest was over. She had found a lovely little girl, four months old. The mother, aged 19, was not only certifiably Jewish but even a college girl, described by the agency as "extremely intelligent." Not so intelligent, evidently, as to avoid being fertilized by a handsome, young air force captain, also Jewish, while he was home on leave in February, 1944. Though he felt remorse over his carelessness he was unwilling to marry the victim of his lusts, and was now on active duty in the Pacific, where, so far as the girl's parents were concerned, he should only be shot down ten times over. They had forced her to give the child out for adoption. David wondered why Martha hadn't brought the baby home with her that very afternoon, but soon he discovered that several weeks of legal formalities lay ahead, and April was well along before his mother finally announced, "Dad and I have a wonderful surprise for you, Duvid."

They named her Judith Hannah Selig, after her adoptive father's recently deceased mother. David hated her instantly. He had been afraid they were going to move her into his bedroom, but no, they set up her crib in their own room; nevertheless, her crying filled the whole apartment night after night, unending raucous wails. It was incredible how much noise she could emit. Paul and Martha spent practically all their time feeding her or playing with her or changing her diapers, and David didn't mind that very much, for it kept them busy and took some of the pressure off him. But he loathed having Judith around. He saw nothing cute about her pudgy limbs and curly hair and dimpled cheeks. Watching her while she was being changed, he found some academic interest in observing her little pink suit, so alien to his experience; but once he had seen it his curiosity was assuaged. *So they have a slit instead of a thing. Okay, but so what?* In general she was an irritating distraction. He couldn't read properly because of the noise she made, and reading was his one pleasure. The apartment was always full of relatives or friends, paying ceremonial visits to the new baby, and their stupid conventional minds flooded the place with blunt thoughts that impinged like mallets on David's vulnerable consciousness. Now and then he tried to read the baby's mind, but there was nothing in it except vague blurry formless globs of cloudy sensation; he had had more rewarding insights reading the minds of dogs and cats. She didn't appear to have any thoughts. All he could pick up were feelings of hunger, of drowsiness, and of dim orgasmic release as she wet her diaper. About ten days after she arrived, he decided to try to kill her telepathically. While his parents were busy elsewhere he went to their room, peered into his sister's bassinet, and concentrated as hard as he could

on draining her unformed mind out of her skull. If only
he could manage somehow to suck the spark of intellect
from her, to draw her consciousness into himself, to
transform her into an empty mindless shell, she would
surely die. He sought to sink his hooks into her soul.
He stared into her eyes and opened his power wide,
taking her entire feeble output and pulling for more.
*Come.... come.... your mind is sliding toward me....
I'm getting it, I'm getting all of it.... zam! I have your
whole mind!* Unmoved by his conjurations, she continued to gurgle and wave her arms about. He stared
more intensely, redoubling the vigor of his concentration. Her smile wavered and vanished. Her brows
puckered into a frown. Did she know he was attacking
her, or was she merely bothered by the faces he was
making? *Come.... come.... your mind is sliding toward
me....*

For a moment he thought he might actually succeed.
But then she shot him a look of frosty malevolence,
incredibly fierce, truly terrifying coming from an infant,
and he backed away, frightened, fearing some sudden
counterattack. An instant later she was gurgling again.
She had defeated him. He went on hating her, but he
never again tried to harm her. She, by the time she was
old enough to know what the concept of hatred meant,
was well aware of how her brother felt about her. And
she hated back. She proved to be a far more efficient
hater than he was. Oh, was she ever an expert at
hating.

TEN.

The subject of this composition is My Very First Acid
Trip.

My first and my last, eight years ago. Actually it
wasn't my trip at all, but Toni's. D-lysergic acid
diethlyamide has never passed through my digestive
tract, if truth be told. What I did was hitchhike on

Toni's trip. In a sense I'm still a hitchhiker on that trip, that very bad trip. Let me tell you.

This happened in the summer of '68. That summer was a bad trip all in itself. Do you remember '68 at all? That was the year we all woke up to the fact that the whole business was coming apart. I mean American society. That pervasive feeling of decay and imminent collapse, so familiar to us all—it really dates from '68, I think. When the world around us became a metaphor for the process of violent entropic increase that had been going on inside our souls—inside my soul, at any rate—for some time.

That summer Lyndon Baines MacBird was in the White House, just barely, serving out his time after his abdication in March. Bobby Kennedy had finally met the bullet with his name on it, and so had Martin Luther King. Neither killing was any surprise; the only surprise was that they had been so long in coming. The blacks were burning down the cities—back then, it was their *own* neighborhoods they burned, remember? Ordinary everyday people were starting to wear freaky clothes to work, bells and body shirts and mini-miniskirts, and hair was getting longer even for those over 25. It was the year of sideburns and Buffalo Bill mustachios. Gene McCarthy, a Senator from—where? Minnesota? Wisconsin?—was quoting poetry at news conferences as part of his attempt to gain the Democratic presidential nomination, but it was a sure bet that the Democrats would give it to Hubert Horatio Humphrey when they got together for their convention in Chicago. (And wasn't that convention a lovely festival of American patriotism?) Over in the other camp Rockefeller was running hard to catch up with Tricky Dick, but everybody knew where that was going to get him. Babies were dying of malnutrition in a place called Biafra, which you don't remember, and the Russians were moving troops into Czechoslovakia in yet another demonstration of socialist brotherhood. In a place called Vietnam, which you probably wish you didn't remember either, we were dumping napalm on everything in sight for the sake of promoting peace and democracy,

and a lieutenant named William Calley had recently
coordinated the liquidation of 100-odd sinister and dangerous old men, women, and children at the town of
Mylai, only we didn't know anything about that yet.
The books everybody was reading were *Couples*, *Myra
Breckinridge*, *The Confessions of Nat Turner*, and *The
Money Game*. I forget that year's movies. *Easy Rider*
hadn't happened yet and *The Graduate* was the year
before. Maybe it was the year of *Rosemary's Baby*. Yes,
that sounds right: 1968 was the devil's year for sure. It
was also the year when a lot of middle-class middle-
aged people started using, self-consciously, terms like
"pot" and "grass" when they meant "marijuana." Some
of them were smoking it as well as talking it. (Me.
Finally turning on at the age of 33.) Let's see, what
else? President Johnson nominated Abe Fortas to re-
place Earl Warren as Chief Justice of the Supreme
Court. Where are you now, Chief Justice Fortas, when
we need you? The Paris peace talks, believe it or not,
had just begun that summer. In later years it came to
seem that the talks had been going on since the beginning of time, as eternal and everlasting as the Grand
Canyon and the Republican Party, but no, they were
invented in 1968. Denny McLain was on his way
toward winning 31 games that season. I guess McLain
was the only human being who found 1968 a worth-
while experience. His team lost the World Series,
though. (No. What am I saying? The Tigers *won*, 4
games to 3. But Mickey Lolich was the star, not McLain.)
That was the sort of year it was. Oh, Christ, I've
forgotten one significant chunk of history. In the spring
of '68 we had the riots at Columbia, with radical
students occupying the campus (*"Kirk Must Go!"*) and
classes being suspended (*"Shut It Down!"*) and final
exams called off and nightly confrontations with the
police, in the course of which a good many undergraduate skulls were laid open and much high-quality blood
leaked into the gutters. How funny it is that I pushed
that event out of my mind, when of all the things I've
listed here it was the only one I actually experienced at
first hand. Standing at Broadway and 116th Street

watching platoons of cold-eyed fuzz go racing toward
Butler Library. ("Fuzz" is what we called policemen
before we started calling them "pigs," which happened
a little later that same year.) Holding my hand aloft in
the forked V-for-Peace gesture and screaming idiotic
slogans with the best of them. Cowering in the lobby of
Furnald Hall as the blue-clad nightstick brigade went
on its rampage. Debating tactics with a ragged-bearded
SDS gauleiter who finally spat in my face and called me
a stinking liberal fink. Watching sweet Barnard girls
ripping open their blouses and waving their bare breasts
at horny, exasperated cops, while simultaneously shrieking
ferocious Anglo-Saxonisms that the Barnard girls of my
own remote era hadn't ever heard. Watching a group of
young shaggy Columbia men ritualistically pissing on a
pile of research documents that had been liberated
from the filing cabinet of some hapless instructor going
for his doctorate. It was then that I knew there could be
no hope for mankind, when even the best of us were
capable of going berserk in the cause of love and peace
and human equality. On those dark nights I looked into
many minds and found only hysteria and madness, and
once, in despair, realizing I was living in a world where
two factions of lunatics were battling for control of the
asylum, I went off to vomit in Riverside Park after a
particularly bloody riot and was caught unawares (me,
caught unawares!) by a lithe 14-year-old black mugger
who smilingly relieved me of $22.

I was living near Columbia in '68, in a seedy residence
hotel on 114th Street, where I had one medium-big
room plus kitchen and bathroom privileges, cock-
roaches at no extra charge. It was the very same place
where I had lived as an undergraduate in my junior and
senior years, 1955–56. The building had been going
downhill even then and was an abominable hellhole
when I came back to it twelve years later—the courtyard was littered with broken hypodermic needles the
way another building's courtyard might be littered with
cigarette butts—but I have an odd way, maybe masoch-
istic, of not letting go of bits of my past however ugly
they may be, and when I needed a place to live I

picked that one. Besides, it was cheap—$14.50 a week—
and I had to be close to the University because of the
work I was doing, researching that Israel book. Are you
still following me? I was telling you about my first acid
trip, which was really Toni's trip.

We had shared our shabby room nearly seven weeks—
a bit of May, all of June, some of July—through thick
and thin, heat waves and rainstorms, misunderstand-
ings and reconciliations, and it had been a happy time,
perhaps the happiest of my life. I loved her and I think
she loved me. I haven't had much love in my life. That
isn't intended as a grab for your pity, just as a simple
statement of fact, objective and cool. The nature of my
condition diminishes my capacity to love and be loved.
A man in my circumstances, wide open to everyone's
innermost thoughts, really isn't going to experience a
great deal of love. He is poor at giving love because he
doesn't much trust his fellow human beings: he knows
too many of their dirty little secrets, and that kills his
feelings for them. Unable to give, he cannot get. His
soul, hardened by isolation and ungivingness, becomes
inaccessible, and so it is not easy for others to love him.
The loop closes upon itself and he is trapped within.
Nevertheless I loved Toni, having taken special care not
to see too deeply into her, and I didn't doubt my love
was returned. What defines love, anyway? We preferred each other's company to the company of anyone
else. We excited one another in every imaginable way.
We never bored each other. Our bodies mirrored our
souls' closeness: I never failed of erection, she never
lacked for lubrication, our couplings carried us both to
ecstasy. I'd call these things the parameters of love.

On the Friday of our seventh week Toni came home
from her office with two small squares of white blotting
paper in her purse. In the center on each square was a
faint blue-green stain. I studied them a moment or two,
without comprehending.

"Acid," she said finally.

"Acid?"

"You know. LSD. Teddy gave them to me."

Teddy was her boss, the editor-in-chief. LSD, yes. I

knew. I had read Huxley on mescaline in 1957. I was fascinated and tempted. For years I had flirted with the psychedelic experience, even once attempting to volunteer for an LSD research program at the Columbia Medical Center. I was too late signing up, though; and then, as the drug became a fad, came all the horror stories of suicides, psychoses, bad trips. Knowing my vulnerabilities, I decided it was the part of wisdom to leave acid to others. Though still I was curious about it. And now these squares of blotting paper sitting in the palm of Toni's hand.

"It's supposed to be dynamite stuff," she said. "Absolutely pure, laboratory quality. Teddy's already tripped on a tab from this batch and he says it's very smooth, very clean, no speed in it or any crap like that. I thought we could spend tomorrow tripping, and sleep it off on Sunday."

"Both of us?"

"Why not?"

"Do you think it's safe for both of us to be out of our minds at the same time?"

She gave me a peculiar look. "Do you think acid drives you out of your mind?"

"I don't know. I've heard a lot of scary stories."

"You've never tripped?"

"No," I said. "Have you?"

"Well, no. But I've watched friends of mine while they were tripping." I felt a pang at this reminder of the life she had led before I met her. "They don't go out of their minds, David. There's a kind of wild high for an hour or so when things sometimes get jumbled up, but basically somebody who's tripping sits there as lucid and as calm as—well, Aldous Huxley. Can you imagine Huxley out of his mind? Gibbering and drooling and smashing furniture?"

"What about the fellow who killed his mother-in-law while he was on acid, though? And the girl who jumped out of a window?"

Toni shrugged. "They were unstable," she said loftily. "Perhaps murder or suicide was where they were really at, and the acid just gave them the push they needed to go and do it. But that doesn't mean you would, or me. Or maybe the doses were too strong, or the stuff was cut with some other drug. Who knows? Those are one-in-a-million cases. I have friends who've tripped fifty, sixty times, and they've never had any trouble." She sounded impatient with me. There was a patronizing, lecturing tone in her voice. Her esteem for me seemed clearly diminished by these old-maid hesitations of mine; we were on the threshold of a real rift. "What's the matter, David? Are you afraid to trip?"

"I think it's unwise for both of us to trip at once, that's all. When we aren't sure where the stuff is going to take us."

"Tripping together is the most loving thing two people can do," she said.

"But it's a risky thing. We just don't know. Look, you can get more acid if you want it, can't you?"

"I suppose so."

"Okay, then. Let's do this thing in an orderly way, one step at a time. There's no hurry. You trip tomorrow and I'll watch. I'll trip on Sunday and you'll watch. If we both like what the acid does to our heads, we can trip together next time. All right, Toni? All right?"

It wasn't all right. I saw her begin to speak, begin to frame some argument, some objection; but also I saw her catch herself, back up, rethink her position, and decide not to make an issue of it. Although I at no time entered her mind, her facial expressions made her sequence of thoughts wholly evident to me. "All right," she said softly. "It isn't worth a hassle."

Saturday morning she skipped breakfast—she'd been told to trip on an empty stomach—and, after I had eaten, we sat for a time in the kitchen with one of the squares of blotting paper lying innocently on the table between us. We pretended it wasn't there. Toni seemed a little clutched; I didn't know whether she was bothered about my insisting that she trip without me or just troubled, here at the brink of it, by the whole idea of tripping. There wasn't much conversation. She filled an ashtray with a great dismal mound of half-smoked cigarettes. From time to time she grinned nervously. From time to time I took her hand and smiled encouragingly. During this touching scene various of the tenants with whom we shared the kitchen on this floor of the hotel drifted in and out. First Eloise, the sleek black hooker. Then Miss Theotokis, the grim-faced nurse who worked at St. Luke's. Mr. Wong, the mysterious little roly-poly Chinese who always walked around in his underwear. Aitken, the scholarly fag from Toledo, and his cadaverous mainlining roommate, Donaldson. A couple of them nodded to us but no one actually said anything, not even "Good morning." In this place it was proper to behave as though your neighbors were invisible. The fine old New York tradition. About half past ten in the morning Toni said, "Get me some orange juice, will you?" I poured a glass from the container in the refrigerator that was labeled with my name. Giving me a wink and a broad toothy smile, all false bravado, she wadded up the blotting paper and pushed it into her mouth, bolting it and gulping the orange juice as a chaser.

"How long will it take to hit?" I asked.

"About an hour and a half," she said.

In fact it was more like fifty minutes. We were back in our own room, the door locked, faint scratchy sounds of Bach coming from the portable phonograph. I was trying to read, and so was Toni; the pages weren't turning very fast. She looked up suddenly and said, "I'm starting to feel a little funny."

"Funny how?"

"Dizzy. A slight touch of nausea. There's a prickling at the back of my neck."

"Can I get you anything? Glass of water? Juice?"

"Nothing, thanks. I'm fine. Really I am." A smile, timid but genuine. She seemed a little apprehensive but not at all frightened. Eager for the voyage. I put down my book and watched her vigilantly, feeling protective, almost wishing that I'd have some occasion to be of service to her. I didn't want her to have a bad trip but I wanted her to need me.

She gave me bulletins on the progress of the acid through her nervous system. I took notes until she indicated that the scratching of pencil against paper was distracting her. Visual effects were beginning. The walls looked a trifle concave to her, and the flaws in the plaster were taking on extraordinary texture and complexity. The color of everything was unnaturally bright. The shafts of sunlight coming through the dirty window were prismatic, shattering and spewing pieces of the spectrum over the floor. The music—I had a stack of her favorite records on the changer—had acquired a curious new intensity; she was having difficulty following melodic lines, and it seemed to her that the turntable kept stopping and starting, but the sound itself, as sound, had some indescribable quality of density and tangibility that fascinated her. There was a whistling sound in her ears, too, as of air rushing past her cheeks. She spoke of a pervading sense of strangeness—"I'm on some other planet," she said twice. She looked flushed, excited, happy. Remembering the terrible tales I had heard of acid-induced descents into hell, harrowing accounts of grueling bummers lovingly recounted for the delight of the millions by the diligent anonymous journalists of *Time* and *Life*, I nearly wept in relief at this evidence that my Toni would come through her journey unscathed. I had feared the worst. But she was making out all right. Her eyes were closed, her face was serene and exultant, her breathing was deep and relaxed. Lost in transcendental realms of mystery was my Toni. She was barely speaking to me now, breaking her silences only every few minutes to murmur something indistinct and oblique. Half an hour had passed since she first had reported strange sensations. As she drifted deeper into her trip, my love for her grew deeper also. Her ability to cope with acid was proof of the basic toughness of her personality, and that delighted me. I admire capable women. Already I was planning my own trip for the next day—selecting the musical accompaniment, trying to imagine the sort of interesting distortions of reality I'd experience, looking forward to comparing notes with Toni afterward. I was regretting the cowardice that had deprived me of the pleasure of tripping with Toni this day.

But what is this, now? What's happening to my head? Why this sudden feeling of suffocation? The pounding in my chest? The dryness in my throat? The walls are flexing; the air seems close and heavy; my right arm is suddenly a foot longer than the left one. These are effects Toni had noticed and described a little while ago. Why do I feel them now? I tremble. Muscles leap about of their own accord in my thighs. Is this what they call a contact high? Merely being so close to Toni while she trips—did she breathe particles of LSD at me, have I inadvertently turned on through some contagion of the atmosphere?

"My dear Selig," says my armchair smugly, "how can you be so foolish? Obviously you're picking these phenomena right out of her mind!"

Obviously? Is it so obvious? I consider the possibility. Am I reading Toni without knowing it? Apparently I am. In the past some effort of concentration, however slight, has always been necessary in order for me to manage a fine-focus peep into another head. But it seems that the acid must intensify her outputs and bring them to me unsolicited. What other explanation can there be? She is broadcasting her trip; and somehow I have tuned to her wavelength, despite all my noble resolutions about respecting her privacy. And now the acid's strangenesses, spreading across the gap between us, infect me as well.

Shall I get out of her mind?

The acid effects distract me. I look at Toni and she seems transformed. A small dark mole on her lower cheek, near the corner of her mouth, flashes a vortex of blazing color: red, blue, violet, green. Her lips are too full, her mouth too wide. All those teeth. Row upon row upon row, like a shark. Why have I never noticed that predatory mouth before? She frightens me. Her neck elongates; her body compresses; her breasts move about like restless cats beneath her familiar red sweater, which itself has taken on an ominous, threatening purplish tinge. To escape her I glance toward the window. A pattern of cracks that I have never been aware of before runs through the soiled panes. In a moment, surely, the shattered window will implode and shower us with fiery fragments of glass. The building across the street is unnaturally squat today. There is menace in its altered form. The ceiling is coming toward me, too. I hear muffled drumbeats overhead—the footsteps of my upstairs neighbor, I tell myself—and I imagine cannibals preparing their dinner. Is this what tripping is like? Is this what the young of our nation have been doing to themselves, voluntarily, even eagerly, for the sake of amusement?

I should turn this off, before it freaks me altogether. I want out.

Well, easily done. I have my ways of stopping down the inputs, of blocking the flow. Only they don't work this time. I am helpless before the power of the acid. I try to shut myself away from these unfamiliar and unsettling sensations, and they march onward into me all the same. I am wide open to everything emanating from Toni. I am caught up in it. I go deeper and deeper. This is a trip. This is a bad trip. This is a very bad trip. How odd: Toni was having a good trip, wasn't she? So it seemed to one outside observer. Then why do I, accidentally hitchhiking on her trip, find myself having a bad one?

Whatever is in Toni's mind floods into mine. Receiving another's soul is no new experience for me, but this is a transfer such as I have never had before, for the information, modulated by the drug, comes to me in ghastly distortions. I am an unwilling spectator in Toni's soul, and what I see is a feast of demons. Can such darkness really live within her? I saw nothing like this those other two times: has the acid released some level of nightmare not accessible to me before? Her past is on parade. Gaudy images, bathed in a lurid light. Lovers. Copulations. Abominations. A torrent of menstrual blood, or is that scarlet river something more sinister? Here is a clot of pain: what is that, cruelty to others, cruelty to self? And look how she gives herself to that army of monstrous men! They advance mechanically, a thundering legion. Their rigid cocks blaze with a terrible red light. One by one they plunge into her, and

I see the light streaming from her loins as they plow
her. Their faces are masks. I know none of them. Why
am I not on line too? Where am I? Where am I? Ah,
there: off to one side, insignificant, irrelevant. Is that
thing me? Is that how she really sees me? A hairy
vampire bat, a crouching huddled bloodsucker? Or is
that merely David Selig's own image of David Selig,
bouncing between us like the reflections in a barber
shop's parallel mirrors? God help me, am I laying my
own bad trip on her, then reading it back from her and
blaming her for harboring nightmares not of her own
making?

How can I break this link?

I stumble to my feet. Staggering, splay-footed, nauseated. The room whirls. Where is the door? The
doorknob retreats from me. I lunge for it.

"David?" Her voice reverberates unendingly. "David
David David David David David—"

"Some fresh air," I mutter. "Just stepping outside a
minute—"

It does no good. The nightmare images pursue me
through the door. I lean against the sweating wall,
clinging to a flickering sconce. The Chinaman drifts by
me as though a ghost. Far away I hear the telephone
ringing. The refrigerator door slams, and slams again,
and slams again, and the Chinaman goes by me a
second time from the same direction, and the doorknob
retreats from me, as the universe folds back upon itself,
locking me into a looped moment. Entropy decreases.
The green wall sweats green blood. A voice like thistles
says, "Selig? Is something wrong?" It's Donaldson, the
junkie. His face is a skull's face. His hand on my
shoulder is all bones. "Are you sick?" he asks. I shake
my head. He leans toward me until his empty eye-
sockets are inches from my face, and studies me a long
moment. He says, "You're *tripping*, man! Isn't that
right? Listen, if you're freaking out, come on down the
hall, we've got some stuff that might help you."

"No. No problem."

I go lurching into my room. The door, suddenly
flexible, will not close; I push it with both hands,

holding it in place until the latch clicks. Toni is sitting where I left her. She looks baffled. Her face is a monstrous thing, pure Picasso; I turn away from her, dismayed.

"David?"

Her voice is cracked and harsh, and seems to be pitched in two octaves at once, with a filling of scratchy wool between the top tone and the bottom. I wave my hands frantically, trying to get her to stop talking, but she goes on, expressing concern for me, wanting to know what's happening, why I've been running in and out of the room. Every sound she makes is torment for me. Nor do the images cease to flow from her mind to mine. That shaggy toothy bat, wearing my face, still glowers in a corner of her skull. Toni, I thought you loved me. Toni, I thought I made you happy. I drop to my knees and explore the dirt-encrusted carpet, a million years old, a faded thinning threadbare piece of the Pleistocene. She comes to me, bending down solicitously, she who is tripping looking after the welfare of her untripping companion, who mysteriously is tripping also. "I don't understand," she whispers. "You're crying, David. Your face is all blotchy. Did I say something wrong? Please don't carry on, David. I was having such a good trip, and now—I just don't understand—"

The bat. The bat. Spreading its rubbery wings. Baring its yellow fangs.

Biting. Sucking. Drinking.

I choke a few words out: "I'm—tripping—too—"

My face pushed against the carpet. The smell of dust in my dry nostrils. Trilobites crawling through my brain. A bat crawling through hers. Shrill laughter in the hallway. The telephone. The refrigerator door: slam, slam, slam! The cannibals dancing upstairs. The ceiling pressing against my back. My hungry mind looting Toni's soul. He who peeps through a hole may see what will vex him. Toni says, "You took the other acid? When?"

"I didn't."

"Then how can you be tripping?"

I make no reply. I crouch, I huddle, I sweat, I moan.

This is the descent into hell. Huxley warned me. I didn't want Toni's trip. I didn't ask to see any of this. My defenses are destroyed now. She overwhelms me. She engulfs me.

Toni says, "Are you reading my mind, David?"

"Yes." The miserable ultimate confession. "I'm reading your mind."

"What did you say?"

"I said I'm reading your mind. I can see every thought. Every experience. I see myself the way you see me. Oh, Christ, Toni, Toni, Toni, it's so awful!"

She tugs at me and tries to pull me up to look at her. Finally I rise. Her face is horribly pale; her eyes are rigid. She asks for clarifications. What's this about reading minds? Did I really say it, or is it something her acid-blurred mind invented? I really said it, I tell her. You asked me if I was reading your mind and I said yes, I was.

"I never asked any such thing," she says.

"I heard you ask it."

"But I didn't—" Trembling, now. Both of us. Her voice is bleak. "You're trying to bum-trip me, aren't you, David? I don't understand. Why would you want to hurt me? Why are you messing me up? It was a good trip. *It was a good trip.*"

"Not for me," I say.

"You weren't tripping."

"But I was."

She gives me a look of total incomprehension and pulls away from me and throws herself on the bed, sobbing. Out of her mind, cutting through the grotesqueries of the acid images, comes a blast of raw emotion: fear, resentment, pain, anger. She thinks I've deliberately tried to injure her. Nothing I can say now will repair things. Nothing can ever repair things. She despises me. I am a vampire to her, a bloodsucker, a leech; she knows my gift for what it is. We have crossed some fatal threshold and she will never again think of me without anguish and shame. Nor I her. I rush from the room, down the hall to the room shared by Donaldson

and Aitken. "Bad trip," I mutter. "Sorry to trouble you,
but—"

* * *

I stayed with them the rest of the afternoon. They
gave me a tranquilizer and brought me gently through
the downslope of the trip. The psychedelic images
still came to me out of Toni for half an hour or so, as
though an inexorable umbilical chain linked us across
all the length of the hallway; but then to my relief the
sense of contact began to slip and fade, and suddenly,
with a kind of audible click at the moment of severance, it was gone altogether. The flamboyant phan-
toms ceased to vex my soul. Color and dimension and
texture returned to their proper states. And at last I
was free from that merciless reflected self-image. Once
I was fully alone in my own skull again I felt like
weeping to celebrate my deliverance, but no tears
would come, and I sat passively, sipping a Bromo-
Seltzer. Time trickled away. Donaldson and Aitken
and I talked in a peaceful, civilized, burned-out way
about Bach, medieval art, Richard M. Nixon, pot, and
a great many other things. I hardly knew these two,
yet they were willing to surrender their time to ease a
stranger's pain. Eventually I felt better. Shortly before
six o'clock, thanking them gravely, I went back to my
room. Toni was not there. The place seemed oddly
altered. Books were gone from the shelves, prints
from the walls; the closet door stood open and half the
things in it were missing. In my befuddled, fatigued
state it took me a moment or two to grasp what had
happened. At first I imagined burglary, abduction, but
then I saw the truth. She had moved out.

Eleven.

Today there is a hint of encroaching winter in the air: it takes tentative nips at the cheeks. October is dying too quickly. The sky is mottled and unhealthy-looking, cluttered by sad, heavy, low-hanging clouds. Yesterday it rained, skinning yellow leaves from the trees, and now they lie pasted to the pavement of College Walk, their tips fluttering raggedly in the harsh breeze. There are puddles everywhere. As I settled down beside Alma Mater's massive green form I primly spread newspaper sheets, selected portions of today's issue of *The Columbia Daily Spectator*, over the cold damp stone steps. Twenty-odd years ago, when I was a foolishly ambitious sophomore dreaming of a career in journalism—how sly, a reporter who reads minds!—*Spec* seemed central to my life; now it serves only for keeping my rump dry.

Here I sit. Office hours. On my knees rests a thick manila folder, held closed by a ballsy big rubber band. Within, neatly typed, each with its own coppery paperclip, are five term papers, the products of my busy week. *The Novels of Kafka. Shaw as Tragedian. The Concept of Synthetic A Priori Statements. Odysseus as a Symbol of Society. Aeschylus and the Aristotelian Tragedy.* The old academic bullshit, confirmed in its hopeless fecality by the cheerful willingness of these bright young men to let an old grad turn the stuff out for them. This is the day appointed for delivering the goods and, perhaps, picking up some new assignments. Five minutes to eleven. My clients will be arriving soon. Meanwhile I scan the passing parade. Students hurrying by, clutching mounds of books. Hair rippling in the wind, breasts bobbling. They all look frighteningly young to me, even the bearded ones. Especially the bearded ones. Do you realize that each year there are more and more young

52

people in the world? Their tribe ever increases as the old farts drop off the nether end of the curve and I shuttle graveward. Even the professors look young to me these days. There are people with doctorates who are fifteen years younger than I am. Isn't that a killer? Imagine a kid born in 1950 who has a doctorate already. In 1950 I was shaving three times a week, and masturbating every Wednesday and Saturday; I was a hearty pubescent *bulyak* five feet nine inches tall, with ambitions and griefs and knowledge, with an identity. In 1950 today's newly fledged Ph.D.'s were toothless infants just squirting from the womb, their faces puckered, their skins sticky with amniotic juices. How can those infants have doctorates so soon? Those infants have lapped me as I plod along the track.

I find my own company wearisome when I descend into self-pity. To divert myself I try to touch the minds of passers-by and learn what I can learn. Playing my old game, my only game. Selig the voyeur, the soul-vampire, ripping off the intimacies of innocent strangers to cheer his chilly heart. But no: my head is full of cotton today. Only muffled murmurs come to me, indistinct, content-free. No discrete words, no flashes of identity, no visions of soul's essence. This is one of the bad days. All inputs converge into unintelligibility; each bit of information is identical to all others. It is the triumph of entropy. I am reminded of Forster's Mrs. Moore, listening tensely for revelation in the echoing Marabar caves, and hearing only the same monotonous noise, the same meaningless all-dissolving sound: *Boum*. The sum and essence of mankind's earnest strivings: *Boum*. The minds flashing past me on College Walk now give me only: *Boum*. Perhaps it is all I deserve. Love, fear, faith, churlishness, hunger, self-satisfaction, every species of interior monolog, all come to me with identical content. *Boum*. I must work to correct this. It is not too late to wage war against entropy. Gradually, sweating, struggling, scrabbling for solid purchase, I widen the aperture, coaxing my perceptions to function. Yes. Yes. Come back to life. Get it up, you miserable spy!

Give me my fix! Within me the power stirs. The inner
murk clears a bit; stray scraps of isolated but coherent
thought find their way into me. *Neurotic but not
altogether psycho yet. Going to see the department
head and tell him to shove it up. Tickets for the opera,
but I have to. Fucking is fun, fucking is very important, but there's more. Like standing on a very high
diving board about to take a plunge.* This scratchy
chaotic chatter tells me nothing except that the power
is not yet dead, and I take comfort enough in that. I
visualize the power as a sort of worm wrapped around
my cerebrum, a poor tired worm, wrinkled and shrunk-
en, its once-glossy skin now ulcerous with shabby,
flaking patches. That is a relatively recent image, but
even in happier days I always thought of the gift as
something apart from myself, something intrusive. An
inhabitant. It and me, me and it. I used to discuss
such things with Nyquist. (Has he entered these exha-
lations yet? Perhaps not. A person I once knew, a
certain Tom Myquist, a former friend of mine. Who
carried a somewhat similar intruder within his skull.)
Nyquist didn't like my outlook. "That's schizoid, man,
setting up a duality like that. Your power is you. You
are your power. Why try to alienate yourself from
your own brain?" Probably Nyquist was right, but it's
much too late. It and me is how it will be, till death
do us part.

Here is my client, the bulky halfback, Paul F.
Bruno. His face is swollen and purple, and he is
unsmiling, as though Saturday's heroics have cost him
some teeth. I flip the rubber band down, extract *The
Novels of Kafka*, and offer the paper to him. "Six
pages," I say. He has given me a ten-dollar advance.
"You owe me another eleven bucks. Do you want to
read it first?"

"How good is it?"

"You won't be sorry."

"I'll take your word for it." He manages a painful,
close-mouthed grin. Pulling forth his thick wallet, he
crosses my palm with greenbacks. I slip quickly into
his mind, just for the hell of it now that my power is

working again, a fast psychic rip-off, and pick up the
surface levels: loose teeth at the football game, a
sweet compensatory blow-job at the frat house Saturday night, vague plans for getting laid after next
Saturday's game, etc., etc. Concerning the present
transaction I detect guilt, embarrassment, even some
annoyance with me for having helped him. Oh, well:
the gratitude of the *goy*. I pocket his money. He favors
me with a curt nod and tucks *The Novels of Kafka*
under his immense forearm. Hastily, in shame, he
goes hustling down the steps and off in the direction
of Hamilton Hall. I watch his broad retreating back. A
sudden gust of malevolent wind, rising off the Hudson,
comes knifing eastward and cuts me bone-deep.

Bruna has paused at the sundial, where a slender
black student close to seven feet tall has intercepted
him. A basketball player, obviously. The black wears a
blue varsity jacket, green sneakers, and tight tubular
yellow slacks. His legs alone seem five feet long. He
and Bruno talk for a moment. Bruno points toward
me. The black nods. I am about to gain a new client, I
realize. Bruno vanishes and the black trots springlegged
across the walk, up the steps. He is very dark, almost
purple-skinned, yet his features have a Caucasian
sharpness, fierce cheekbones, proud aquiline nose,
thin frosty lips. He is formidably handsome, some
kind of walking statuary, some sort of idol. Perhaps his
genes are not Negroid at all: an Ethiopan, maybe,
some tribesman of the Nile bulrushes? Yet he wears
his midnight mass of kinky hair in a vast aggressive
Afro halo a foot in diameter or more, fastidiously
trimmed. I would not have been surprised by scarified
cheeks, a bone through the nostrils. As he nears me,
my mind, barely slit-wide, picks up peripheral generalized emanations of his personality. Everything is
predictable, even stereotyped: I expect him to be
touchy, cocky, defensive, hostile, and what comes to
me is a bouillabaisse of ferocious racial pride, overwhelming physical self-satisfaction, explosive mistrust
of others—especially whites. All right. Familiar
patterns.

His elongated shadow falls suddenly upon me as the sun momentarily pierces the clouds. He sways bouncily on the balls of his feet. "Your name Selig?" he asks. I nod. "Yahya Lumumba," he says.

"Pardon me?"

"*Yahya Lumumba.*" His eyes, glossy white against glossy purple, blaze with fury. From the impatience of his tone I realize that he is telling me his name, or at least the name he prefers to use. His tone indicates also that he assumes it's a name everyone on this campus will recognize. Well, what would I know of college basketball stars? He could throw the ball through the hoop fifty times a game and I'd still not have heard of him. He says, "I hear you do term papers, man."

"That's right."

"You got a good recommend from my pal Bruno there. How much you charge?"

"$3.50 a page. Typed, double-spaced."

He considers it. He shows many teeth and says, "What kind of fucking rip-off is that?"

"It's how I earn my living, Mr. Lumumba." I hate myself for that toadying, cowardly *mister.* "That's about $20 for an average-length paper. A decent job takes a fair amount of time, right?"

"Yeah. Yeah." An elaborate shrug. "Okay, I'm not hassling you, man. I got need for your work. You know anything about Europydes?"

"Euripides?"

"That's what I said." He's baiting me, coming on with exaggerated black mannerisms, talking watermelon-nigger at me with his *Europydes.* "That Greek cat who wrote plays."

"I know who you mean. What sort of paper do you need, Mr. Lumumba?"

He pulls a scrap of a notebook sheet from a breast pocket and makes a great show of consulting it. "The prof he want us to compare the 'Electra' theme in Europydes, Sophocles, and Eesk—Aysk—"

"Aeschylus?"

"Him, yeah. Five to ten pages. It due by November 10. Can you swing it?"

"I think so," I say, reaching for my pen. "It shouldn't be any trouble at all," especially since there resides in my files a paper of my own, vintage 1952, covering this very same hoary old humanities theme. "I'll need some information about you for the heading. Exact spelling of your name, the name of your professor, the course number—" He starts to tell me these things. As I jot them down, I simultaneously open the aperture of my mind for my customary scan of the client's interior, to give me some idea of the proper tone to use in the paper. Will I be able to do a convincing job of faking the kind of essay Yahya Lumumba is like to turn in? It will be a taxing technical challenge if I have to write in black hipster jargon, coming on all cool and jazzy and snotty, every line laughing in the ofay prof's fat face. I imagine I could do it: but does Lumumba want me to? Will he think I'm mocking *him* if I adopt the jiveass style and seem to be putting him on as he might put on the prof? I must know these things. So I slip my snaky tendrils past his woolly scalp into the hidden gray jelly. Hello, big black man. Entering, I pick up a somewhat more immediate and vivid version of the generalized persona he constantly projects: the hyped-up black pride, the mistrust of the paleface stranger, the chuckling enjoyment of his own lean long-legged muscular frame. But these are mere residual attitudes, the standard furniture of his mind. I have not yet reached the level of this-minute thought. I have not penetrated to the essential Yahya Lumumba, the unique individual whose style I must assume. I push deeper. As I sink in, I sense a distinct warming of the psychic temperature, an outflow of heat, comparable perhaps to what a miner might experience five miles down, tunneling toward the magmatic fires at the earth's core. This man Lumumba is constantly boiling within, I realize. The glow from his tumultuous soul warns me to be careful, but I have not yet gained the information I seek, and so I go onward, until abruptly the molten frenzy of his stream of consciousness hits me with terrible force. *Fucking Jew*

*bigbrain shithead Christ how I hate the little bald
mother conning me three-fifty a page I ought to jew
him down I ought to bust his teeth the exploiter the
oppressor he wouldn't charge a Jew that much I bet
special price for niggers sure well I ought to jew him
down that's a good one jew him down I ought to bust
his teeth pick him up throw him into the trash what if I
wrote the fucking paper myself show him but I can't
shit I can't that's the whole fucking trouble mom I can't
Europydes Sophocles Eeskilus who knows shit about
them I got other stuff on my mind the Rutgers game
one-on-one down the court gimme the ball you dumb
prick that's it and it's up and in for Lumumba! and wait
folks he was fouled in the act of shooting now he goes to
the line big confident easy six feet ten inches tall holder
of every Columbia scoring record bounces the ball once
twice up, swish! Lumumba on his way to another big
evening tonight folks Europydes Sophocles Eeskilus why
the fuck do I have to know anything about them write
anything about them what good is it to a black man
those old dead Greek fuckers how are they relevant to
the black experience relevant relevant relevant not to
me just to the Jews shit what do any of them know four
hundred years of slavery we got other stuff on our
minds what do any of them know especially this shithead
mother here I got to pay him twenty bucks to do
something I'm not good enough to do for myself who
says I have to what good is any of it why why why why*

A roaring furnace. The heat is overwhelming. I've
been in contact with intense minds before, far more
intense even than this one, but that was when I was
younger, stronger, more resilient. I can't handle this
volcanic blast. The force of his contempt for me is
magnified factorially by the force of the self-contempt
that needing my services makes him feel. He is a pillar
of hatred. And my poor enfeebled power can't take it.
Some sort of automatic safety device cuts in to protect
me from an overload: the mental receptors shut themselves down. This is a new experience for me, a strange
one, this load-shedding phenomenon. It is as though
limbs are dropping off, ears, balls, anything disposable,
leaving nothing but a smooth torso. The inputs fall

away, the mind of Yahya Lumumba retreats and is inaccessible to me, and I find myself involuntarily reversing the process of penetration until I can feel only his most superficial emanations, then not even those, only a gray furry exudation marking the mere presence of him alongside me. All is indistinct. All is muffled. *Boum.* We are back to that again. There is a ringing in my ears: it is an artifact of the sudden silence, a silence loud as thunder. A new stage on my downward path. Never have I lost my grip and slipped from a mind like this. I look up, dazed, shattered. Yahya Lumumba's thin lips are tightly compressed; he stares down at me in distaste, having no inkling of what has occurred. I say faintly, "I'd like ten dollars now in advance. The rest you pay when I deliver the paper." He tells me coldly that he has no money to give me today. His next check from the scholarship fund isn't due until the beginning of the coming month. I'll just have to do the job on faith, he says. Take it or leave it, man. "Can you manage five?" I ask. "As a binder. Faith isn't enough. I have expenses." He glares. He draws himself to his full height; he seems nine or ten feet tall. Without a word he takes a five-dollar bill from his wallet, crumples it, scornfully tosses it into my lap. "I'll see you here the morning of November 9," I call after him, as he stalks away. Europydes, Sophocles, Eeskilus. I sit stunned, shivering, listening to the bellowing silence. *Boum. Boum. Boum.*

TWELVE.

In his more flamboyantly Dostoevskian moments, David Selig liked to think of his power as a curse, a savage penalty for some unimaginable sin. The mark of Cain, perhaps. Certainly his special ability had caused a lot of trouble for him, but in his saner moments he knew that calling it a curse was sheer self-indulgent melodramatic bullshit. The power was a divine gift. The

power brought ecstasy. Without the power he was
nothing, a schmendrick; with it he was a god. Is that a
curse? Is that so terrible? Something funny happens
when gamete meets gamete, and destiny cries, Here,
Selig-baby: be a god! This you would spurn? Sophocles,
age 88 or so, was heard to express his great relief at
having outlived the pressures of the physical passions. I
am freed at last from a tyrannical master, said the wise
and happy Sophocles. Can we then assume that Sophocles,
had Zeus given him a chance retroactively to alter the
entire course of his days, would have opted for lifelong
impotence? Don't kid yourself, Duvid: no matter how
badly the telepathy stuff fucked you up, and it fucked
you up pretty badly, you wouldn't have done without it
for a minute. Because the power brought ecstasy.

The power brought ecstasy. That's the whole megil-
lah in a single crisp phrase. Mortals are born into a vale
of tears and they get their kicks wherever they can.
Some, seeking pleasure, are compelled to turn to sex,
drugs, booze, television, movies, pinochle, the stock
market, the racetrack, the roulette wheel, whips and
chains, collecting first editions, Caribbean cruises, Chinese snuff bottles, Anglo-Saxon poetry, rubber garments,
professional football games, whatever. Not him, not the
accursed David Selig. All he had to do was sit quietly
with his apparatus wide open and drink in the thought-
waves drifting on the telepathic breeze. With the greatest
of ease he lived a hundred vicarious lives. He heaped
his treasurehouse with the plunder of a thousand souls.
Ecstasy. Of course, the ecstatic part was all quite some
time ago.

The best years were those between the ages of
fourteen and twenty-five. Younger, and he was still too
naive, too unformed, to wring much appreciation from
the data he took in. Older, and his growing bitterness,
his sour sense of isolation, damped his capacity for joy.
Fourteen to twenty-five, though. The golden years. Ah!

It was so very much more vivid then. Life was like a
waking dream. There were no walls in his world; he
could go anywhere and see anything. The intense flavor
of existence. Steeped in the rich juices of perception.

Not until Selig was past forty did he realize how much he had lost, over the years, in the way of fine focus and depth of field. The power had not begun detectibly to dim until he was well along in his thirties, but it obviously must have been fading by easy stages all through his manhood, dwindling so gradually that he remained unaware of the cumulative loss. The change had been absolute, qualitative rather than quantitative. Even on a good day, now, the inputs did not begin to approach the intensity of those he remembered from his adolescence. In those remote years the power had brought him not only bits of subcranial conversation and scattered snatches of soul, as now, but also a gaudy universe of colors, textures, scents, densities: the world through an infinity of other sensory intakes, the world captured and played out for his delight on the glassy radiant spherical screen within his mind.

* * *

For instance. He lies propped against an itchy August haystack in a hot Brueghelesque landscape, shortly past noon. This is 1950 and he hangs becalmed midway between his fifteenth birthday and his sixteenth. Some sound effects, Maestro: Beethoven's Sixth, bubbling up gently, sweet flutes and playful piccolos. The sun dangles in a cloudless sky. A gentle wind stirs the willows bordering the cornfield. The young corn trembles. The brook burbles. A starling circles overhead. He hears crickets. He hears the drone of a mosquito, and watches calmly as it zeroes in on his bare, hairless, sweat-shiny chest. His feet are bare too; he wears only tight, faded blue jeans. City boy, digging the country.

The farm is in the Catskills, twelve miles north of Ellenville. It is owned by the Schieles, a tribe of tawny Teutons, who produce eggs and an assortment of vegetable crops and who supplement their earnings every summer by renting out their guest house to some family of urban Yids looking for rural solace. This year the tenants are Sam and Annette Stein of Brooklyn, New York, and their daughter Barbara. The Steins have invited their close friends, Paul and Martha Selig, to spend a week on the farm with their son David and their daughter Judith. (Sam Stein and Paul Selig are hatching a scheme, destined ultimately to empty their bank accounts and destroy the friendship between the two families, to enter into a partnership and act as jobbers for replacement parts for television sets. Paul Selig is forever attempting unwise business ventures.) Today is the third day of the visit, and this afternoon, mysteriously, David finds himself utterly alone. His father has gone on an all-day hike with Sam Stein: in the serenity of the nearby hills they will plot the details of their commercial coup. Their wives have driven off, taking five-year-old Judith with them, to explore the antique shops of Ellenville. No one remains on the premises except the tightlipped Schieles, going somberly about their unending chores, and sixteen-year-old Barbara Stein, who has been David's classmate from the third grade on through high school. Willy-nilly, David and Barbara are thrown together for the day. The Steins and the Seligs evidently have some unvoiced hope that romance will blossom between their offspring. This is naive of them. Barbara, a lush and reasonably beautiful dark-haired girl, sleek-skinned and long-legged, sophisticated and smooth of manner, is six months older than David chronologically, and three or four years ahead of him in social development. She does not actually dislike him, but she regards him as strange, disturbing, alien, and repellent. She has no knowledge of his special gift—no one does; he's seen to that—but she's had seven years to observe him at close range, and she knows there's something fishy about him. She is a conventional girl, plainly destined to marry early (a doctor, a lawyer, an insurance broker) and have lots of babies, and the chances of romance flowering between her and anyone as dark-souled and odd as David Selig are slight. David knows this very well and he is not at all surprised, or even dismayed, when Barbara slips away in mid-morning. "If anyone asks," she says, "tell them I went for a stroll in the woods." She carries a paperback poetry anthology. David is not deceived by

it. He knows she goes off to screw 19-year-old Hans
Schiele at every chance she gets.

So he is left to his own resources. No matter. He has
ways of entertaining himself. He wanders the farm for a
while, peering at the hen-coop and the combine, and
then settles down in a quiet corner of the fields. Time
for mind-movies. Lazily he casts his net. The power
rises and goes forth, looking for emanations. What shall
I read, what shall I read? Ah. A sense of contact. His
questing mind has snared another mind, a buzzing one,
small, dim, intense. It is a bee's mind, in fact: David is
not limited only to contact with humans. Of course
there are no verbal outputs from the bee, nor any
conceptual ones. If the bee thinks at all, David is
incapable of detecting those thoughts. But he does get
into the bee's head. He experiences a strong sense of
what it is like to be tiny and compact and winged and
fuzzy. How *dry* the universe of a bee is: bloodless,
desiccated, arid. He soars. He swoops. He evades a
passing bird, as monstrous as a winged elephant. He
burrows deep into a steamy, pollen-laden blossom. He
goes aloft again. He sees the world through the bee's
faceted eyes. Everything breaks into a thousand fragments, as though seen through a cracked glass; the
essential color of everything is gray, but odd hues lurk
at the corners of things, peripheral blues and scarlets
that do not correspond in any way to the colors he
knows. The effect, he might have said twenty years
later, is an extremely trippy one. But the mind of a bee
is a limited one. David bores easily. He abandons the
insect abruptly and, zooming his perceptions barnward,
clicks into the soul of a hen. She is laying an egg!
Rhythmic internal contractions, pleasurable and painful, like the voiding of a mighty turd. Frenzied squawks.
The smarmy hen-coop odor, sharp and biting. A sense
of too much straw all about. The world looks dark and
dull to this bird. *Heave. Heave.* Oooh! Orgasmic excitement! The egg slides through the hatch and lands
safely. The hen subsides, fulfilled, exhausted. David
departs from her in this moment of rapture. He plunges
deep into the adjoining woods, finds a human mind,

enters it. How much richer and more intense it is to make communion with his own species. His identity blurs into that of his communicant who is Barbara Stein, who is getting laid by Hans Schiele. She is naked and lying on a carpet of last year's fallen leaves. Her legs are spread and her eyes are closed. Her skin is damp with sweat. Hans' fingers dig into the soft flesh of her shoulders and his cheek, rough with blond stubble, abrades her cheek. His weight presses down on her chest, flattening her breasts and emptying her lungs. With steady thrusts and unvarying tempo he penetrates her, and as his long stiff member slowly and patiently rams into her again and again, throbbing sensation spreads in eddying ripples outward from her loins, growing less intense with distance. Through her mind David observes the impact of the hard penis against the tender, slippery internal membranes. He picks up her clamorous heartbeat. He notices her hammering her heels against the calves of Hans' legs. He is aware of the slickness of her own fluids on her buttocks and thighs. And now he senses the first dizzying spasms of orgasm. David struggles to remain with her, but he knows he won't succeed; clinging to the consciousness of someone who's coming is like trying to ride a wild horse. Her pelvis bucks and heaves, her fingernails desperately rake her lover's back, her head twists to one side, she gulps for air, and, as she erupts with pleasure, she catapults David from her unsaddled mind. He travels only a short way, into the stolid soul of Hans Schiele, who unknowingly grants the virgin voyeur a few instants of knowledge of what it is like to be stoking the furnace of Barbara Stein, thrust and thrust and thrust and thrust, her inner muscles clamping fiercely against the swollen prod, and then, almost immediately, comes the tickle of Hans' onrushing climax. Hungry for information, David holds on with all his strength, hoping to keep contact right through the tumult of fulfillment, but no, he is flipped free, he tumbles uncontrollably, the world goes swinging past him in giddy streaks of color, until—click!—he finds a new sanctuary. All is calm here. He glides through a dark cold environment.

He has no weight; his body is long and slender and agile; his mind is nearly a void, but through it run faint chilly flickering perceptions of a low order. He has entered the consciousness of a fish, perhaps a brook trout. Downstream he moves in the swiftly rushing creek, taking delight in the smoothness of his motions and the delicious texture of the pure icy water flowing past his fins. He can see very little and smell even less; information comes to him in the form of minute impacts on his scales, tiny deflections and interferences. Easily he responds to each incoming news item, now twisting to avoid a fang of rock, now fluttering his fins to seize some speedy subcurrent. The process is fascinating, but the trout itself is a dull companion, and David, having extracted the troutness of the experience in two or three minutes, leaps gladly to a more complex mind the moment he approaches one. It is the mind of gnarled old Georg Schiele, Hans' father, who is at work in a remote corner of the cornfield. David has never entered the elder Schiele's mind before. The old man is a grim and forbidding character, well past sixty, who says little and stalks dourly through his day-long round of chores with his heavy-jowled face perpetually locked in a frosty scowl. David occasionally wonders whether he once might have been a concentration-camp attendant, though he knows the Schieles came to America in 1935. The farmer gives off so unpleasant a psychic aura that David has steered clear of him, but so bored is he with the trout that he slips into Schiele now, slides down through dense layers of unintelligible Deutsch ruminations, and strikes bottom in the basement of the farmer's soul, the place where his essence lives. Astonishment: old Schiele is a mystic, an ecstatic! No dourness here. No dark Lutheran vindictiveness. This is pure Buddhism: Schiele stands in the rich soil of his fields, leaning on his hoe, feet firmly planted, communing with the universe. God floods his soul. He touches the unity of all things. Sky, trees, earth, sun, plants, brook, insects, birds—everything is one, part of a seamless whole, and Schiele resonates in perfect harmony with it. How can this be? How can such a bleak, inaccessible man entertain such raptures

in his depths? Feel his joy! Sensations drench him!
Birdsong, sunlight, the scent of flowers and clods of
upturned earth, the rustling of the sharp-bladed green
cornstalks, the trickle of sweat down the reddened
deep-channeled neck, the curve of the planet, the
fleecy premature outline of the full moon—a thousand
delights enfold this man. David shares his pleasure. He
kneels in his mind, reverent, awed. The world is a
mighty hymn. Schiele breaks from his stasis, raises his
hoe, brings it down; heavy muscles go taut and metal
digs into earth, and everything is as it should be, all
conforms to the divine plan. Is this how Schiele goes
through his days? Is such happiness possible? David is
surprised to find tears bulging in his eyes. This simple
man, this narrow man, lives in daily grace. Suddenly
sullen, bitterly envious, David rips his mind free, whirls,
projects it toward the woods, drops down into Barbara
Stein again. She lies back, sweat-sticky, exhausted.
Through her nostrils David receives the stink of semen
already going sour. She rubs her hands over her skin,
plucking stray bits of leaf and grass from herself. Idly
she touches her softening nipples. Her mind is slow,
dull, almost as empty as the trout's, just now: sex seems
to have drained her of personality. David shifts to Hans
and finds him no better. Lying by Barbara's side, still
breathing hard after his exertions, he is torpid and
depressed. His wad is shot and all desire is gone from
him; peering sleepily at the girl he has just possessed,
he is conscious mainly of body odors and the untidiness
of her hair. Through the upper levels of his mind
wanders a wistful thought, in English punctuated by
clumsy German, of a girl from an adjoining farm who
will do something to him with her mouth that Barbara
refuses to do. Hans will be seeing her on Saturday
night. Poor Barbara, David thinks, and wonders what
she would say if she knew what Hans is thinking. Idly
he tries to bridge their two minds, entering both
in the mischievous hope that thoughts may flow from
one to the other, but he miscalculates his span and
finds himself returning to old Schiele, deep in his
ecstasy, while holding contact with Hans as well.

Father and son, old and young, priest and profaner. David
sustains the twin contact a moment. He shivers. He is
filled with a thundering sense of the wholeness of life.

* * *

It was like that all the time, in those years: an endless
trip, a gaudy voyage. But powers decay. Time leaches
the colors from the best of visions. The world becomes
grayer. Entropy beats us down. Everything fades. Everything goes. Everything dies.

THIRTEEN.

Judith's dark, rambling apartment fills with pungent
smells. I hear her in the kitchen, bustling, dumping
spices into the pot: hot chili, oregano, tarragon, cloves,
garlic, powdered mustard, sesame oil, curry powder,
God knows what else. Fire burn and cauldron bubble.
Her famous fiery spaghetti sauce is in the making, a
compound product of mysterious antecedents, part
Mexican in inspiration, part Szechuan, part Madras,
part pure Judith. My unhappy sister is not really much of
a domestic type, but the few dishes she can cook she
does extraordinarily well, and her spaghetti is celebrated
on three continents; I'm convinced there are men who go
to bed with her just to have dining-in privileges here.
I have arrived unexpectedly early, half an hour before
the appointed time, catching Judith unprepared, not
even dressed; so I am on my own while she readies
dinner. "Fix yourself a drink," she calls to me. I go to the
sideboard and pour a shot of dark rum, then into the
kitchen for ice cubes. Judith, flustered, wearing housecoat and headband, flies madly about, breathlessly selecting
spices. She does everything at top speed. "Be with you
in another ten minutes," she gasps, reaching for the
pepper mill. "Is the kid making a lot of trouble for you?"
My nephew, she means. His name is Paul, in honor

of our father which art in heaven, but she never calls
him that, only "the baby," "the kid." Four years old.
Child of divorce, destined to be as taut-strung as his
mother. "He's not bothering me at all," I assure her,
and go back to the livingroom.

The apartment is one of those old, immense West
Side jobs, roomy and high-ceilinged, which carries with
it some sort of aura of intellectual distinction simply
because so many critics, poets, playwrights, and chore-
ographers have lived in similar apartments in this very
neighborhood. Giant livingroom with many windows
looking out over West End Avenue; formal dining room;
big kitchen; master bedroom; child's room; maid's room;
two bathrooms. All for Judith and her cub. The rent is
cosmic, but Judith can manage it. She gets well over a
thousand a month from her ex, and earns a modest but
decent living of her own as an editor and translator; aside
from that she has a small income from a portfolio of
stocks, shrewdly chosen for her a few years ago by a lover
from Wall Street, which she purchased with her inherited
share of our parents' surprisingly robust savings. (My
share went to clean up accumulated debts; the whole
thing melted like June snow.) The place is furnished half
in 1960 Greenwich Village and half in 1970 Urban
Elegance—black pole-lamps, gray string chairs, red brick
bookcases, cheap prints, and wax-encrusted Chianti bottles on the one hand; leather couches, Hopi pottery,
psychedelic silkscreens, glass-topped coffee-tables, and
giant potted cacti on the other. Bach harpischord sonatas
tinkle from the thousand-dollar speaker system. The
floor, ebony-dark and mirror-bright, gleams between the
lush, thick area rugs. A pile of broken-backed paperbacks
clutters one wall. Opposite it stand two rough unopened
wooden crates, wine newly arrived from her vintner. A
good life my sister leads here. Good and miserable.

The kid eyes me untrustingly. He sits twenty feet
away, by the window, fiddling with some intricate plastic toy but keeping close watch on me. A dark child,
slender and tense like his mother, aloof, cool. No love is
lost between us: I've been inside his head and I know
what he thinks of me. To him I'm one of the many men

in his mother's life, a real uncle being not very different from the innumerable uncle-surrogates forever sleeping over; I suppose he thinks I'm just one of her lovers who shows up more often than most. An understandable error. But while he resents the others merely because they compete with him for her affection, he looks coldly upon me because he thinks I've caused his mother pain; he dislikes me for her sake. How shrewdly he's discerned the decades-old network of hostilities and tensions that shapes and defines my relationship with Judith! So I'm an enemy. He'd gut me if he could.

I sip my drink, listen to Bach, smile insincerely at the kid, and inhale the aroma of spaghetti sauce. My power is practically quiescent; I try not to use it much here, and in any case its intake is feeble today. After some time Judith emerges from the kitchen and, flashing across the livingroom, says, "Come talk to me while I get dressed, Duv." I follow her to her bedroom and sit down on the bed; she takes her clothes into the adjoining bathroom, leaving the door open only an inch or two. The last time I saw her naked she was seven years old. She says, "I'm glad you decided to come."

"So am I."

"You look awfully peaked though."

"Just hungry, Jude."

"I'll fix that in five minutes." Sounds of water running. She says something else; the sink drowns her out. I look idly around the bedroom. A man's white shirt, much too big for Judith, hangs casually from the doorknob of the closet. On the night-table sit two fat textbooky-looking books. *Analytical Neuroendocrinology* and *Studies in the Physiology of Thermoregulation*. Unlikely reading for Judith. Maybe she's been hired to translate them into French. I observe that they're brand new copies, though one book was published in 1964 and the other in 1969. Both by the same author: K. F. Silvestri, M.D., Ph.D.

"You going to medical school these days?" I ask.

"The books, you mean? They're Karl's."

Karl? A new name. Dr. Karl F. Silvestri. I touch her mind lightly and extract his image: a tall hefty sober-faced man, broad shoulders, strong dimpled chin, flow-

ing mane of graying hair. About fifty, I'd guess. Judith
digs older men. While I raid her consciousness she tells
me about him. Her current "friend," the kid's latest
"uncle." He's someone very big at Columbia Medical
Center, a real authority on the human body. Including
her body, I assume. Newly divorced after a 25-year
marriage. Uh-huh: she likes getting them on the re-
bound. He met her three weeks ago through a mutual
friend, a psychoanalyst. They've only seen each other
four or five times; he's always busy, committee meetings
at this hospital or that, seminars, consultations. It wasn't
very long ago that Judith told me she was between
men, maybe off men altogether. Evidently not. It must
be a serious affair if she's trying to read his books. They
look absolutely opaque to me, all charts and statistical
tables and heavy Latinate terminology.

She comes out of the bathroom wearing a sleek
purple pants-suit and the crystal earrings I gave her for
her 29th birthday. When I visit she always tries to
register some little sentimental touch to tie us together;
tonight it's the earrings. There is a convalescent quality
to our friendship nowadays, as we tiptoe gently through
the garden where our old hatred lies buried: We embrace, a brother-sister hug. A pleasant perfume. "Hello," she says. "I'm sorry I was such a mess when you
walked in."

"It's my fault. I was too early. Anyway, you weren't a
mess at all."

She leads me to the livingroom. She carries herself
well. Judith is a handsome woman, tall and extremely
slender, exotic-looking, with dark hair, dark complex-
ion, sharp cheekbones. The slim sultry type. I suppose
she'd be considered very sexy, except that there is
something cruel about her thin lips and her quick
glistening brown eyes, and that cruelty, which grows
more intense in these years of divorce and discontent,
turns people off. She's had lovers by the dozen, by the
gross, but not much love. You and me, sis, you and me.
Chips off the old block.

She sets the table while I fix a drink for her, the
usual, Pernod on the rocks. The kid, thank God, has

already eaten; I hate having him at the table. He plays with his plastic thingy and favors me with occasional sour glares. Judith and I clink our cocktail glasses together, a stagy gesture. She produces a wintry smile. "Cheers," we say. Cheers.

"Why don't you move back downtown?" she asks. "We could see more of each other."

"It's cheap up there. Do we want to see more of each other?"

"Who else do we have?"

"You have Karl."

"I don't *have* him or anybody. Just my kid and my brother."

I think of the time when I tried to murder her in her bassinet. She doesn't know about that. "Are we really friends, Jude?"

"Now we are. At last."

"We haven't exactly been fond of each other all these years."

"People change, Duv. They grow up. I was dumb, a real shithead, so wrapped up in myself that I couldn't give anything but hate to anybody around me. That's over now. If you don't believe me, look into my head and see."

"You don't want me poking around in there."

"Go ahead," she says. "Take a good look and see if I haven't changed toward you."

"No. I'd rather not." I deal myself another two ounces of rum. The hand shakes a little. "Shouldn't you check the spaghetti sauce? Maybe it's boiling over."

"Let it boil. I haven't finished my drink. Duv, are you still having trouble? With your power, I mean."

"Yes. Still. Worse than ever."

"What do you think is happening?"

I shrug. Insouciant old me. "I'm losing it, that's all. It's like hair, I suppose. A lot of it when you're young, then less and less, and finally none. Fuck it. It never did me any good anyway."

"You don't mean that."

"Show me any good it did me, Jude."

"It made you someone special. It made you unique. When everything else went wrong for you, you could always fall back on that, the knowledge that you could go into minds, that you could see the unseeable, that you could get close to people's souls. A gift from God."

"A useless gift. Except if I'd gone into the sideshow business."

"It made you a richer person. More complex, more interesting. Without it you might have been someone quite ordinary."

"With it I turned out to be someone quite ordinary. A nobody, a zero. Without it I might have been a happy nobody instead of a dismal one."

"You pity yourself a lot, Duv."

"I've got a lot to pity myself for. More Pernod, Jude?"

"Thanks, no. I ought to look after dinner. Will you pour the wine?"

She goes into the kitchen. I do the wine thing; then I carry the salad bowl to the table. Behind me the kid begins to chant derisive nonsense syllables in his weirdly mature baritone. Even in my current state of dulled deceptivity I feel the pressure of the kid's cold hatred against the back of my skull. Judith returns, toting a well-laden tray: spaghetti, garlic bread, cheese. She flashes a warm smile, evidently sincere, as we sit down. We clink wine-glasses. We eat in silence a few minutes. I praise the spaghetti. She says, finally, "Can I do some mindreading on you, Duv?"

"Be my guest."

"You say you're glad the power's going. Is that snow-job directed at me or at yourself? Because you're snowing somebody. You hate the idea of losing it, don't you?"

"A little."

"A lot, Duv."

"All right, a lot. I'm of two minds. I'd like it to vanish completely. Christ, I wish I'd never had it. But on the other hand, if I lose it, who am I? Where's my identity? I'm Selig the Mindreader, right? The Amazing Mental Man. So if I stop being him—you see, Jude?"

"I see. The pain's all over your face. I'm so sorry, Duv."

"For what?"

"That you're losing it."

"You despised my guts for using it on you, didn't you?"

"That's different. That was a long time ago. I know what you must be going through, now. Do you have any idea why you're losing it?"

"No. A function of aging, I guess."

"Is there anything that might be done to stop it from going?"

"I doubt it, Jude. I don't even know why I have the gift in the first place, let alone how to nurture it now. I don't know how it works. It's just something in my head, a genetic fluke, a thing I was born with, like freckles. If your freckles start to fade, can you figure out a way of making them stay, if you want them to stay?"

"You've never let yourself be studied, have you?"

"No."

"Why not?"

"I don't like people poking in my head any more than you do," I say softly. "I don't want to be a case history. I've always kept a low profile. If the world ever found out about me, I'd become a pariah. I'd probably be lynched. Do you know how many people there are to whom I've openly admitted the truth about myself? In my whole life, how many?"

"A dozen."

"Three," I say. "And I wouldn't willingly have told any of them."

"Three?"

"You. I suppose you suspected it all along, but you didn't find out for sure till you were sixteen, remember? Then there's Tom Nyquist, who I don't see any more. And a girl named Kitty, who I don't see any more either."

"What about the tall brunette?"

"Toni? I never explicitly told her. I tried to hide it from her. She found out indirectly. A lot of people may have found out indirectly. But I've only told three. I don't want to be known as a freak. So let it fade. Let it die. Good riddance."

"You want to keep it, though."

"To keep it and lose it both."

"That's a contradiction."

"Do I contradict myself? Very well, then I contradict myself. I am large, I contain multitudes. What can I say, Jude? What can I tell you that's true?"

"Are you in pain?"

"Who isn't in pain?"

She says, "Losing it is almost like becoming impotent, isn't it, Duv? To reach into a mind and find out that you can't connect? You said there was ecstasy in it for you, once. That flood of information, that vicarious experience. And now you can't get it as much, or at all. Your mind can't get it up. Do you see it that way, as a sexual metaphor?"

"Sometimes." I give her more wine. For a few minutes we sit silently, shoveling down the spaghetti, exchanging tentative grins. I almost feel warmth toward her. Forgiveness for all the years when she treated me like a circus attraction. *You sneaky fucker, Duv, stay out of my head or I'll kill you! You voyeur. You peeper. Keep away, man, keep away.* She didn't want me to meet her fiancé. Afraid I'd tell him about her other men, I guess. *I'd like to find you dead in the gutter some day, Duv, with all my secrets rotting inside you.* So long ago. Maybe we love each other a little now, Jude. Just a little, but you love me more than I love you.

"I don't come any more," she says abruptly. "You know, I used to come, practically every time. The original Hot Pants Kid, me. But around five years ago something happened, around the time my marriage was first breaking up. A short circuit down below. I started coming every fifth time, every tenth time. Feeling the ability to respond slip away from me. Lying there waiting for it to happen, and of course that doused it every time. Finally I couldn't come at all. I still can't. Not in three years. I've laid maybe a hundred men since the divorce, give or take five or ten, and not one brought me off, and some of them were studs, real bulls. It's one of the things Karl's going to work on with me. So I know what it's like, Duv. What you must be going through. To lose your best way of making contact with others. To lose contact gradually with yourself. To become a stranger in your own head." She smiles. "Did you know that about me? About the troubles I've been having in bed?"

I hesitate briefly. The icy glare in her eyes gives her
away. The aggressiveness. The resentment she feels.
Even when she tries to be loving she can't help hating.
How fragile our relationship is! We're locked in a kind
of marriage, Judith and I, an old burned-out marriage
held together with skewers. What the hell, though.
"Yes," I tell her. "I knew about it."

"I thought so. You've never stopped probing me."
Her smile is all hateful glee now. She's glad I'm losing
it. She's relieved. "I'm always wide open to you, Duv."

"Don't worry, you won't be much longer." Oh, you
sadistic bitch! Oh, you beautiful ball-buster! And you're
all I've got. "How about some more spaghetti, Jude?"
Sister. Sister. Sister.

FOURTEEN.

Yahya Lumumba
Humanities 2A, Dr. Katz
November 10, 1976

The "Electra" Theme in Aeschylus,
Sophocles, and Euripides

The use of the "Electra" motif by Aeschylus, Sophocles,
and Euripides is a study in varying dramatic methods
and modes of attack. The plot is basically the same in
Aeschylus' *Choephori* and the *Electras* of Sophocles and
Euripides: Orestes, exiled son of murdered Agamemnon,
returns to his native Mycenae, where he discovers his
sister Electra. She persuades him to avenge Agamemnon's
murder by killing Clytemnestra and Aegisthus, who had
slain Agamemnon on his return from Troy. The treat-
ment of the plot varies greatly at the hands of each
dramatist.

Aeschylus, unlike his later rivals, held as prime
consideration the ethical and religious aspects of Orestes'
crime. Characterization and motivation in *The Choephori*

are simple to the point of inviting ridicule—as, indeed, can we see when the more worldly-minded Euripides ridicules Aeschylus in the recognition scene of his *Electra*. In Aeschylus' play Orestes appears accompanied by his friend Pylades and places an offering on Agamemnon's tomb: a lock of his hair. They withdraw, and lamenting Electra comes to the tomb. Noticing the lock of hair, she recognizes it as being "like unto those my father's children wear," and decides Orestes has sent it to the tomb as a token of mourning. Orestes then reappears, and identifies himself to Electra. It is this implausible means of identification which was parodied by Euripides.

Orestes reveals that Apollo's oracle had commanded him to avenge Agememnon's murder. In a long poetic passage, Electra steels Orestes' courage, and he goes forth to kill Clytemnestra and Aegisthus. He obtains entrance to the palace by deception, pretending to his mother Clytemnestra that he is a messenger from far-off Phocis, bearing news of Orestes' death. Once inside, he slays Aegisthus, and then, confronting his mother, he accuses her of the murder and kills her.

The play ends with Orestes, maddened by his crime, seeing the Furies coming to pursue him. He takes refuge in the temple of Apollo. The mystic and allegorical sequel, *The Eumenides*, sees Orestes absolved of blame.

Aeschylus, in short, was not overly concerned with the credibility of his play's action. His purpose in the *Oresteia* trilogy was a theological one: to examine the actions of the gods in placing a curse upon a house, a curse stemming from murder and leading to further murder. The keynote of his philosophy is perhaps the line, " 'Tis Zeus alone who shows the perfect way of knowledge: He hath ruled, men shall learn wisdom, by affliction schooled." Aeschylus sacrifices dramatic technique, or at least holds it in secondary importance, in order to focus attention on the religious and psychological aspects of the matricide.

The *Electra* of Euripides is virtually at an opposite pole from the concept of Aeschylus; though he uses the same plot, he elaborates and innovates to provide far richer texture. Electra and Orestes stand out in relief in Euripides: Electra a near-mad woman, banished from the court, married to a peasant, craving vengeance; Orestes a coward, sneaking into Mycenae the back way, abjectly stabbing Aegisthus from behind, luring Clytemnestra to her doom by a ruse. Euripides is concerned with dramatic credibility, whereas Aeschylus is not. After the famous parody of the Aeschylean recognition scene, Orestes makes himself known to Electra not by his hair or the size of his foot, but rather by

* * *

Oh God. Oh shit. Shit shit shit. This is deadly. This is no fucking good at all. Could Yahya Lumumba have written any of this crap? Phony from Word One. Why should Yahya Lumumba give a shit about Greek tragedy? Why should I? What's Hecuba to him or he to Hecuba, that he should weep for her? I'll tear this up and start again. I'll write it jivey, man. I'll give it dat ole watermelon rhythm. God help me to think black. But I can't. But I can't. But I can't. Christ, I'd like to throw up. I think I'm getting a fever. Wait. Maybe a joint would help some. Yeah. Let's get high and try again. A lil ole stick of mootah. Get some soul into it, man. Smartass white Jew-bastard, get some soul into it, you hear? Okay, now. There was this cat Agamemnon, he was one big important fucker, you hear, he was The Man, but he got fucked all the same. His old lady Clytemnestra, she was makin' it with this chickenshit muthafuck Aegisthus, and one day she say, Baby, let's waste old Aggie, you and me, and then you gonna be king—gwine be king?—gonna—and we have a high ole time. Aggie, he off in the Nam runnin' the show, but he come home for some R & R and before he know what happenin' they stick him good, right, they really cut him, and that all for *him*. Now there this crazy cunt Electra, dig, she the daughter of ole Aggie, and she get real uptight when they use him up, so she say to her brother, his name Orestes, she say, listen, Orestes, I want you to *get* them two muthafucks, I want you to get them real good. Now, this cat Orestes he been out of town for a while, he don't know the score, but—

Yeah, that's it, man! You're digging it! Now go on to explain about Euripides' use of the *deus ex machina* and the cathartic virtues of Sophocles' realistic dramatic technique. Sure. What a dumb schmuck you are, Selig. What a dumb schmuck.

FIFTEEN.

I tried to be good to Judith, I tried to be kind and loving, but our hatred kept coming between us. I said to myself, She's my kid sister, my only sibling, I must love her more. But you can't will love. You can't conjure it into existence on nothing more than good intentions. Besides, my intentions had never been that good. I saw her as a rival from the word go. I was the firstborn, I was the difficult one, the maladjusted one. I was supposed to be the center of everything. Those were the terms of my contract with God: I must suffer because I am different, but by way of compensation the entire universe will revolve about me. The girlbaby who was brought into the household was intended to be nothing more than a thera- peutic aid designed to help me relate better to the human race. That was the deal: she wasn't supposed to have independent reality as a person, she wasn't supposed to have her own needs or make demands or drain away their love. Just a thing, an item of furni- ture. But I knew better than to believe that. I was ten years old, remember, when they adopted her. Your ten-year-old, he's no fool. I knew that my par- ents, no longer feeling obliged now to direct all their concern exclusively toward their mysteriously intense and troubled son, would rapidly and with great relief transfer their attention and their love—yes, particu- larly their love—to the cuddly, uncomplicated infant. She would take my place at the center; I'd become a quirky obsolescent artifact. I couldn't help resenting that. Do you blame me for trying to kill her in her

bassinet? On the other hand you can understand the
origin of her life-long coldness toward me. I offer no
defense at this late date. The cycle of hatred began
with me. With me, Jude, with me, with me, with me.
You could have broken it with love, though, if you
wanted to. You didn't want to.

On a Saturday afternoon in May, 1961, I went out
to my parents' house. In those years I didn't go there
often, though I lived twenty minutes away by subway. I was outside the family circle, autonomous and
remote, and I felt powerful resistance to any kind of
reattachment. For one thing I had free-floating hostilities toward my parents: it was their fluky genes, after
all, that had sent me into the world this way. And then
too there was Judith, shriveling me with her disdain:
did I need more of that? So I stayed away from the
three of them for weeks, months, at a time, until the
melancholy maternal phonecalls became too much for
me, until the weight of my guilt overcame my resistances.

I was happy to discover, when I got there, that
Judith was still in her bedroom, asleep. At three in
the afternoon? Well, my mother said, she was out
very late last night on a date. Judith was sixteen, I
imagined her going to a high school basketball game
with some skinny pimply kid and sipping milkshakes
afterwards. Sleep well, sister, sleep on and on. But
of course her absence put me into direct and
unshielded confrontation with my sad depleted parents. My mother, mild and dim; my father, weary
and bitter. All my life they had steadily grown smaller.
They seemed very small now. They seemed close to
the vanishing point.

I had never lived in this apartment. For years Paul
and Martha had struggled with the upkeep of a three-
bedroom place they couldn't afford, simply because it
had become impossible for Judith and me to share the
same bedroom once she was past her infancy. The
moment I left for college, taking a room near campus,
they found a smaller and far less expensive one. Their
bedroom was to the right of the entry foyer, and Judith's,
down a long hall and past the kitchen, was to the left;

straight ahead was the livingroom, in which my father sat dreamily leafing through the *Times*. He read nothing but the newspaper these days, though once his mind had been more active. From him came a dull sludgy emanation of fatigue. He was making some decent money for the first time in his life, actually would end up quite prosperous, yet he had conditioned himself to the poor-man psychology: poor Paul, you're a pitiful failure, you deserved so much better from life. I looked at the newspaper through his mind as he turned the pages. Yesterday Alan Shepard had made his epochal sub-orbital flight, the first manned venture into space by the United States. U.S. HURLS MAN 115 MILES INTO SPACE, cried the banner headline. SHEPARD WORKS CONTROLS IN CAPSULE, REPORTS BY RADIO IN 15-MINUTE FLIGHT. I groped for some way to connect with my father. "What did you think of the space voyage?" I asked. "Did you listen to the broadcast?" He shrugged. "Who gives a damn? It's all crazy. A mishigos. A waste of everybody's time and money." ELIZABETH VISITS POPE IN VATICAN. Fat Pope John, looking like a well-fed rabbi. JOHNSON TO MEET LEADERS IN ASIA ON U.S. TROOP USE. He skimmed onward, skipping pages. HELP OF GOLDBERG ASKED ON ROCKETS. KENNEDY SIGNS WAGE-FLOOR BILL. Nothing registered on him, not even KENNEDY TO SEEK INCOME TAX CUTS. He lingered at the sports pages. A faint flicker of interest. MUD MAKES CARRY BACK STRONGER FAVORITE FOR 87th KENTUCKY DERBY TODAY. YANKS OPPOSE ANGELS IN OPENER OF 3-GAME SERIES BEFORE 21,000 ON COAST. "Who do you like in the Derby?" I asked. He shook his head. "What do I know about horses?" he said. He was, I realized, already dead, although in fact his heart would beat for another decade. He had stopped responding. The world had defeated him.

I left him to his brooding and made polite talk with my mother: her Hadassah reading group was discussing *To Kill a Mockingbird* next Thursday and she wanted to know if I had read it. I hadn't. What was I doing with myself? Had I seen any good movies? *L'Avventura*, I said. Is that a French film? she asked. Italian, I said. She wanted me to describe the plot. She listened patiently, looking troubled, not following anything. "Who did you go with?" she asked. "Are you seeing any nice girls?" My son the bachelor. Already 26 and not even engaged. I deflected the tiresome question with patient skill born of long experience. Sorry, Martha. I won't give you the grandchildren you're waiting for. You'll have to get them from Judith; it won't be all that long.

"I have to baste the chicken now," she said, and disappeared. I sat with my father for a while, until I couldn't stand that and went down the hall to the john, next to Judith's room. Her door was ajar. I glanced in. Lights off, blinds drawn, but I touched her mind and found that she was awake and thinking of getting up. All right, make a gesture, be friendly, Duvid. It won't cost you anything. I knocked lightly. "Hi, it's me," I said. "Okay if I come in?"

She was sitting up, wearing a frilly white bathrobe over dark-blue pajamas. Yawning, stretching. Her face, usually so taut, was puffy from too much sleep. Out of force of habit I went into her mind, and saw something new and surprising there. My sister's erotic inauguration. The night before. The whole thing: the scurry in the parked car, the rise of excitement, the sudden realization that this was going to be more than an interlude of petting, the panties coming down, the awkward shiftings of position, the fumble with the condom, the moment of ultimate hesitation giving way to total willingness, the hasty inexpert fingers coaxing lubrication out of the virgin crevice, the cautious clumsy poking, the thrust, the surprise of discovering that penetration was accomplished without pain, the pistoning of body against body, the boy's quick explosion, the messy aftermath, the guilt and confusion and disappointment as it ended with Judith still unsatisfied. The drive home, silent, shamefaced. Into the house, tiptoe, hoarsely greeting the vigilant, unsleeping parents. The late-night shower. Inspection and cleansing of the deflowered and slightly

swollen vulva. Uneasy sleep, frequently punctured. A
long stretch of wakefulness, in which the night's event
is considered: she is pleased and relieved to have
entered womanhood, but also frightened. Unwillingness
to rise and face the world the next day, especially to
face Paul and Martha. Judith, your secret is no secret to
me.

"How are you?" I asked.

Stagily casual, she drawled, "Sleepy. I was out very
late. How come you're here?"

"I drop in to see the family now and then."

"Nice to have seen you."

"That isn't friendly, Jude. Am I that loathsome to
you?"

"Why are you bothering me, Duv?"

"I told you, I'm trying to be sociable. You're my only
sister, the only one I'll ever have. I thought I'd stick my
head in the door and say hello."

"You've done that. So?"

"You might tell me what you've been doing with
yourself since the last time I saw you."

"Do you care?"

"If I didn't care, would I ask?"

"Sure," she said. "You don't give a crap about what
I've been doing. You don't give a crap about anybody
but David Selig, and why pretend otherwise? You don't
need to ask me polite questions. It isn't natural coming
from you."

"Hey, hold on!" Let's not be dueling so fast, sister.
"What gives you the idea that—"

"Do you think of me from one week to the next?
I'm just furniture to you. The drippy little sister.
The brat. The inconvenience. Have you ever talked
to me? About anything? Do you even know the
name of the school I go to? I'm a total stranger to
you."

"No, you're not."

"What the hell *do* you know about me?"

"Plenty."

"For example."

"Quit it, Jude."

"One example. Just one. One thing about me. For example—"

"For example. All right. For example, I know that you got laid last night."

We were both amazed by that. I stood in shocked silence, not believing that I had allowed those words to pass my lips; and Judith jerked as though electrified, her body stiffening and rearing, her eyes blazing with astonishment. I don't know how long we remained frozen, unable to speak.

"What?" she said finally. "What did you say, Duv?"

"You heard it."

"I heard it but I think I must have dreamed it. Say it again."

"No."

"Why not?"

"Leave me alone, Jude."

"Who told you?"

"Please, Jude—"

"Who told you?"

"Nobody," I muttered.

Her smile was terrifyingly triumphant. "You know something? I believe you. I honestly believe you. Nobody told you. You pulled it right out of my mind, didn't you, Duv?"

"I wish I had never come in here."

"Admit it. Why won't you admit it? You see into people's minds, don't you, Duvid? You're some kind of circus freak. I've suspected that a long time. All those little hunches you have, and they always turn out to be right, and the embarrassed phony way you cover up for yourself when you're right. Talking about your 'luck' at guessing things. Sure! Sure, luck! I knew the real scoop. I said to myself, This fucker is reading my mind. But I told myself it was crazy, there aren't any such people, it has to be impossible. Only it's true, isn't it? You don't guess. You look. We're wide open to you and you read us like books. Spying on us. Isn't that so?"

I heard a sound behind me. I jumped, frightened. But it was only Martha, poking her head into Judith's bedroom. A vague, dreamy grin. "Good morning, Judith. Or good afternoon, I should say. Having a nice chat, children? I'm so glad. Don't forget to have breakfast, Judith." And she drifted on her way.

Judith said sharply, "Why didn't you tell her? Describe the whole thing. Who I was with last night, what I did with him, how it felt—"

"Stop it, Jude."

"You didn't answer my other question. You've got this weird power, don't you? *Don't you?*"

"Yes."

"And you've been secretly spying on people all your life."

"Yes. Yes."

"I knew it. I didn't know, but I really did, all along. And it explains so much. Why I always felt dirty when I was a kid and you were around. Why I felt as if anything I did was likely to show up in tomorrow's newspapers. I never had any privacy, even when I was locked in the bathroom. I didn't *feel* private." She shuddered. "I hope I never see you again, Duv. Now that I know what you are. I wish I never *had* seen you. If I ever catch you poking around in my head after this, I'll cut your balls off. Got that? I'll cut your balls off. Now clear out of here so I can get dressed."

I stumbled away. In the bathroom I gripped the cold edge of the sink and leaned close to the mirror to study my flushed, flustered face. I looked stunned and dazed, my features as rigid as though I had had a stroke. *I know that you got laid last night.* Why had I told her that? An accident? The words spilling out of me because she had goaded me past the point of prudence? But I had never let anyone push me into a revelation like that before. There are no accidents, Freud said. There are never any slips of the tongue. Everything's deliberate, on one level or another. I must have said what I did to Judith because I wanted her at last to know the truth about me. But why? Why her? I had already told Nyquist, yes; there could be no risk in that; but I had never admitted it to anyone else. Always taken such great pains to conceal it, eh, Miss Mueller?

And now Judith knew. I had given her a weapon with which she could destroy me.

* * *

I had given her a weapon. How strange that she never chose to use it.

SIXTEEN.

Nyquist said, "The real trouble with you, Selig, is that you're a deeply religious man who doesn't happen to believe in God." Nyquist was always saying things like that, and Selig never could be sure whether he meant them or was just playing verbal games. No matter how deeply Selig penetrated the other man's soul, he never could be sure of anything. Nyquist was too wily, too elusive.

Playing it safe, Selig said nothing. He stood with his back to Nyquist, looking out the window. Snow was falling. The narrow streets below were choked with it; not even the municipal snowplows could get through, and a strange serenity prevailed. High winds whipped the drifts about. Parked cars were disappearing under the white blanket. A few janitors from the apartment houses on the block were out, digging manfully. It had been snowing on and off for three days. Snow was general all over the Northeast. It was falling on every filthy city, on the arid suburbs, falling softly upon the Appalachians and, farther eastward, softly falling into the dark mutinous Atlantic waves. Nothing was moving in New York City. Everything was shut down: office buildings, schools, the concert halls, the theaters. The railroads were out of commission and the highways were blocked. There was no action at the airports. Basketball games were being canceled at Madison Square Garden. Unable to get to work, Selig had waited out most of the blizzard in Nyquist's apartment, spending so much time with him that by now he had come to find his friend's company stifling and oppressive. What earlier had seemed amusing and charming in Nyquist had become abrasive and tricksy. Nyquist's bland self-assurance conveyed itself now as smugness; his casual forays into Selig's mind were no longer affectionate gestures of intimacy, but rather, conscious acts of aggression. His habit of repeating aloud what Selig was thinking was increasingly irritating, and there seemed to be no deterring him from that. Here he was doing it again, plucking a quotation from Selig's head and declaiming it in half-mocking tones: "Ah. How pretty. 'His soul swooned slowly as he heard the snow falling faintly through the universe and faintly falling, like the descent of their last end, upon all the living and the dead.' I like that. What is it, David?"

"James Joyce," said Selig sourly. " 'The Dead,' from *Dubliners*. I asked you yesterday not to do that."

"I envy the breadth and depth of your culture. I like to borrow fancy quotations from you."

"Fine. Do you always have to play them back at me?"

Nyquist, gesturing broadly as Selig stepped away from the window, humbly turned his palms outward. "I'm sorry. I forgot you didn't like it."

"You never forget a thing, Tom. You never do anything accidentally." Then, guilty over his peevishness: "Christ, I've had about enough snow!"

"Snow is general," said Nyquist. "It isn't ever going to stop. What are we going to do today?"

"The same as yesterday and the day before, I imagine. Sitting around watching the snowflakes fall and listening to records and getting sloshed."

"How about getting laid?"

"I don't think you're my type," Selig said.

Nyquist flashed an empty smile. "Funny man. I mean finding a couple of ladies marooned somewhere in this building and inviting them to a little party. You don't think there are two available ladies under this roof?"

"We could look, I suppose," Selig said, shrugging. "Is there any more bourbon?"

"I'll get it," Nyquist said.

He brought the bottle over. Nyquist moved with a strange slowness, like a man moving through a dense reluctant atmosphere of mercury or some other viscous fluid. Selig had never seen him hurry. He was heavy without being fat, a thick-shouldered, thick-necked man with a square head, close-cropped yellow hair, a flat wide-flanged nose, and an easy, innocent grin. Very, very Aryan: he was Scandinavian, a Swede perhaps, raised in Finland and transplanted to the United States at the age of 10. He still had the elusive traces of an accent. He said he was 28 and looked a few years older than that to Selig, who had just turned 23. This was February, 1958, in an era when Selig still had the delusion that he was going to make it in the adult world. Eisenhower was President, the stock market had gone to hell, the post-Sputnik emotional slump was troubling everybody even though the first American space satellite had just been orbited, and the latest feminine fashion was the gunny-sack chemise. Selig was living in Brooklyn Heights, on Pierrepont Street, commuting several days a week to the lower Fifth Avenue office of a publishing company for which he was doing freelance copy-editing at $3 an hour. Nyquist lived in the same building, four floors higher.

He was the only other person Selig knew who had the power. Not only that, having it hadn't crippled him at all. Nyquist used his gift as simply and naturally as he did his eyes or his legs, for his own advantage, without apologies and without guilt. Perhaps he was the least neurotic person Selig had ever met. By occupation he was a predator, skimming an income by raiding the minds of others; but, like any jungle cat, he pounced only when hungry, never for sheer love of pouncing. He took what he needed, never questioning the providence that had made him so superbly fitted for taking, yet he did not take more than he needed, and his needs were moderate. He held no job and apparently never had. Whenever he wanted money he made the ten-minute subway ride to Wall Street, sauntered through the gloomy canyons of the financial district, and rummaged about freely in the minds of the moneymen cloistered in the lofty boardrooms. On any given day there was always some major development hatching that would have an impact on the market—a merger, a stock split, an ore discovery, a favorable earnings report—and Nyquist had no difficulty learning the essential details. This information he swiftly sold at handsome but reasonable fees to some twelve or fifteen private investors who had learned in the happiest possible way that Nyquist was a reliable tout. Many of the unaccountable leaks on which quick fortunes had been made in the bull market of the '50's were his doing. He earned a comfortable living this way, enough to support himself in a congenial style. His apartment was small and agreeable—black Naugahyde upholstery, Tiffany lamps, Picasso wallpaper, a well-stocked liquor closet, a superb music system that emitted a seamless flow of Monteverdi and Palestrina, Bartok and Stravinsky. He lived a gracious bachelor life, going out often, making the rounds of his favorite restaurants, all of them obscure and ethnic—Japanese, Pakistani, Syrian, Greek. His circle of friends was limited but distinguished: painters, writers, musicians, poets, mainly. He slept with many women, but Selig rarely saw him with the same one twice.

Like Selig, Nyquist could receive but was unable to send; he was, however, able to tell when his own mind was being probed. That was how they had happened to meet. Selig, newly arrived in the building, had indulged himself in his hobby, letting his consciousness rove freely from floor to floor by way of getting acquainted with his neighbors. Bouncing about, surveying this head and that, finding nothing of any special interest, and then suddenly:

—Tell me where you are.

A crystalline string of words glimmering at the periphery of a sturdy, complacent mind. The statement came through with the immediacy of an explicit message. Yet Selig realized that no act of active transmission had taken place; he had simply found the words lying passively in wait. He made quick reply:

—35 Pierrepont Street.

—No, I know that. I mean, where are you in the building?

—Fourth floor.

—I'm on the eighth. What's your name?

—Selig.

—Nyquist.

The mental contact was stunningly intimate. It was almost a sexual thing, as though he were slicing into a body, not a mind, and he was abashed by the resonant masculinity of the soul he had entered; he felt that there was something not quite permissible about such closeness with another man. But he did not draw back. That rapid interplay of verbal communication across the gap of darkness was a delicious experience, too rewarding to reject. Selig had the momentary illusion of having expanded his powers, of having learned how to send as well as to draw forth the contents of other minds. It was, he knew, only an illusion. He was sending nothing, nor was Nyquist. He and Nyquist were merely picking information out of each other's minds. Each planted phrases for the other to find, which was not quite the same thing, in terms of the situational dynamics, as sending messages to one another. It was a fine and possibly pointless distinction, though; the net effect of the juxtaposition of two wide-open receivers was an efficient send/receive circuit as reliable as a telephone. The marriage of true minds, to which let no impediments be admitted. Tentatively, self-consciously, Selig reached into the lower levels of Nyquist's consciousness, seeking the man as well as the messages, and as he did so he was vaguely aware of disquiet in the depths of his own mind, probably indicating that Nyquist was doing the same to him. For long minutes they explored each other like lovers entwined in the first discovering caresses, although there was nothing loving about Nyquist's touch, which was cool and impersonal. Nevertheless Selig quivered; he felt as if he stood at the edge of an abyss. At last he gently withdrew, as did Nyquist. Then, from the other:

—Come upstairs. I'll meet you by the elevator.

He was bigger than Selig expected, a fullback of a

man, his blue eyes uninviting, his smile a purely formal one. He was remote without actually being cold. They went into his apartment: soft lights, unfamiliar music playing, an atmosphere of unostentatious elegance. Nyquist offered him a drink and they talked, keeping out of one another's minds as much as possible. It was a subdued visit, unsentimental, no tears of joy at having come together at last. Nyquist was affable, inaccessible, pleased that Selig had appeared, but not at all delirious with excitement at the discovery of a fellow freak. Possibly it was because he had discovered fellow freaks before. "There are others," he said. "You're the third, fourth, fifth I've met since I came to the States. Let's see: one in Chicago, one in San Francisco, one in Miami, one in Minneapolis. You're the fifth. Two women, three men."

"Are you still in touch with the others?"

"No."

"What happened?"

"We drifted apart," Nyquist said. "What did you expect? That we'd be clannish? Look, we talked, we played games with our minds, we got to know each other, and after a while we got bored. I think two of them are dead now. I don't mind being isolated from the rest of my kind. I don't think of myself as one of a tribe."

"I never met another one," said Selig. "Until today."

"It isn't important. What's important is living your own life. How old were you when you found out you could do it?"

"I don't know. Five, six years old, maybe. And you?"

"I didn't realize I had anything special until I was eleven. I thought everybody could do it. It was only after I came to the States and heard people thinking in a different language that I knew there was something out of the ordinary about my mind."

"What kind of work do you do?" Selig asked.

"As little as I can," said Nyquist. He grinned and thrust his perceptors brusquely into Selig's mind. It seemed like an invitation of sorts; Selig accepted it and pushed forth his own antennae. Roaming the other man's consciousness, he quickly grasped the picture of Nyquist's Wall Street sorties. He saw the entire balanced, rhythmic, unobsessive life of the man. He was amazed by Nyquist's coolness, his wholeness, his clarity of spirit. How limpid Nyquist's soul was! How unmarred by life! Where did he keep his anguish? Where did he hide his loneliness, his fear, his insecurity? Nyquist, withdrawing, said, "Why do you feel so sorry for yourself?"

"Do I?"

"It's all over your head. What's the problem, Selig? I've looked into you and I don't see the problem, only the pain."

"The problem is that I feel isolated from other human beings."

"Isolated? You? You can get right inside people's heads. You can do something that 99.999% of the human race can't do. They've got to struggle along using words, approximations, semaphore signals, and you go straight to the core of meaning. How can you pretend you're isolated?"

"The information I get is useless," Selig said. "I can't act on it. I might just as well not be reading it in."

"Why?"

"Because it's just voyeurism. I'm spying on them."

"You feel guilty about that?"

"Don't you?"

"I didn't ask for my gift," Nyquist said. "I just happen to have it. Since I have it, I use it. I like it. I like the life I lead. I like myself. Why don't you like yourself, Selig?"

"You tell me."

But Nyquist had nothing to tell him, and when he finished his drink he went back downstairs. His own apartment seemed so strange to him as he re-entered it that he spent a few minutes handling familiar artifacts: his parents' photograph, his little collection of adolescent love-letters, the plastic toy that the psychiatrist had given him years ago. The presence of Nyquist continued to buzz in his mind—a residue of the visit, nothing more, for Selig was certain that Nyquist was not now probing him. He felt so jarred by their meeting, so intruded upon, that he resolved never to see him again, in fact to move somewhere else as soon as possible, to Manhattan, to Philadelphia, to Los Angeles, anywhere that might be beyond Nyquist's reach. All his life he had yearned to meet someone who shared his gift, and now that he had, he felt threatened by it. Nyquist was so much in control of his life that it was terrifying. He'll humiliate me, Selig thought. He'll devour me. But that panic faded. Two days later Nyquist came around to ask him out to dinner. They ate in a nearby Mexican restaurant and got smashed on Carta Blanca. It still appeared to Selig that Nyquist was toying with him, teasing him, holding him at arm's length and tickling him; but it was all done so amiably that Selig felt no resentment. Nyquist's charm was irresistible, and his strength was worth taking as a model of behavior. Nyquist was like an older brother who had preceded him through this same vale of traumas and had emerged unscathed long ago; now he was jollying Selig into an acceptance of the terms of his existence. The superhuman condition, Nyquist called it.

They became close friends. Two or three times a week they went out together, ate together, drank together. Selig had always imagined that a friendship with someone else of his kind would be uniquely intense, but this was not; after the first week they took their specialness for granted and rarely discussed the gift they shared, nor did they ever congratulate each other on having formed an alliance against the ungifted world around them. They communicated sometimes by words, sometimes by the direct contact of minds; it became an easy, cheerful relationship, strained only when Selig slipped into his habitual brooding mood and Nyquist mocked him for such self-indulgence. Even that was no difficulty between them until the days of the blizzard, when all tensions became exaggerated because they were spending so much time together.

"Hold out your glass," Nyquist said.

He poured an amber splash of bourbon. Selig settled back to drink while Nyquist set about finding girls for

them. The project took him five minutes. He scanned
the building and turned up a pair of roommates on the
fifth floor. "Take a look," he said to Selig. Selig entered
Nyquist's mind. Nyquist had attuned himself to the
consciousness of one of the girls—sensual, sleepy,
kittenish—and was looking through her eyes at the
other, a tall gaunt blonde. The doubly refracted mental
image nevertheless was quite clear: the blonde had a
leggy voluptuousness and fashion-model poise. "That
one's mine," Nyquist said. "Now tell me if you like
yours." He jumped, Selig following along, to the mind
of the blonde. Yes, a fashion model, more intelligent
than the other girl, cold, selfish, passionate. From her
mind, via Nyquist, came the image of her roommate,
sprawled out on a sofa in a pink housecoat: a short
plump redhead, breasty, full-faced. "Sure," Selig said.
"Why not?" Nyquist, rummaging through minds, found
the girls' phone number, called, worked his charm.
They came up for drinks. "This awful snowstorm," the
blonde said, shuddering. "It can drive you crazy!" The
four of them went through a lot of liquor to a tinkling
jazz accompaniment: Mingus, MJQ, Chico Hamilton.
The redhead was better-looking than Selig expected,
not quite so plump or coarse—the double refraction
must have introduced some distortions—but she giggled too much, and he found himself disliking her to
some degree. Still, there was no backing out now.
Eventually, very late in the evening, they coupled off,
Nyquist and the blonde in the bedroom, Selig and the
redhead in the livingroom. Selig grinned selfconsciously
at her when they were finally alone. He had never
learned how to suppress that infantile grin, which he
knew must reveal a mingling of gawky anticipation and
plummeting terror. "Hello," he said. They kissed and
his hands went to her breasts, and she pushed herself
up against him in an unashamedly hungry way. She
seemed a few years older than he was, but most women
seemed that way to him. Their clothes dropped away. "I
like lean men," she said, and giggled as she pinched his
sparse flesh. Her breasts rose to him like pink birds.
He caressed her with a virgin's timid intensity. During

the months of their friendship Nyquist had occasionally supplied him with his own discarded women, but it was weeks since he had been to bed with anyone, and he was afraid that his abstinence would rush him into an embarrassing calamity. No: the liquor cooled his ardor just enough, and he held himself in check, ploughing her solemnly and energetically with no fears of going off too fast.

About the time he realized the redhead was too drunk to come, Selig felt a tickle in his skull: Nyquist was probing him! This show of curiosity, this voyeurism, seemed an odd diversion for the usually self-contained Nyquist. Spying's *my* trick, Selig thought, and for a moment he was so disturbed by being observed in the act of love that he began to soften. Through conscious effort he reconstituted himself. This has no deep significance, he told himself. Nyquist is wholly amoral and does what he pleases, peeks here and peeks there without regard for propriety, and why should I let his scanning bother me? Recovering, he reached toward Nyquist and reciprocated the probe. Nyquist welcomed him:

—How you doing, Davey?

—Fine. Just fine.

—I got me a hot one here. Take a look.

Selig envied Nyquist's cool detachment. No shame, no guilt, no hangups of any kind. No trace of exhibitionistic pride nor voyeuristic panting, either: it seemed altogether natural to him to exchange such contacts now. Selig, though, could not help feeling queasy as he watched, through closed eyes, Nyquist busily working over the blonde, and watched Nyquist similarly watching him, echoing images of their parallel copulations reverberating dizzily from mind to mind. Nyquist, pausing a moment to detect and isolate Selig's sense of uneasiness, mocked it gently. You're worried that there's some kind of latent gayness in this thing, Nyquist told him. But I think what really scares you is contact, any sort of contact. Right? Wrong, Selig said, but he had felt the point hit home. For five minutes more they monitored each other's minds, until Nyquist decided the time had come to come, and the tempestuous tremors of his nervous system flung Selig, as usual, from his consciousness. Soon after, growing bored with humping the jiggling, sweaty redhead, Selig let his own climax overwhelm him and slumped down, shivering, weary.

Nyquist came into the livingroom half an hour later, the blonde with him, both of them naked. He didn't bother to knock, which surprised the redhead a little; Selig had no way of telling her that Nyquist had known they were finished. Nyquist put some music on and they all sat quietly, Selig and the redhead working on the bourbon, Nyquist and the blonde nipping into the Scotch, and toward dawn, as the snow began to slacken, Selig tentatively suggested a second round of lovemaking with a change of partners. "No," the redhead said. "I'm all fucked out. I want to go to sleep. Some other time, okay?" She fumbled for her clothes. At the door, wobbling and staggering, making a boozy farewell, she let something slip. "I can't help thinking there's something peculiar about you two guys," she said. *In vino veritas*. "You aren't a couple of queers, by any chance, are you?"

SEVENTEEN.

I remain on dead center. Becalmed, static, anchored. No, that's a lie, or if not a lie then at the very least a benign misstatement, a faulty cluster of metaphors. I am ebbing. Ebbing all the time. My tide is going out. I am revealed as a bare rocky shore, iron-hard, with trailing streamers of dirty brown seaweed dangling toward the absenting surf. Green crab scuttling about. Yes, I ebb, which is to say I diminish, I attenuate. Do you know, I feel quite calm about it now? Of course my moods fluctuate but

I feel

Quite calm

About it now.

This is the third year since first I began to recede
from myself. I think it started in the spring of 1974. Up
till then it worked faultlessly, I mean the power, always
there when I had occasion to call upon it, always
dependable, doing all its customary tricks, serving me
in all my dirty needs; and then without warning, without reason, it began dying. Little failures of input. Tiny
episodes of psychic impotence. I associate these events
with early spring, blackened wisps of late snow still
clinging to the streets, and it could not have been '75
nor was it '73, which leads me to place the onset of
outgo in the intermediate year. I would be snug and
smug inside someone's head, scanning scandals thought
to be safely hidden, and suddenly everything would
blur and become uncertain. Rather like reading the
Times and having the text abruptly turn to Joycean
dream-gabble between one line and the next, so that a
straightforward dreary account of the latest Presidential
fact-finding commission's finding of futile facts has meta-
morphosed into a foggy impenetrable report on old
Earwicker's borborygmi. At such times I would falter
and pull out in fear. What would you do if you believed
you were in bed with your heart's desire and awakened
to find yourself screwing a starfish? But these unclarities
and distortions were not the worst part: I think the
inversions were, the total reversal of signal. Such as
picking up a flash of love when what is really being
radiated is frosty hatred. Or vice versa. When that
happens I want to pound on walls to test reality. From
Judith one day I got strong waves of sexual desire, an
overpowering incestuous yearning, which cost me a fine
dinner as I ran nauseated and retching to the bowl. All
an error, all a deception; she was aiming spears at me
and I took them for Cupid's arrows, more fool I. Well,
after that I got blank spaces, tiny deaths of perception
in mid-contact, and after that came mingled inputs,
crossed wires, two minds coming in at once and me
unable to tell the which from the which. For a time the
color appercept dropped out, though that has come
back, one of the many false returns. And there were
other losses, barely discernible ones but cumulative in

their effect. I make lists now of the things I once could do that I can no longer. Inventories of the shrinkage. Like a dying man confined to his bed, paralyzed but observant, watching his relatives pilfer his goods. This day the television set has gone, and this day the Thackeray first editions, and this day the spoons, and now they have made off with my Piranesi, and tomorrow it will be the pots and pans, the Venetian blinds, my neckties, and my trousers, and by next week they will be taking toes, intestines, corneas, testicles, lungs, and nostrils. What will they use my nostrils for? I used to fight back with long walks, cold showers, tennis, massive doses of Vitamin A, and other hopeful, implausible remedies, and more recently I experimented with fasting and pure thoughts, but such struggling now seems to me inappropriate and even blasphemous; these days I strive toward cheerful acceptance of loss, with such success as you may have already perceived. Aeschylus warns me not to kick against the pricks, also Euripides and I believe Pindar, and if I were to check the New Testament I think I would find the injunction there as well, and so I obey, I kick not, even when the pricks are fiercest. I accept, I accept. Do you see that quality of acceptance growing in me? Make no mistake, I am sincere. This morning, at least, I am well on my way to acceptance, as golden autumn sunlight floods my room and expands my tattered soul. I lie here practicing the techniques that will make me invulnerable to the knowledge that it's all fleeing from me. I search for the joy that I know lies buried in the awareness of decline. Grow old along with me! The best is yet to be, The last of life, for which the first was made. Do you believe that? I believe that. I'm getting better at believing all sorts of things. Why, sometimes I've believed as many as six impossible things before breakfast. Good old Browning! How comforting he is:

> Then welcome each rebuff
> That turns earth's smoothness rough,
> Each sting that bids not sit nor stand, but go!

> Be our joys three parts pain!
> Strive, and hold cheap the strain.

Yes. Of course. And be our pains three parts joy, he might have added. Such joy this morning. And it's all fleeing from me, all ebbing. Going out of me from every pore.

* * *

Silence is coming over me. I will speak to no one after it's gone. And no one will speak to me.

* * *

I stand here over the bowl patiently pissing my power away. Naturally I feel some sorrow over what's happening, I feel regret, I feel—why crap around?—I feel anger and frustration and despair, but also, strangely, I feel shame. My cheeks burn, my eyes will not meet other eyes, I can hardly face my fellow mortals for the shame of it, as if something precious has been entrusted to me and I have failed in my trusteeship. I must say to the world, I've wasted my assets, I've squandered my patrimony, I've let it slip away, going, going, I'm a bankrupt now, a bankrupt. Perhaps this is a family trait, this embarrassment when disaster comes. We Seligs like to tell the world we are orderly people, captains of our souls, and when something external downs us we are abashed. I remember when my parents briefly owned a car, a dark-green 1948 Chevrolet purchased at some absurdly low price in 1950, and we were driving somewhere deep in Queens, perhaps on our way to my grandmother's grave, the annual pilgrimage, and a car emerged from a blind alley and hit us. A schvartze at the wheel, drunk, giddy. Nobody hurt, but our fender badly crumpled and our grille broken, the distinctive T-bar that identified the 1948 model hanging loose. Though the accident was in no way his fault my father reddened and reddened, transmitting feverish embarrassment, as though he were apologizing to the universe for having done anything so thoughtless as allowing his car to be hit. How he apologized to the other driver, too, my grim bitter father! It's all right, it's all right, accidents can happen, you mustn't feel upset about it, see, we're all okay! Looka mah car, man, looka mah car, the other driver kept saying, evidently aware that he was on to a soft touch, and I feared my father was going to give him money for the repairs, but my mother, fearing the same thing, headed him off at the pass. A week later he was still embarrassed; I popped into his mind while he was talking with a friend and heard him trying to pretend my mother had been driving, which was absurd—she never had a license—and then I felt embarrassed for him. Judith, too, when her marriage broke up, when she walked out on an impossible situation, registered enormous grief over the shameful fact that someone so purposeful and effective in life as Judith Hannah Selig should have entered into a lousy, murderous marriage which had to be terminated vulgarly in the divorce courts. Ego, ego, ego. I the miraculous mindreader, entering upon a mysterious decline, apologizing for my carelessness. I have misplaced my gift somewhere. Will you forgive me?

* * *

Good, to forgive;
Best, to forget!
Living, we fret;
Dying, we live.

* * *

Take an imaginary letter, Mr. Selig. Harrumph. Miss Kitty Holstein, Something West Sixty-something Street, New York City. Check the address later. Don't bother about the zipcode.

Dear Kitty:

I know you haven't heard from me in ages but I think now it's appropriate to try to get in touch with you again. Thirteen years have passed and a certain maturity must have come over both of us, I think, healing old wounds and making communication possible. Despite all hard feelings that may once have existed between us

*I never lost my fondness for you, and you remain bright
in my mind.*

*Speaking of my mind, there's something I ought to
tell you. I no longer do things very well with it. By
"things" I mean the mental thing, the mindreading
trick, which of course I couldn't do on you in any case,
but which defined and shaped my relationship to everybody else in the world. This power seems to be
slipping away from me now. It caused us so much grief,
remember? It was what ultimately split us up, as I tried
to explain in my last letter to you, the one you never
answered. In another year or so—who knows, six months,
a month, a week?—it will be totally gone and I will be
just an ordinary human being, like yourself. I will be a
freak no longer. Perhaps then there will be an opportu-
nity for us to resume the relationship that was interrupted
in 1963 and to reestablish it on a more realistic footing.*

*I know I did dumb things then. I pushed you
mercilessly. I refused to accept you for yourself, and
tried to make something else out of you, something
freakish, in fact, something just like myself. I had good
reasons in theory for attempting that, I thought then,
but of course they were wrong, they had to be wrong,
and I never saw that until it was too late. To you I
seemed domineering, overpowering, dictatorial—me, mild
self-effacing me! Because I was trying to transform you.
And eventually I bored you. Of course you were very
young then, you were—shall I say it?—shallow, unformed, and you resisted me. But now that we're both
adults we might be able to make a go of it.*

*I hardly know what my life will be like as an ordi-
nary human being unable to enter minds. Right now
I'm floundering, looking for definitions of myself, looking
for structures. I'm thinking seriously of entering the
Roman Catholic Church.* (Good Christ, am I? That's
the first I've heard of that! The stink of incense, the
mumble of priests, is that what I want?) *Or perhaps the
Episcopalians, I don't know. It's a matter of affiliating
myself with the human race. And also I want to fall in
love again. I want to be part of someone else. I've
already begun tentatively, timidly getting in touch with*

my sister Judith again, after a whole lifetime of war-
fare; we're starting to relate to each other for the first
time, and that's encouraging to me. But I need more: a
woman to love, not just sexually but in all ways. I've
really had that only twice in my life, once with you,
once about five years later with a girl named Toni who
wasn't very much like you, and both times this power of
mine ruined things, once because I got too close with it,
once because I couldn't get close enough. As the power
slips away from me, as it dies, perhaps there's a chance
for an ordinary human relationship between us at last,
of the kind that ordinary human beings have all the
time. For I will be ordinary. For I will be very ordinary.

I wonder about you. You're 35 years old now, I think.
That sounds very old to me, even though I'm 41. (41
doesn't sound old, somehow!) I still think of you as
being 22. You seemed even younger than that: sunny,
open, naive. Of course that was my fantasy-image of
you; I had nothing to go by but externals, I couldn't do
my usual number on your psyche, and so I made up a
Kitty who probably wasn't the real Kitty at all. Anyway,
so you're 35. I imagine you look younger than that
today. Did you marry? Of course you did. A happy
marriage? Lots of kids? Are you still married? What's
your married name, then, and where do you live, and
how can I find you? If you're married, will you be able
to see me anyway? Somehow I don't think you'd be a
completely faithful wife—does that insult you?—and so
there ought to be room in your life for me, as a friend,
as a lover. Do you ever see Tom Nyquist? Did you go on
seeing him for long, after you and I broke up? Were
you bitter toward me for the things I told you about
him in that letter? If your marriage has broken up, or
if somehow you never married, would you live with me
now? Not as a wife, not yet, just as a companion. To
help me get through the last phases of what's happening
to me? I need help so much. I need love. I know that's a
lousy way to go about making a proposition, let alone a
proposal, that is, saying, Help me, comfort me, stay
with me. I'd rather reach to you in strength than in
weakness. But right now I'm weak. There's this globe of

silence growing in my head, expanding, expanding, filling my whole skull, creating this big empty place. I'm suffering a slow reality leakage. I can only see the edges of things, not their substance, and now the edges are getting indistinct too. Oh, Christ. Kitty I need you. Kitty how will I find you? Kitty I hardly knew you. Kitty Kitty Kitty

* *.*

Twang. The plangent chord. *Twing.* The breaking string. *Twong.* The lyre untuned. Twang. Twing. Twong.

* * *

Dear children of God, my sermon this morning will be a very short one. I wish only that you should ponder and meditate the deep meaning and mystery of a few lines I intend to rip off the saintly Tom Eliot, a thoughtful guide for troubled times. Beloved, I direct you to his *Four Quartets*, to his paradoxical line, "In my beginning is my end," which he amplifies some pages later with the comment, "What we call the beginning is often the end/ And to make an end is to make a beginning." Some of us are ending right now, dear children; that is to say, aspects of their lives that once were central to them are drawing to a close. Is this an end or is it a beginning? Can the end of one thing not be the beginning of another? I think so, beloved. I think that the closing of a door does not preclude the opening of a different door. Of course, it takes courage to walk through that new door when we do not know what may lie beyond it, but one who has faith in Our Lord who died for us, who trusts fully in Him who came for the salvation of man, need have no fears. Our lives are pilgrimages toward Him. We may die small deaths every day, but we are reborn from death to death, until at last we go into the dark, into the vacant interstellar spaces where He awaits us, and why should we fear that, if He is there? And until that time comes let us live our lives without giving way to the temptation to grieve for ourselves. Remember always that the world still is full of wonders, that there are always new quests, that seeming ends are not ends in truth, but only transitions, stations of the way. Why should we mourn? Why should we give ourselves over to sorrow, though our lives be daily subtractions? If we lose *this*, do we also lose *that*? If sight goes, does love go also? If feeling grows faint, may we not return to old feelings and draw comfort from them? Much of our pain is mere confusion.

Be then of good cheer on this Our Lord's day, beloved, and spin no snares in which to catch yourselves, nor allow yourselves the self-indulgent sin of misery, and make no false distinctions between ends and beginnings, but go onward, ever searching, to new ecstasies, to new communions, to new worlds, and give no space in your soul to fear, but yield yourself up to the Peace of Christ and await that which must come. In the Name of the Father, and of the Son, and of the Holy Ghost. Amen.

* * *

Now comes a dark equinox out of its proper moment. The bleached moon glimmers like a wretched old skull. The leaves shrivel and fall. The fires die down. The dove, wearying, flutters to earth. Darkness spreads. Everything blows away. The purple blood falters in the narrowing veins; the chill impinges on the straining heart; the soul dwindles; even the feet become untrustworthy. Words fail. Our guides admit they are lost. That which has been solid grows transparent. Things pass away. Colors fade. This is a gray time, and I fear it will be grayer still, one of these days. Tenants of the house, thoughts of a dry brain in a dry season.

EIGHTEEN.

When Toni moved out of my place on 114th Street I waited two days before I did anything. I assumed she would come back when she calmed down; I figured she'd call, contrite, from some friend's house and say she was sorry she panicked and would I come get her in a cab. Also, in those two days I was in no shape to take any sort of action, because I was still suffering the aftereffects of my vicarious trip; I felt as though someone had seized my head and pulled on it, stretching my neck like a rubber band, letting it finally snap back into place with a sharp *thwock!* that addled my brains. I spent those two days in bed, dozing mostly, occasionally reading, and rushing madly out into the hall every time the telephone rang.

But she didn't come back and she didn't call, and on the Tuesday after the acid trip I started searching for her. I phoned her office first. Teddy, her boss, a bland sweet scholarly man, very gentle, very gay. No, she hadn't been to work this week. No, she hadn't been in touch at all. Was it urgent? Would I like to have her home number? "I'm *calling* from her home number," I said. "She isn't here and I don't know where she's gone. This is David Selig, Teddy." "Oh," he said. Very faintly, with great compassion. "Oh." And I said, "If she happens to call in, will you tell her to get in touch with me?" Next I started to phone her friends, those whose numbers I could find: Alice, Doris, Helen, Pam, Grace. Most of them, I knew, didn't like me. I didn't have to be telepathic to realize that. They thought she was throwing herself away on me, wasting her life with a man without career, prospects, money, ambition, talent, or looks. All five of them told me they hadn't heard from her. Doris, Helen, and Pam sounded sincere. The other two, it seemed to me, were lying. I took a taxi

over to Alice's place in the Village and shot a probe
upward, *zam!* nine stories into her head, and I learned
a lot of things about Alice that I hadn't really wanted to
know, but I didn't find out where Toni was. I felt dirty
about spying and didn't probe Grace. Instead I called
my employer, the writer, whose book Toni was editing,
and asked if he'd seen her. Not in weeks, he told me,
all ice. Dead end. The trail had run out.

I dithered on Wednesday, wondering what to do, and
finally, melodramatically, called the police. Gave a bored
desk sergeant her description: tall, thin, long dark hair,
brown eyes. No bodies found in Central Park lately? In
subway trash cans? The basements of Amsterdam Avenue tenements? No. No. No. Look, buddy, if we hear
anything we'll let you know, but it don't sound serious
to me. So much for the police. Restless, hopelessly
strung out, I walked down to the Great Shanghai for a
miserable half-eaten dinner, good food gone to waste.
(Children are starving in Europe, Duv. Eat. Eat.) Afterwards, sitting around over the sad scattered rem-
nants of my shrimp with sizzling rice and feeling myself
drop deep into bereavement, I scored a cheap pickup
in a manner I've always despised: I scanned the various
single girls in the big restaurant, of whom there were
numerous, looking for one who was lonely, thwarted,
vulnerable, sexually permissive, and in generally urgent need of ego reinforcement. It's no trick getting
laid if you have a sure way of knowing who's available,
but there's not much sport in the chase. She was, this
fish in the barrel, a passably attractive married lady in
her mid-20's, childless, whose husband, a Columbia
instructor, evidently had more interest in his doctoral
thesis than in her. He spent every night immured in
the stacks of Butler Library doing research, creeping
home late, exhausted, irritable, and generally impotent. I took her to my room, couldn't get it up either—
that bothered her; she assumed it was a sign of rejection—
and spent two tense hours listening to her life story.
Ultimately I managed to screw her, and I came almost
instantly. Not my finest hour. When I returned from
walking her home—110th and Riverside Drive—the

phone was ringing. Pam. "I've heard from Toni," she said, and suddenly I was slimy with guilt over my sleazy consolatory infidelity. "She's staying with Bob Larkin at his place over on East 83rd Street."

Jealousy, despair, humiliation, agony.

"Bob who?"

"Larkin. He's that high-bracket interior decorator she always talks about."

"Not to me."

"One of Toni's oldest friends. They're very close. I think he used to date her when she was in high school." A long pause. Then Pam chuckled warmly into my numb silence. "Oh, relax, relax, David! He's *gay*! He's just a kind of father-confessor for her. She goes to him when there's trouble."

"I see."

"You two have broken up, haven't you?"

"I'm not sure. I suppose we have. I don't know."

"Is there anything I can do to help?" This from Pam, who I had always thought regarded me as a destructive influence of whom Toni was well advised to be quit.

"Just give me his phone number," I said.

I phoned. It rang and rang and rang. At last Bob Larkin picked up. Gay, all right, a sweet tenor voice complete with lisp, not very different from the voice of Teddy-at-work. Who teaches them to speak with the homo accent? I asked, "Is Toni there?" A guarded response: "Who's calling, please?" I told him. He asked me to wait, and a minute or so passed while he conferred with her, hand over the mouthpiece. At last he came back and said Toni was there, yes, but she was very tired and resting and didn't want to talk to me right now. "It's urgent," I said. "Please tell her it's urgent." Another muffled conference. Same reply. He suggested vaguely that I call back in two or three days. I started to wheedle, to whine, to beg. In the middle of that unheroic performance the phone abruptly changed hands and Toni said to me, "Why did you call?"

"That ought to be obvious. I want you to come back."

"I can't."

She didn't say *I won't*. She said *I can't*.

I said, "Would you like to tell me why?"

"Not really."

"You didn't even leave a note. Not a word of explanation. You ran out so fast."

"I'm sorry, David."

"It was something you saw in me while you were tripping, wasn't it?"

"Let's not talk about it," she said. "It's over."

"I don't want it to be over."

"I do."

I do. That was like the sound of a great gate clanging shut in my face. But I wasn't going to let her throw home the bolts just yet. I told her she had left some of her things in my room, some books, some clothing. A lie; she had made a clean sweep. But I can be persuasive when I'm cornered, and she began to think it might be true. I offered to bring the stuff over right now. She didn't want me to come. She preferred never to see me again, she told me. Less painful all around, that way. But her voice lacked conviction; it was higher in pitch and much more nasal than it was when she spoke with sincerity. I knew she still loved me, more or less; even after a forest fire, some of the burned snags live on, and green new shoots spring from them. So I told myself. Fool that I was. In any case she couldn't entirely turn me away. Just as she had been unable to refrain from picking up the telephone, now she found it impossible to refuse me access to her. Talking very fast, I bludgeoned her into yielding. All right, she said. Come over. Come over. But you're wasting your time.

It was close to midnight. The summer air was clinging and clammy, with a hint of rain on the way. No stars visible. I hurried crosstown, choked with the vapors of the humid city and the bile of my shattered love. Larkin's apartment was on the nineteenth floor of an immense new terraced white-brick tower, far over on York Avenue. Admitting me, he gave me a tender, compassionate smile, as if to say, You poor bastard, you've been hurt and you're bleeding and now you're going to get ripped open again. He was about 30, a stocky, boyish-faced man with long unruly curly brown hair and large uneven teeth. He radiated warmth and sympathy and kindness. I could understand why Toni ran to him at times like this. "She's in the livingroom," he said. "To the left."

It was a big, impeccable place, somewhat freaky in decor, with jagged blurts of color dancing over the walls, pre-Columbian artifacts in spotlighted showcases, bizarre African masks, chrome-steel furniture—the kind of implausible apartment you see photographed in the Sunday *Times*' magazine section. The livingroom was the core of the spectacle, a vast white-walled room with a long curving window that revealed all the splendors of Queens across the East River. Toni sat at the far end, near the window, on an angular couch, dark blue flecked with gold. She wore old, dowdy clothes that clashed furiously with the splendor around her: a motheaten red sweater that I detested, a short frumpy black skirt, dark hose—and she was slumped down sullenly on her spine, leaning on one elbow, her legs jutting awkwardly forward. It was a posture that made her look bony and ungraceful. A cigarette drooped in her hand and there was a huge pile of butts in the ashtray beside her. Her eyes were bleak. Her long hair was tangled. She didn't move as I walked toward her. Such an aura of hostility came from her that I halted twenty feet away.

"Where's the stuff you were bringing?" she asked.

"There wasn't any. I just said that to have an excuse to see you."

"I figured that."

"What went wrong, Toni?"

"Don't ask. Just don't ask." Her voice had dropped into its lowest register, a bitter husky contralto. "You shouldn't have come here at all."

"If you'd tell me what I did—"

"You tried to hurt me," she said. "You tried to bum-trip me." She stubbed out her cigarette and immediately lit another. Her eyes, somber and hooded, refused to meet mine. "I realized finally that you were my enemy, that I had to escape from you. So I packed and got out."

"Your enemy? You know that isn't true."

"It was strange," she said. "I didn't understand what was happening, and I've talked to some people who've dropped a lot of acid and they can't understand it either. It was like our minds were linked, David. Like a telepathic channel had opened between us. And all sorts of stuff was pouring from you into me. Hateful stuff. Poisonous stuff. I was thinking your thoughts. Seeing myself as you saw me. Remember, when you said you were tripping too, even though you hadn't had any acid? And then you told me you were, like, reading my mind. That was what scared me. The way our minds seemed to blur together, to overlap. To become one. I never knew acid could do that to people."

This was my cue to tell her that it wasn't only the acid, that it hadn't been some druggy delusion, that what she had felt was the impingement of a special power granted me at birth, a gift, a curse, a freak of nature. But the words congealed in my mouth. They sounded insane to me. How could I confess such stuff? I let the moment pass. Instead I said lamely, "Okay, it was a strange moment for both of us. We were a little out of our heads. But the trip's over. You don't have to hide from me now. Come back, Toni."

"No."

"In a few days, then?"

"No."

"I don't understand this."

"Everything's changed," she said. "I couldn't ever live with you now. You scare me too much. The trip's over, but I look at you and I see demons. I see some kind of thing that's half-bat, half-man, with big rubbery wings and long yellow fangs and—oh, Jesus, David, I can't help any of this! I *still* feel as if our minds are linked. Stuff creeping out of you into my head. I should never have touched the acid." Carelessly she crushed her cigarette and found another. "You make me uncomfortable now. I wish you'd go. It gives me a headache just being this close to you. Please. Please. I'm sorry, David."

I didn't dare look into her mind. I was afraid that what I'd find there would blast and shrivel me. But in those days my power was still so strong that I couldn't help picking up, whether I sought it or not, a generalized low-level mental radiation from everyone I came close to, and what I picked up now from Toni confirmed what she was saying. She hadn't stopped loving me. But the acid, though lysergic and not sulfuric, had scarred and corroded our relationship by opening that terrible gateway between us. It was torment for her to be in the same room with me. No resources of mine could deal with that. I considered strategies, looked for angles of approach, ways to reason with her, to heal her through soft earnest words. No way. No way at all. I ran a dozen trial dialogs in my head and they all ended with Toni begging me to get out of her life. So. The End. She sat there all but motionless, downcast, dark-faced, her wide mouth clapped in pain, her brilliant smile extinguished. She seemed to have aged twenty years. Her odd, exotic desert-princess beauty had wholly fled from her. Suddenly she was more real to me, in her shroud of pain, than ever before. Ablaze with suffering, alive with anguish. And no way for me to reach her. "All right," I said quietly. "I'm sorry too." Over, done with, swiftly, suddenly, no warning, the bullet singing through the air, the grenade rolling treacherously into the tent, the anvil falling from the placid sky. Done with. Alone again. Not even any tears. Cry? What shall I cry?

Bob Larkin had tactfully remained outside, in his long foyer papered with dazzling black and white optical illusions, during our brief muffled conversation. Again the gentle sorrowing smile from him as I emerged.

"Thanks for letting me bother you this late," I said.

"No trouble at all. Too bad about you and Toni."

I nodded. "Yes. Too bad."

We faced each other uncertainly, and he moved toward me, digging his fingers momentarily into the muscle of my arm, telling me without words to shape up, to ride out the storm, to get myself together. He was so open that my mind sank unexpectedly into his, and I saw him plain, his goodness, his kindness, his sorrow. Out of him an image rose to me, a sharp encapsulated memory: himself and a sobbing, demolished Toni, the night before last, lying naked together on his modish round bed, her head cradled against his muscular hairy chest, his hands fondling the pale heavy globes of her breasts. Her body trembling with need. His unwilling drooping manhood struggling to offer her the consolation of sex. His gentle spirit at war with itself, flooded with pity and love for her but dismayed by her disturbing femaleness, those breasts, that cleft, her softness. You don't have to, Bob, she keeps saying, you don't have to, you really don't have to, but he tells her he wants to, it's about time we made it after knowing each other all these years, it'll cheer you up, Toni, and anyway a man needs a little variety, right? His heart goes out to her but his body resists, and their lovemaking, when it happens, is a hurried, pathetic, fumbled thing, a butting of troubled reluctant bodies, ending in tears, tremors, shared distress, and, finally, laughter, a triumph over pain. He kisses her tears away. She thanks him gravely for his efforts. They fall into childlike sleep, side by side. How civilized, how tender. My poor Toni. Goodbye. Goodbye. "I'm glad she went to you," I said. He walked me to the elevator. What shall I cry? "If she snaps out of it I'll make sure she calls you," he told me. I put my hand to his arm as he had to mine, and gave him the best smile in my repertoire. Goodbye.

NINETEEN.

This is my cave. Twelve floors high in the Marble Hill Houses, Broadway and 228th Street, formerly a middle-income municipal housing project, now a catch-all for classless and deracinated urban detritus. Two rooms plus bathroom, kitchenette, hallway. Once upon a time you couldn't get into this project unless you were married and had kids. Nowadays a few singles have slipped in, on the grounds that they're destitute. Things change as the city decays; regulations break down. Most of the building's population is Puerto Rican, with a sprinkling of Irish and Italian. In this den of papists a David Selig is a great anomaly. Sometimes he thinks he owes his neighbors a daily lusty rendition of the *Shma Yisroel*, but he doesn't know the words. *Kol Nidre*, perhaps. Or the *Kaddish*. This is the bread of affliction which our forefathers ate in the land of Egypt. He is lucky to have been led out of Egypt into the Promised Land.

Would you like the guided tour of David Selig's cave? Very well. Please come this way. No touching anything, please, and don't park your chewing gum on the furniture. The sensitive, intelligent, amiable, neurotic man who will be your guide is none other than David Selig himself. No tipping allowed. Welcome, folks, welcome to my humble abode. We'll begin our tour in the bathroom. See, this is the tub—that yellow stain in the porcelain was already there when he moved in—this is the crapper, this is the medicine chest. Selig spends a great deal of time in here; it's a room significant to any in-depth understanding of his existence. For example, he sometimes takes two or three showers a day. What is it, do you think, that he's trying to wash away? Leave that toothbrush alone, sonny. All right, come with me. Do you see these posters in the hallway? They are artifacts of the 1960's. This one shows the poet Allen Ginsberg in the costume of Uncle Sam. This one is a crude vulgarization of a subtle topological paradox by the Dutch printmaker M. C. Escher. This one shows a nude young couple making love in the Pacific surf. Eight to ten years ago, hundreds of thousands of young people decorated their rooms with such posters. Selig, although he was not exactly young even then, did the same. He often has followed current fads and modes in an attempt to affiliate himself more firmly with the structures of contemporary existence. I suppose these

posters are quite valuable now; he takes them with him
from one cheap rooming house to the next.

This room is the bedroom. Dark and narrow, with
the low ceiling typical of municipal construction a
generation ago. I keep the window closed at all times
so that the elevated train, roaring through the adjacent
sky late at night, doesn't awaken me. It's hard enough
to get some sleep even when things are quiet around
you. This is his bed, in which he dreams uneasy
dreams, occasionally, even now, involuntarily reading
the minds of his neighbors and incorporating their
thoughts in his fantasies. On this bed he has fornicated
perhaps fifteen women, one or two or occasionally three
times each, during the two and a half years of his
residence here. Don't look so abashed, young lady! Sex
is a healthy human endeavor and it remains an essential
aspect of Selig's life, even now in middle age! It may
become even more important to him in the years
ahead, for sex is, after all, a way of establishing communication with other human beings, and certain other
channels of communication appear to be closing for
him. Who are these girls? Some of them are not girls;
some are women well along in life. He charms them in
his diffident way and persuades them to share an hour
of joy with him. He rarely invites any of them back, and
those whom he does invite back often refuse the invitation, but that's all right. His needs are met. What's
that? Fifteen girls in two and a half years isn't very
many for a bachelor? Who are you to judge? He finds it
sufficient. I assure you, he finds it sufficient. Please
don't sit on his bed. It's an old one, bought second-
hand at an upstairs bargain basement that the Salvation
Army runs in Harlem. I picked it up for a few bucks
when I moved out of my last place, a furnished room on
St. Nicholas Avenue, and needed some furniture of my
own. Some years before that, around 1971, 1972, I had
a waterbed, another example of my following of transient fads, but I couldn't ever get used to the swooshing
and gurgling and I gave it, finally, to a hip young lady
who dug it the most. What else is in the bedroom? Very
little of interest, I'm afraid. A chest of drawers containing

commonplace clothing. A pair of worn slippers. A cracked mirror: are you superstitious? A lopsided bookcase packed tight with old magazines that he will never look at again—*Partisan Review, Evergreen, Paris Review, New York Review of Books, Encounter,* a mound of trendy literary stuff, plus a few journals of psychoanalysis and psychiatry, which Selig reads sporadically in the hope of increasing his self-knowledge; he always tosses them aside in boredom and disappointment. Let's get out of here. This room must be depressing you. We go past the kitchenette—four-burner stove, half-size refrigerator, formica-topped table—where he assembles very modest breakfasts and lunches (dinner he usually eats out) and enter the main focus of the apartment, the L-shaped blue-walled jam-packed livingroom/study.

Here you can observe the full range of David Selig's intellectual development. This is his record collection, about a hundred well-worn disks, some of them purchased as far back as 1951. (Archaic monophonic records!) Almost entirely classical music, although you will note two intrusive deposits: five or six jazz records dating from 1959 and five or six rock records dating from 1969, both groups acquired in vague, abortive efforts at expanding the horizons of his taste. Otherwise, what you will find here, in the main, is pretty austere stuff, thorny, inaccessible: Schoenberg, late Beethoven, Mahler, Berg, the Bartok quartets, Bach passacaglias. Nothing that you'd be likely to whistle after one hearing. He doesn't know a lot about music, but he knows what he likes; you wouldn't much care for it.

And these are his books, accumulated since the age of ten and hauled lovingly about with him from place to place. The archaeological strata of his reading can readily be isolated and examined. Jules Verne, H. G. Wells, Mark Twain, Dashiell Hammett at the bottom. Sabatini. Kipling. Sir Walter Scott. Van Loon, *The Story of Mankind*. Verrill, *Great Conquerors of South and Central America*. The books of a sober, earnest, alienated little boy. Suddenly, with adolescence, a quantum leap: Orwell, Fitzgerald, Hemingway, Hardy, the easier Faulkner. Look at these rare paperbacks of the 1940's and early 1950's, in odd off-sized formats, with laminated plastic covers! See what you could buy then for only 25¢! Look at the prurient paintings, the garish lettering! These science-fiction books date from that era too. I gobbled the stuff whole, hoping to find some clues to my own dislocated self's nature in the fantasies of Bradbury, Heinlein, Asimov, Sturgeon, Clarke. Look, here's Stapledon's *Odd John*, here's Beresford's *Hampdenshire Wonder*, here's a whole book called *Outsiders: Children of Wonder*, full of stories of little superbrats with freaky powers. I've underlined a lot of passages in that last one, usually places where I quarreled with the writers. *Outsiders?* Those writers, gifted as they were, were the outsiders, trying to imagine powers they'd never had; and I, who was on the inside, I the youthful mind-prowler (the book is dated 1954), had bones to pick with them. They stressed the angst of being supernormal, forgot about the ecstasy. Although, thinking about angst vs. ecstasy now, I have to admit they knew whereof they writ. Fellows, I have fewer bones to pick these days. This is rats' alley, where the dead men lost their bones.

Observe how Selig's reading becomes more rarefied as we reach the college years. Joyce, Proust, Mann, Eliot, Pound, the old avant-garde hierarchy. The French period: Zola, Balzac, Montaigne, Celine, Rimbaud, Baudelaire. This thick slug of Dostoevsky occupying half a shelf. Lawrence. Woolf. The mystical era: Augustine, Aquinas, the *Tao Te Ching*, the *Upanishads*, the *Bhagavad-Gita*. The psychological era: Freud, Jung, Adler, Reich, Reik. The philosophical era. The Marxist era. All that Koestler. Back to literature: Conrad, Forster, Beckett. Moving onward toward the fractured '60's: Bellow, Pynchon, Malamud, Mailer, Burroughs, Barth. *Catch*-22 and *The Politics of Experience*. Oh, yes, ladies and gentlemen, you are in the presence of a well-read man!

Here we have his files. A treasure-trove of personalia, awaiting a biographer yet unknown. Report cards, always with low marks for conduct. ("David shows little interest in his work and frequently disrupts the class.")

Crudely crayoned birthday cards for his mother and
father. Old photographs: can this fat freckled boy be the
gaunt individual who stands before you now? This man
with the high forehead and the forced rigid smile is the
late Paul Selig, father of our subject, deceased (*olav
hasholom!*) 11 August 1971 of complications following
surgery for a perforated ulcer. This gray-haired woman
with the hyperthyroid eyes is the late Martha Selig,
wife of Paul, mother of David, deceased (*oy, veh,
mama!*) 15 March 1973 of mysterious rot of internal
organs, probably cancerous. This grim young lady with
cold knifeblade face is Judith Hannah Selig, adopted
child of P. and M., unloving sister of D. Date on back of
photo: July 1963. Judith is therefore 18 years old and in
the summertime of her hate for me. How much she
looks like Toni in this picture! I never noticed the
resemblance before, but they've got the same dusky
Yemenite look, the same long black hair. But Toni's eyes
were always warm and loving, except right at the very
end, and Jude's eyes never held anything for me other
than ice, ice, Plutonian ice. Let us continue with the
examination of David Selig's private effects. This is his
collection of essays and term papers, written during his
college years. ("Carew is a courtly and elegant poet,
whose work reflects influences both of Jonson's precise
classicism and Donne's grotesque fancy—an interesting
synthesis. His poems are neatly constructed and sharp
of diction; in a poem such as 'Ask me no more where
Jove bestows,' he captures Jonson's harmonious austeri-
ty perfectly, while in others, such as 'Mediocrity in
Love Rejected' or 'Ingrateful Beauty Threatened,' his
wit is akin to that of Donne.") How fortunate for D.
Selig that he kept all this literary twaddle: here in his
later years these papers have become the capital on
which he lives, for you know, of course, how the central
figure of our investigations earns his livelihood nowadays. What else do we find in these archives? The
carbon copies of innumerable letters. Some of them are
quite impersonal missives. *Dear President Eisenhower.
Dear Pope John. Dear Secretary-General Hammarskjold.*
Quite often, once, though rarely in recent years, he

launched these letters to far corners of the globe. His fitful unilateral efforts at making contact with a deaf world. His troubled futile attempts at restoring order in a universe plainly tumbling toward the ultimate thermodynamic doom. Shall we look at a few of these documents? *You say, Governor Rockefeller, that "with nuclear weapons multiplying, our security is dependent on the credibility of our willingness to resort to our deterrent. It is our heavy responsibility as public officials and as citizens to save the lives and to protect the health of our people. A lagging civil-defense effort cannot be excused by our conviction that nuclear war is a tragedy and that we must strive by all honorable means to assure peace." Permit me to disagree. Your bomb-shelter program, Governor, is the project of a morally impoverished mind. To divert energy and resources from the search for a lasting peace to this ostrich-in-the-sand scheme is, I think, a foolish and dangerous policy that . . . .* The Governor, by way of replying, sent his thanks and an offprint of the very speech which Selig was protesting. Can one expect more? *Mr. Nixon, your entire campaign is pitched to the theory that America never had it so good under President Eisenhower, and so let's have four more years of the same. To me you sound like Faust, crying out to the passing moment, Bleibe doch, du bist so schoen! (Am I too literate for you, Mr. Vice-President?) Please bear in mind that when Faust utters those words, Mephistopheles arrives to collect his soul. Does it honestly seem to you that this instant in history is so sweet that you would stop the clocks forever? Listen to the anguish in the land. Listen to the voices of Mississippi's Negroes, listen to the cries of the hungry children of factory workers thrown out of work by a Republican recession, listen to. . . . Dear Mrs. Hemingway: Please allow me to add my words to the thousands expressing sorrow at the death of your husband. The bravery he showed in the face of a life-situation that had become unendurable and intolerable is indeed an example for those of us who . . . . Dear Dr. Buber. . . . Dear Professor Toynbee. . . . Dear President Nehru. . . . Dear Mr. Pound:*

The whole civilized world rejoices with you upon your liberation from the cruel and unnatural confinement which. . . .Dear Lord Russell. . . .Dear Chairman Khrushchev. . . .Dear M. Malraux. . . .dear. . . .dear. . . .dear . . . . A remarkable collection of correspondence, you must agree. With equally remarkable replies. See, this answer says, *You may be right,* and this one says, *I am grateful for your interest,* and this one says, *Of course time does not permit individual replies to all letters received, but nevertheless please be assured that your thoughts will receive careful consideration,* and this one says, *Send this bastard the bedbug letter.*

Unfortunately we do not have the imaginary letters which he dictates constantly to himself but never sends. *Dear Mr. Kierkegaard: I agree entirely with your celebrated dictum equating "the absurd" with "the fact that with God all things are possible," and declaring, "The absurd is not one of the factors which can be discriminated within the proper compass of the understanding: it is not identical with the improbable, the unexpected, the unforeseen." In my own experiences with the absurd. . . .Dear Mr. Shakespeare: How aptly you put it when you say, "Love is not love Which alters when it alteration finds, Or bends with the remover to remove." Your sonnet, however, begs the question: If love is not love, what then is it, that feeling of closeness which can be so absurdly and unexpectedly destroyed by a trifle? If you could suggest some alternate existential mode of relating to others that. . . .* Since they are transient, the product of vagrant impulses, and often incomprehensible, we have no satisfactory access to such communications, which Selig sometimes produces at a rate of hundreds per hour. *Dear Mr. Justice Holmes: In Southern Pacific Co. v. Jensen, 244 U.S. 205, 221 [1917], you ruled, "I recognize without hesitation that judges do and must legislate, but they can do so only interstitially; they are confined from molar to molecular motions." This splendid metaphor is not entirely clear to me, I must confess, and. . . .*

* * *

Dear Mr. Selig:

The present state of the world and the whole of life is diseased. If I were a doctor and were asked for my advice, I should reply, "Create silence."

Yours very sincerely,
Sören Kierkegaard
(1813–1855)

* * *

And then there are these three folders here, thick beige cardboard. They are not available for public inspection, since they contain letters of a rather more personal kind. Under the terms of our agreement with the David Selig Foundation, I am forbidden to quote, though I may paraphrase. These are his letters to and occasionally from the girls he has loved or has wanted to love. The earliest is dated 1950 and bears the notation at the top in large red letters, NEVER SENT. *Dear Beverly*, it begins, and it is full of embarrassingly graphic sexual imagery. What can you tell us about this Beverly, Selig? Well, she was short and cute and freckled, with big headlights and a sunny disposition, and sat in front of me in my biology class, and had a creepy twin sister, Estelle, who scowled a lot and through some fluke of genetics was as flat as Beverly was bosomy. Maybe that was why she scowled so much. Estelle liked me in her bitter murky way and I think might eventually have slept with me, which would have done my 15-year-old ego a lot of good, but I despised her. She seemed like a blotchy, badly done imitation of Beverly, whom I loved. I used to wander barefoot in Beverly's mind while the teacher, Miss Mueller, droned on about mitosis and chromosomes. She had just yielded her cherry to Victor Schlitz, the big rawboned green-eyed red-haired boy who sat next to her, and I learned a lot about sex from her at one remove, with a 12-hour time-lag, as she radiated every morning her adventure of the night before with Victor. I wasn't jealous of him. He was handsome and self-confident and deserved her, and I was too shy and insecure to lay anybody anyway, then. So I rode secretly piggyback on their romance and fantasized doing with Beverly the gaudy things Victor was doing with her, until I desperately wanted to get into her myself, but my explorations of her head told me that to her I was just an amusing gnomish child, an oddity, a jester. How then to score? I wrote her this letter describing in vivid sweaty detail everything that she and Victor had been up to, and said, Don't you wonder how I know all this, heh heh heh? The implication being that I'm some kind of superman with the power to penetrate the intimacies of a woman's mind. I figured that would topple her right into my arms in a swoon of awe, but some second thoughts led me to see that she'd either think I was crazy or a peeping tom, and would in either case be wholly turned off me, so I filed the letter away undelivered. My mother found it one night but she didn't dare say anything about it to me, hopelessly blocked as she was on the entire subject of sexuality; she just put it back in my notebook. I picked her thoughts that night and discovered she'd sneaked a look. Was she shocked and disturbed? Yes, she was, but also she felt very proud that her boy was a man at last, writing smutty stuff to pretty girls. My son the pornographer.

Most of the letters in this file date between 1954 and 1968. The most recent was written in the autumn of 1974, after which time Selig began to feel less and less in touch with the rest of the human race and stopped writing letters, except in his head. I don't know how many girls are represented here, but there must have been quite a few. Generally these were all superficial affairs, for Selig, as you know, never married or even had many serious involvements with women. As in the case of Beverly, the ones he loved most deeply he usually never had actual relationships with, though he was capable of pretending he felt love for someone who was in fact a casual pickup. At times he made use of his special gifts knowingly to exploit women sexually, especially about the age of 25. He is not proud of that period. Wouldn't you like to read these letters, you stinking voyeurs? But you won't. You won't get your paws on them. Why have I invited you in here, anyway? Why do I let you peer at my books and my photographs and my unwashed dishes and my stained bathtub? It must be that my sense of self is slipping. Isolation is choking me; the windows are closed but at least I've opened the door. I need you to bolster my grip on reality by looking into my life, by incorporating parts of it into your own experience, by discovering that I'm real, I exist, I suffer, I have a past if not a future. So that you can go away from here saying, Yes, I know David Selig, actually I know him quite well. But that doesn't mean I have to show you everything. Hey, here's a letter to Amy! Amy who relieved me of my festering virginity in the spring of 1953. Wouldn't you like to know the story of how that happened? Anybody's first time has an irresistible fascination. Well, fuck you: I don't feel like discussing it. It isn't much of a story anyway. I put it in her and I came and she didn't, that's how it was, and if you want to know the rest, who she was, how I seduced her, make up the details yourself. Where's Amy now? Amy's dead. How do you like that? His first lay, and he's outlived her already. She died in an auto accident at the age of 23 and her husband, who knew me vaguely, phoned me to tell me, since I had once been a friend of hers. He was still in trauma because the police had made him come down to identify the body, and she had really been destroyed, mangled, mutilated. Like something from another planet, that's how she looked, he told me. Catapulted through the windshield and into a tree. And I told him, "Amy was the first girl I ever slept with," and he started consoling me. He, consoling me, and I had only been trying to be sadistic.

Time passes. Amy's dead and Beverly's a pudgy middle-aged housewife, I bet. Here's a letter to Jackie Newhouse, telling her I can't sleep for thinking about her. Jackie Newhouse? Who that? Oh, yes. Five feet two and a pair of boobs that would have made Marilyn

Monroe feel topheavy. Sweet. Dumb. Puckered lips, baby-blue eyes. Jackie had nothing going for her at all except her bosom, but that was enough for me, 17 years old and hung up on breasts, God knows why. I loved her for her mammaries, so globular and conspicuous in the tight white polo shirts she liked to wear. Summer of 1952. She loved Frank Sinatra and Perry Como, and had FRANKIE written in lipstick down the left thigh of her jeans and PERRY on the right. She also loved her history teacher, whose name, I think, was Leon Sissinger or Zippinger or something like that, and she had LEON on her jeans too, from hip to hip. I kissed her twice but that was all, not even my tongue in her mouth; she was even more shy than I, terrified that some hideous male hand would violate the purity of those mighty knockers. I followed her around, trying not to get into her head because it depressed me to see how empty it was. How did it end? Oh, yes: her kid brother Arnie was telling me how he sees her naked at home all the time, and I, desperate for a vicarious glimpse of her bare breasts, plunged into his skull and stole a second-hand peek. I hadn't realized until then how important a bra can be. Unbound, they hung to her plump little belly, two mounds of dangling meat crisscrossed by bulging blue veins. Cured me of my fixation. So long ago, so unreal to me now, Jackie.

Here. Look. Spy on me. My fervid frenzied outpourings of love. Read them all, what do I care? Donna, Elsie, Magda, Mona, Sue, Lois, Karen. Did you think I was sexually deprived? Did you think my lame adolescence sent me stumbling into manhood incapable of finding women? I quarried for my life between their thighs. Dear Connie, what a wild night that was! Dear Chiquita, your perfume still lingers in the air. Dear Elaine, when I woke this morning the taste of you was on my lips. Dear Kitty, I—

Oh, God. Kitty. *Dear Kitty, I have so much to explain to you that I don't know where to begin. You never understood me, and I never understood you, and so the love I had for you was fated to bring us to a bad pass sooner or later. Which it now has. The failures of*

communication extended all up and down our relation-
ship, but because you were different from any person I
had ever known, truly and qualitatively different, I
made you the center of my fantasies and could not
accept you as you were, but had to keep hammering
and hammering and hammering away at you, until—
Oh, God. This one's too painful. What the hell are you
doing reading someone else's mail? Don't you have any
decency? I can't show you this. The tour's over. Out!
Out! Everybody out! For Christ's sake, get *out!*

TWENTY.

There was always the danger of being found out. He
knew he had to be on his guard. This was an era of
witch-hunters, when anyone who departed from com-
munity norms was ferreted out and burned at the stake.
Spies were everywhere, probing for young Selig's secret, fishing for the awful truth about him. Even Miss
Mueller, his biology teacher. She was a pudgy little
poodle of a woman, about 40, with a glum face and dark
arcs under her eyes; like a cryptodyke of some sort she
wore her hair cut brutally short, the back of her neck
always showing the stubble of a recent shave, and came
to class every day in a gray laboratory smock. Miss
Mueller was very deep into the realm of extrasensory
and occult phenomena. Of course they didn't use phrases
like "very deep into" in 1949, when David Selig was in
her class, but let the anachronism stand: she was ahead
of her time, a hippie born too soon. She really grooved
behind the irrational, the unknown. She knew her way
around the high-school bio curriculum in her sleep,
which was more or less the way she taught it. What
turned her on, really, were things like telepathy, clairvoyance, telekinesis, astrology, the whole parapsycho-
logical bag. The most slender provocation was enough
to nudge her away from the day's assignment, the study
of metabolism or the circulatory system or whatever,

and onto one of her hobbyhorses. She was the first on
her block to own the *I Ching*. She had done time inside
orgone boxes. She believed that the Great Pyramid of
Gizeh held divine revelations for mankind. She had
sought deeper truths by way of Zen, General Seman-
tics, the Bates eyesight exercises, and the readings of
Edgar Cayce. (How easily I can extend her quest past
the year of my own exposure to her! She must have
gone on to dianetics, Velikovsky, Bridey Murphy, and
Timothy Leary, and ended up, in her old age, as a lady
guru in some Los Angeles eyrie, heavy into psilocybin
and peyote. Poor silly gullible pitiful old bitch.)

Naturally she kept up with the research into extrasensory perception that J. B. Rhine was doing down at
Duke University. It terrified David whenever she spoke
of this. He constantly feared that she was going to give
way to the temptation to run some Rhine experiments
in class, and would thereby flush him out of hiding. He
had read Rhine himself, of course, *The Reach of the
Mind* and *New Frontiers of the Mind*, had even peered
into the opacities of *The Journal of Parapsychology*,
hoping to find something that would explain him to
himself, but there was nothing there except statistics
and foggy conjecture. Okay, Rhine was no threat to him
so long as he went on piddling around in North Carolina.
But muddled Miss Mueller might just strip him naked
and deliver him to the pyre.

Inevitable, the progression toward disaster. The topic
for the week, suddenly, was the human brain, its functions and capabilities. See, this is the cerebrum, this is
the cerebellum, this is the medulla oblongata. A child's
garden of synapses. Fat-cheeked Norman Heimlich,
gunning for a 99, knowing precisely which button to
push, put up his hand: "Miss Mueller, do you think it'll
ever be possible for people really to read minds, I mean
not by tricks or anything but actual mental telepathy?"
Oh, the joy of Miss Mueller! Her lumpy face glowing.
This was her cue to launch into an animated discussion
of ESP, parapsychology, inexplicable phenomena, supernormal modes of communication and perception,
the Rhine researches, et cetera, et cetera, a torrent of

metaphysical irrelevance. David wanted to hide under his desk. The word "telepathy" made him wince. He already suspected that half the class realized what he was. Now a flash of wild paranoia. Are they looking at me, are they staring and pointing and tapping their heads and nodding? Certainly these were irrational fears. He had surveyed every mind in the class again and again, desperately trying to amuse himself during the arid stretches of boredom, and he knew that his secret was safe. His classmates, plodding young Brooklynites all, would never cotton to the veiled presence of a superman in their midst. They thought he was strange, yes, but had no notion of *how* strange. Would Miss Mueller now blow his cover, though? She was talking about conducting parapsychology experiments in class to demonstrate the potential reach of the human brain. Oh where can I hide?

No escape. She had her cards with her the next day. "These are known as Zener cards," she explained solemnly, holding them up, fanning them out like Wild Bill Hickok about to deal himself a straight flush. David had never actually seen a set of the cards before, yet they were as familiar to him as the deck his parents used in their interminable canasta games. "They were devised about twenty-five years ago at Duke University by Dr. Karl E. Zener and Dr. J. B. Rhine. Another name for them is 'ESP cards.' Who can tell me what 'ESP' means?"

Norman Heimlich's stubby hand waving in the air. "Extrasensory perception, Miss Mueller!"

"Very good, Norman." Absentmindedly she began to shuffle the cards. Her eyes, normally inexpressive, gleamed with a Las Vegas intenisty. She said, "The deck consists of 25 cards, divided into five 'suits' or symbols. There are five cards marked with a star, five with a circle, five with a square, five with a pattern of wavy lines, and five with a cross or plus sign. Otherwise they look just like ordinary playing cards." She handed the pack to Barbara Stein, another of her favorites, and told her to copy the five symbols on the blackboard. "The idea is for the subject being examined to look at each

card in turn, face down, and try to name the symbol on
the other side. The test can be run in many different
ways. Sometimes the examiner looks briefly at each
card first; that gives the subject a chance to pick the
right answer out of the examiner's mind, if he can.
Sometimes neither the subject nor the examiner sees
the card in advance. Sometimes the subject is allowed
to touch the card before he makes his guess. Sometimes
he may be blindfolded, and other times he may be
permitted to stare at the back of each card. No matter
how it's done, though, the basic aim is always the same:
for the subject to determine, using extrasensory powers, the design on a card that he can't see. Estelle,
suppose the subject has no extrasensory powers at all,
but is simply operating on pure guesswork. How many
right guesses could we expect him to make, out of the
25 cards?"

Estelle, caught by surprise, reddened and blurted,
"Uh—twelve and a half?"

A sour smirk from Miss Mueller, who turned to the
brighter, happier twin. "Beverly?"

"Five, Miss Mueller?"

"Correct. You always have one chance out of five of
guessing the right suit, so five right calls out of 25 is
what luck alone ought to bring. Of course, the results
are never that neat. On one run through the deck you
might have four correct hits, and then next time six,
and then five, and then maybe seven, and then perhaps
only three—but the *average*, over a long series of trials,
ought to be about five. That is, if pure chance is the
only factor operating. Actually, in the Rhine experiments some groups of subjects have averaged 6½ or 7
hits out of 25 over many tests. Rhine believes that this
above-average performance can only be explained as
ESP. And certain subjects have done much better.
There was a man once who called nine straight cards
right, two days in a row. Then a few days later he hit 15
straight cards, 21 out of 25. The odds against that are
fantastic. How many of you think it could have been
nothing but luck?"

About a third of the hands in the class went up. Some

of them belonged to dullards who failed to realize that it was shrewd politics to show sympathy for the teacher's pet enthusiasms. Some of them belonged to incorrigible skeptics who disdained such cynical manipulations. One of the hands belonged to David Selig. He was merely trying to don protective coloration.

Miss Mueller said, "Let's run a few tests today. Victor, will you be our first guinea pig? Come to the front of the room."

Grinning nervously, Victor Schlitz shambled forward. He stood stiffly beside Miss Mueller's desk as she cut the cards and cut them again. Then, peering quickly at the top card, she slid it toward him. "Which symbol?" she asked.

"Circle?"

"We'll see. Class, don't say anything." She handed the card to Barbara Stein, telling her to place a checkmark under the proper symbol on the blackboard. Barbara checked the square. Miss Mueller glanced at the next card. *Star*, David thought.

"Waves," Victor said. Barbara checked the star.

"Plus." *Square, dummy!* Square.

"Circle." *Circle*. Circle. A sudden ripple of excitement in the classroom at Victor's hit. Miss Mueller, glaring, called for silence.

"Star." *Waves*. Waves was what Barbara checked.

"Square." *Square*, David agreed. Square. Another ripple, more subdued.

Victor went through the deck. Miss Mueller had kept score: four correct hits. Not even as good as chance. She put him through a second round. Five. All right, Victor: you may be sexy, but a telepath you aren't. Miss Mueller's eyes roved the room. Another subject? Let it not be me, David prayed. God, let it not be me. It wasn't. She summoned Sheldon Feinberg. He hit five the first time, six the second. Respectable, unspectacular. Then Alice Cohen. Four and four. Stony soil, Miss Mueller. David, following each turn of the cards, had hit 25 out of 25 every time, but he was the only one who knew that.

"Next?" Miss Mueller said. David shrank into his

seat. How much longer until the dismissal bell? "Norman Heimlich." Norman waddled toward the teacher's desk. She glanced at a card. David, scanning her, picked up the image of a star. Bouncing then to Norman's mind, David was amazed to detect a flicker of an image there, a star perversely rounding its points to form a circle, then reverting to being a star. What was this? Did the odious Heimlich have a shred of the power? "Circle," Norman murmured. But he hit the next one—the waves—and the one after that, the square. He did indeed seem to be picking up emanations, fuzzy and indistinct but emanations all the same, from Miss Mueller's mind. Fat Heimlich had the vestiges of the gift. But only the vestiges; David, scanning his mind and the teacher's, watched the images grow ever more cloudy and vanish altogether by the tenth card, fatigue scattering Norman's feeble strength. He scored a seven, though, the best so far. *The bell*, David prayed. *The bell, the bell, the bell!* Twenty minutes away.

A small mercy. Miss Mueller briskly distributed test paper. She would run the whole class at once. "I'll call numbers from 1 to 25," she said. "As I call each number, write down the symbol you think you see. Ready? *One*."

David saw a circle. *Waves*, he wrote.

Star. *Square*.

Waves. *Circle*.

Star. *Waves*.

As the test neared its close, it occurred to him that he might be making a tactical error by muffing every call. He told himself to put down two or three right ones, just for camouflage. But it was too late for that. There were only four numbers left; it would look too conspicuous if he hit several of them correctly after missing all the others. He went on missing.

Miss Mueller said, "Now exchange papers with your neighbor and mark his answers. Ready? Number one: circle. Number two: star. Number three: waves. Number four. . . ."

Tensely she called for results. Had anyone scored ten hits or more? No, teacher. Nine? Eight? Seven? Nor-

man Heimlich had seven again. He preened himself:
Heimlich the mind-reader. David felt disgust at the
knowledge that Heimlich had even a crumb of power.
Six? Four students had six. Five? Four? Miss Mueller
diligently jotted down the results. Any other figures?
Sidney Goldblatt began to snicker. "Miss Mueller, how
about zero?"

She looked startled. *"Zero?* Was there someone who
got all 25 cards *wrong?"*

"David Selig did!"

David Selig wanted to drop through the floor. All
eyes were on him. Cruel laughter assailed him. *David
Selig got them all wrong.* It was like saying, David Selig
wet his pants, David Selig cheated on the exam, David
Selig went into the girls' toilet. By trying to conceal
himself, he had made himself terribly conspicuous.
Miss Mueller, looking stern and oracular, said, "A null
score can be quite significant too, class. It might mean
extremely strong ESP abilities, rather than the total
absence of such powers, as you might think." Oh, God.
Extremely strong ESP abilities. She went on, "Rhine
talks of phenomena such as 'forward displacement' and
'backward displacement,' in which an unusually powerful ESP force might accidentally focus on one card
ahead of the right one, or one card behind it, or even
two or three cards away. So the subject would appear to
get a below-average result when actually he's hitting
perfectly, just off the target! David, let me see your
answers."

"I wasn't getting anything, Miss Mueller. I was just
putting down my guesses, and I suppose they were all
wrong."

"Let me see."

As though marching to the scaffold, he brought her
the sheet. She placed it beside her own list and tried to
realign it, searching for some correlation, some displacement sequence. But the randomness of his deliberately wrong answers protected him. A forward displacement of one card gave him two hits; a backward
displacement of one card gave him three. Nothing
significant there. Nevertheless, Miss Mueller would not

let go. "I'd like to test you again," she said. "We'll run
several kinds of trials. A null score is fascinating." She
began to shuffle the deck. God, God, God, where are
you? Ah. The bell! Saved by the bell! "Can you stay
after class?" she asked. In agony, he shook his head.
"Got to go to geometry next, Miss Mueller." She relented.
Tomorrow, then. We'll run the tests tomorrow. God! He
was up all the night in a turmoil of fear, sweating,
shivering; about four in the morning he vomited. He
hoped his mother would make him stay home from
school, but no luck: at half past seven he was aboard the
bus. Would Miss Mueller forget about the test? Miss
Mueller had not forgotten. The fateful cards were on
her desk. There would be no escape. He found himself
the center of all attention. All right, Duv, be cleverer
this time. "Are you ready to begin?" she asked, tipping
up the first card. He saw a plus sign in her mind.

"Square," he said.

He saw a circle. "Waves," he said.

He saw another circle. "Plus," he said.

He saw a star. "Circle," he said.

He saw a square. "Square," he said. *That's one*.

He kept careful count. Four wrong answers, then a
right one. Three wrong answers, another right one.
Spacing them with false randomness, he allowed himself five hits on the first test. On the second he had
four. On the third, six. On the fourth, four. Am I being
too average, he wondered? Should I give her a one-hit
run, now? But she was losing interest. "I still can't
understand your null score, David," she told him. "But
it does seem to me as if you have no ESP ability
whatever." He tried to look disappointed. Apologetic,
even. Sorry, teach, I ain't got no ESP. Humbly the
deficient boy made his way to his seat.

* * *

In one blazing instant of revelation and communion,
Miss Mueller, I could have justified your whole lifelong
quest for the improbable, the inexplicable, the unknow-
able, the irrational. The miraculous. But I didn't have

the guts to do it. I had to look after my own skin, Miss
Mueller. I had to keep a low profile. Will you forgive
me? Instead of giving you truth, I faked you out, Miss
Mueller, and sent you spinning blindly onward to the
tarot, to the signs of the zodiac, to the flying-saucer
people, to a thousand surreal vibrations, to a million
apocalyptic astral antiworlds, when the touch of my
mind against yours might have been enough to heal
your madness. One touch from me. In a moment. In
the twinkling of an eye.

TWENTY-ONE.

These are the days of David's passion, when he
writhes a lot on his bed of nails. Let's do it in short
takes. It hurts less that way.

* * *

Tuesday. Election Day. For months the clamor of the
campaign has fouled the air. The free world is choosing
its new maximum leader. The sound-trucks rumble
along Broadway, belching slogans. Our next President!
The man for all America! Vote! Vote! Vote! Vote for X!
Vote for Y! The hollow words merge and blur and flow.
Republocrat. Demican. *Boum*. Why should I vote? I
will not vote. I do not vote. I am not plugged in. I am
not part of the circuit. Voting is for *them*. Once, in the
late autumn of 1968, I think it was, I was standing
outside Carnegie Hall, thinking of going over to the
paperback bookshop on the other side of the street,
when suddenly all traffic halted on 57th and scores of
policemen sprang up from the pavement like the dragon's-
teeth warriors sown by Cadmus, and a motorcade came
rumbling out of the east, and lo! in a dark black
limousine rode Richard M. Nixon, President-Elect of
the United States of America, waving jovially to the
assembled populace. My big chance at last, I thought. I

will look into his mind and make myself privy to great secrets of state; I will discover what it is about our leaders that sets them apart from ordinary mortals. And I looked into his mind, and what I found in there I will not tell you, except to say that it was more or less what I should have expected to find. And since that day I have had nothing to do with politics or politicians. Today I stay home from the polls. Let them elect the next President without my help.

* * *

Wednesday. I doodle with Yahya Lumumba's half-finished term paper and other such projects, a few futile lines on each. Getting nowhere. Judith calls. "A party," she says. "You're invited. Everybody'll be there."

"A party? Who? Where? Why? When?"

"Saturday night. Near Columbia. The host is Claude Guermantes. Do you know him? Professor of French Literature." No, the name is not Guermantes. I have changed the name to protect the guilty. "He's one of those charismatic new professors. Young, dynamic, handsome, a friend of Simone de Beauvoir, of Genet. Karl and I are coming. And a lot of others. He always invites the most interesting people."

"Genet? Simone de Beauvoir? Will they be there?"

"No, silly, not them. But it'll be worth your time. Claude gives the best parties of anybody I know. Brilliant combinations of people."

"Sounds like a vampire to me."

"He gives as well as takes, Duv. He specifically asked me to invite you."

"How does he know me at all?"

"Through me," she says. "I've talked of you. He's dying to meet you."

"I don't like parties."

"Duv—"

I know that warning tone of voice. I have no stomach for a hassle just now. "All right," I say, sighing. "Saturday night. Give me the address." Why am I so pliable?

Why do I let Judith manipulate me? Is this how I build my love for her, through these surrenders?

* * *

Thursday, I do two paragraphs, a.m., for Yahya Lumumba. Very apprehensive about his reaction to the thing I'm writing for him. He might just loathe it. If I ever finish it. I *must* finish it. Never missed a deadline yet. Don't dare to. In the p.m. I walk up to the 230th St. bookstore, needing fresh air and wanting, as usual, to see if anything interesting has come out since my last visit, three days before. Compulsively buy a few paperbacks—an anthology of minor metaphysical poets, Updike's *Rabbit Redux,* and a heavy Levi-Straussian anthropological study, folkways of some Amazonian tribe, that I know I'll *never* get around to reading. A new clerk at the cash register: a girl, 19, 20, pale, blond, white silk blouse, short plaid skirt, impersonal smile. Attractive in a vacant-eyed way. She isn't at all interesting to me, sexually or otherwise, and as I think that I chide myself for putting her down—let nothing human be alien to me—and on a whim I invade her mind as I pay for my books, so that I won't be judging her by superficials. I burrow in easily, deep, down through layer after layer of trivia, mining her without hindrance, getting right to the real stuff. Oh! What a sudden blazing communion, soul to soul! She glows. She streams fire. She comes to me with a vividness and a completeness that stun me, so rare has this sort of experience become for me. No dumb pallid mannequin now. I see her full and entire, her dreams, her fantasies, her ambitions, her loves, her soaring ecstasies (last night's gasping copulation and the shame and guilt afterward), a whole churning steaming sizzling human soul. Only once in the last six months have I hit this quality of total contact, only once, that awful day with Yahya Lumumba on the steps of Low Library. And as I remember that searing, numbing experience, something is triggered in me and the same thing happens. A dark curtain falls. I am disconnected. My grip on her consciouness is severed.

Silence, that terrible mental silence, rushes to enfold me. I stand there, gaping, stunned, alone again and frightened, and I start to shake and drop my change, and she says to me, worried, "Sir? *Sir?*" in that sweet fluting little-girl voice.

*   *   *

Friday. Wake up with aches, high fever. Undoubtedly an attack of psychosomatic ague. The angry, embittered mind mercilessly flagellating the defenseless body. Chills followed by hot sweats followed by chills. Empty-gut puking. I feel hollow. Headpiece filled with straw. Alas! Can't work. I scribble a few pseudo-Lumumbesque lines and toss the sheet away. Sick as a dog. Well, a good excuse not to go to that dumb party, anyhow. I read my minor metaphysicals. Some of them not so minor. Traherne, Crashaw, William Cartwright. As for instance, Traherne:

> Pure native Powers that Corruption loathe,
> >   Did, like the fairest Glass
> >   Or, spotless polished Brass,
> Themselves soon in their Object's Image clothe:
> >   Divine Impressions, when they came,
> >   Did quickly enter and my Soul enflame.
> 'Tis not the Object, but the Light,
> That maketh Heav'n: 'Tis a clearer Sight.
> >   Felicity
> Appears to none but them that purely see.

Threw up again after that. Not to be interpreted as an expression of criticism. Felt better for a while. I should call Judith. Have her make some chicken soup for me. Oy, veh. Veh is mir.

*   *   *

Saturday. Without help of chicken soup I recover and decide to go to the party. Veh is mir, in spades. Remember, remember, the sixth of November. Why has David allowed Judith to drag him from his cave? An endless subway ride downtown; spades full of weekend wine add a special *frisson* to the ordinary adventure of Manhattan transportation. At last the familiar Columbia station. I must walk a few blocks, shivering, not dressed properly for the wintry weather, to the huge old apartment house at Riverside Drive and 112th St. where Claude Guermantes is reputed to live. I stand hesitantly outside. A cold, sour breeze ripping malevolently across the Hudson at me, bearing the windborne detritus of New Jersey. Dead leaves swirling in the park. Inside, a mahogany doorman eyes me fishily. "Professor Guermantes?" I say. He jerks a thumb. "Seventh floor, 7-G." Waving me toward the elevator. I'm late; it's almost ten o'clock. Upstairs in the weary Otis, creak creak creak creak, elevator door rolls back, silkscreen poster in the hallway proclaims the route to Guermantes' lair. Not that posters are necessary. A high-decibel roar from the left tells me where the action is. I ring the bell. Wait. Nothing. Ring again. Too loud for them to hear me. Oh, to be able to transmit thoughts instead of just to receive them! I'd announce myself in tones of thunder. Ring again, more aggressively. Ah! Yes! Door opens. Short dark-haired girl, undergraduate-looking, wearing a sort of orange sari that leaves her right breast—small—bare. Nudity a la mode. Flashes her teeth gaily. "Come in, come in, come in!"

A mob scene. Eighty, ninety, a hundred people, everyone dressed in Seventies Flamboyant, gathered in groups of eight to ten, shouting profundities at one another. Those who hold no highballs are busily passing joints, ritualistic hissing intake of breath, much coughing, passionate exhaling. Before I have my coat off someone pops an elaborate ivory-headed pipe in my mouth. "Super hash," he explains. "Just in from Damascus. Come on, man, toke up!" I suck smoke willy-nilly and feel an immediate effect. I blink. "Yeah," my benefactor shouts. "It's got the power to cloud men's minds, don't it?" In this mob my mind is already pretty well clouded, however, sans cannabis, solely from input overload. My power seems to be functioning at reasonably high intensity tonight, only without much differentiation of

persons, and I am involuntarily taking in a thick soup of
overlapping transmissions, a chaos of merging thoughts.
Murky stuff. Pipe and passer vanish and I stumble
stonedly foward into a cluttered room lined from floor
to ceiling with crammed bookcases. I catch sight of
Judith just as she catches sight of me, and from her on a
direct line of contact comes her outflow, fiercely vivid at
first, trailing off in moments into mush: *brother, pain,
love, fear, shared memories, forgiveness, forgetting,
hatred, hostility, murmphness, froomz, zzzhhh, mmmm.
Brother. Love. Hate. Zzzhhh.*

"Duv!" she cries. "Oh, here I am, Duvid!"

Judith looks sexy tonight. Her long lithe body is
sheathed in a purple satiny wrap, skin-tight, throat-
high, plainly showing her breasts and the little bumps
of her nipples and the cleft between her buttocks. On
her bosom nestles a glittering slab of gold-rimmed jade,
intricately carved; her hair, unbound, tumbles gloriously.
I feel pride in her beauty. She is flanked by two
impressive-looking men. On one side is Dr. Karl F.
Silvestri, author of *Studies in the Physiology of Thermoregulation*. He corresponds fairly closely to the image
of him that I had plucked from Judith's mind at her
apartment a week or two ago, though he is older than I
had guessed, at least 55, maybe closer to 60. Bigger,
too—perhaps six feet five. I try to envision his huge
burly body atop Jude's wiry slender self, pressing down.
I can't. He has florid cheeks, a stolid self-satisfied facial
expression, tender intelligent eyes. He radiates something avuncular or even paternal toward her. I see why
Jude is attracted to him: he is the powerful father-figure
that poor beaten Paul Selig never could have been for
her. On Judith's other side is a man whom I suspect to
be Professor Claude Guermantes; I bounce a quick
probe into him and confirm that guess. His mind is
quicksilver, a glittering, shimmering pool. He thinks in
three or four languages at once. His rampaging energy
exhausts me at a single touch. He is about 40, just
under six feet tall, muscular, athletic; he wears his
elegant sandy hair done in swirling baroque waves, and

his short goatee is impeccably clipped. His clothing is
so advanced in style that I lack the vocabulary to
describe it, being unaware of fashions myself: a kind of
mantle of coarse green and gold fabric (linen? muslin?),
a scarlet sash, flaring satin trousers, turned-up pointed-
toed medieval boots. His dandyish appearance and
mannered posture suggest that he might be gay, but he
gives off a powerful aura of heterosexuality, and from
Judith's stance and fond way of looking at him I begin to
realize that he and she must once have been lovers.
May still be. I am shy about probing that. My raids on
Judith's privacy are too sore a point between us.

"I'd like you to meet my brother David," Judith says.

Silvestri beams. "I've heard so much about you, Mr.
Selig."

"Have you really?" (*I've got this freak of a brother,
Karl. Would you believe it, he can actually read minds?
Your thoughts are as clear as a radio broadcast to him.*)
How much has Judith actually revealed about me? I'll
try to probe him and see. "And call me David. You're
Dr. Silvestri, right?"

"That's right. Karl. I'd prefer Karl."

"I've heard a lot about you from Jude," I say. No go
on the probe. My abominable waning gifts; I get only
sputtering bits of static, misty scraps of unintelligible
thought. His mind is opaque to me. My head starts to
throb. "She showed me two of your books. I wish I
could understand things like that."

A pleased chuckle from lofty Silvestri. Judith meanwhile has begun to introduce me to Guermantes. He
murmurs his delight at making any acquaintance. I half
expect him to kiss my cheeks, or maybe my hand. His
voice is soft, purring; it carries an accent, but not a
French one. Something strange, a mixture, Franco-
Italic, maybe, or Franco-Hispanic. Him at least I can
probe, even now; somehow his mind, more volatile
than Silvestri's, remains within my reach. I slither in
and take a look, even while exchanging platitudes about
the weather and the recent election. Christ! Casanova
Redivivus! He's slept with everything that walks or
crawls, masculine feminine neuter, including of course

my accessible sister Judith, whom—according to a neatly filed surface memory—he last penetrated just five hours ago, in this very room. His semen now curdles within her. He is obscurely restless over the fact that she never has come with him; he takes it as a failure of his flawless technique. The professor is speculating in a civilized way on the possibilities of nailing me before the night is out. No hope, professor. I will not be added to your Selig collection. He asks me pleasantly about my degrees. "Just one," I say. "A B.A. in '56. I thought about doing graduate work in English literature but never got around to it." He teaches Rimbaud, Verlain, Mallarmé, Baudelaire, Lautréamont, that whole sick crew, and identifies with them spiritually; his classes are full of adoring Barnard girls whose thighs open gladly for him, although in his Rimbaud facet he is not averse to romping with hearty Columbia men on occasions. As he talks to me he fondles Judith's shoulderblades affectionately, proprietorially. Dr. Silvestri appears not to notice, or else not to care. "Your sister," Guermantes murmurs, "she is a marvel, she is an original, a splendor—a *type*, M'sieu Selig, a *type*." A compliment, in the froggish sense. I poke his mind again and learn that he is writing a novel about a bitter, voluptuous young divorcee and a French intellectual who is an incarnation of the life-force, and expects to make millions from it. He fascinates me: so blatant, so phony, so manipulative, and yet so attractive despite all his transparent failings. He offers me cocktails, highballs, liqueurs, brandies, pot, hash, cocaine, anything I crave. I feel engulfed and escape from him, in some relief, slipping away to pour a little rum.

A girl accosts me at the liquor table. One of Guermantes' students, no more than 20. Coarse black hair tumbling into ringlets; pug nose; fierce perceptive eyes; full fleshy lips. Not beautiful but somehow interesting. Evidently I interest her, too, for she grins at me and says, "Would you like to go home with me?"

"I just got here."

"Later. Later. No hurry. You look like you're fun to fuck."

"Do you say that to everybody you've just met?"

"We haven't even met," she points out. "And no, I don't say it to everybody. To lots, though. What's wrong? Girls can take the initiative these days. Besides, it's leap year. Are you a poet?"

"Not really."

"You look like one. I bet you're sensitive and you suffer a lot." My familiar dopy fantasy, coming to life before my eyes. *Her* eyes are red-rimmed. She's stoned. An acrid smell of sweat rising from her black sweater. Her legs are too short for her torso, her hips too wide, her breasts too heavy. Probably she's got the clap. Is she putting me on? *I bet you're sensitive and you suffer a lot. Are you a poet?* I try to explore her, but it's useless; fatigue is blanking my mind, and the collective shriek of the massed mob of partygoers is drowning out all individual outputs now. "What's your name?" she asks.

"David Selig."

"Lisa Holstein. I'm a senior at Barn—"

"*Holstein?*" The name triggers me. Kitty, Kitty, Kitty! "Is that what you said? Holstein?"

"Holstein, yes, and spare me the cow jokes."

"Do you have a sister named Kitty? Catherine, I guess. Kitty Holstein. About 35 years old. Your sister, maybe your cousin—"

"No. Never heard of her. Someone you know?"

"Used to know," I say. "Kitty Holstein." I pick up my drink and turn away.

"Hey," she calls after me. "Did you think I was kidding? Do you want to go home with me tonight or don't you?"

A black colossus confronts me. Immense Afro nimbus, terrifying jungle face. His clothing a sunburst of clashing colors. *Him*, here? Oh, God. Just who I most need to see. I think guiltily of the unfinished term paper, lame, humpbacked, a no-ass monstrosity, sitting on my desk. What is he doing here? How has Claude Guermantes managed to draw Yahya Lumumba into his orbit? The evening's token black, perhaps. Or the delegate from the world of high-powered sports, summoned here by way of demonstrating our host's intellectual versatility, his eclectic ballsiness. Lumumba stands over me, glowering, coldly examining me from his implausible height like an ebony Zeus. A spectacular black woman has her arm through his, a goddess, a titan, well over six feet tall, skin like polished onyx, eyes like beacons. A stunning couple. They shame us all with their beauty. Lumumba says, finally, "I *know* you, man. I know you from someplace."

"Selig. David Selig."

"Sounds familiar. Where do I know you?"

"Euripides, Sophocles, and Aeschylus."

"What the fuck?" Baffled. Pausing, then. Grinning. "Oh, yeah. Yeah, baby. That fucking term paper. How you coming along on that, man?"

"Coming along."

"You gonna have it Wednesday? Wednesday when it due."

"I'll have it, Mr. Lumumba." *Doin' my best, massa.*

"You better, boy. I counting on you."

"—Tom Nyquist—"

The name leaps suddenly, startlingly, out of the white-noise background hum of party chatter. For an instant it hangs in the smoky air like a dead leaf caught by a lazy October breeze. Who said "Tom Nyquist" just then? Who was it who spoke his name? A pleasant baritone voice, no more than a dozen feet from me. I look for likely owners of that voice. Men all around. You? You? You? No way of telling. Yes, one way. When words are spoken aloud, they reverberate in the mind of the speaker for a short while. (Also in the minds of his hearers, but the reverberations are different in tonality.) I summon my slippery skill and, straining, force needles of inquiry into the nearby consciousnesses, hunting for echoes. The effort is murderously great. The skulls I enter are solid bony domes through whose few crevices I struggle to ram my limp, feeble probes. But I enter. I seek the proper reverberations. *Tom Nyquist? Tom Nyquist?* Who spoke his name? You? You? Ah. There. The echo is almost gone, just a dim hollow clangor at the far end of a cavern. A tall plump man with a comic fringe of blond beard.

"Excuse me," I say. "I didn't mean to eavesdrop, but I heard you mention the name of a very old friend of mine—"

"Oh?"

"—and I couldn't help coming over to ask you about him. Tom Nyquist. He and I were once very close. If you know where he is now, what he's doing—"

"Tom Nyquist?"

"Yes. I'm sure I heard you mention him."

A blank smile. "I'm afraid there's been a mistake. I don't know anyone by that name. Jim? Fred? Can you help?"

"But I'm positive I heard—" The echo. *Boum* in the cave. Was I mistaken? At close range I try to get inside his head, to hunt in his filing system for any knowledge of Nyquist. But I can't function at all, now. They are conferring earnestly. Nyquist? Nyquist? Did anybody hear a Nyquist mentioned? Does anyone know a Nyquist?

One of them suddenly cries: "John Leibnitz!"

"Yes," says the plump one happily. "Maybe that's who you heard me mention. I was talking about John Leibnitz a few moments ago. A mutual friend. In this racket that might very well have sounded like Nyquist to you."

Leibnitz. Nyquist. Leibnitz. Nyquist. *Boum. Boum.* "Quite possibly," I agree. "No doubt that's what happened. Silly of me." John Leibnitz. "Sorry to have bothered you."

Guermantes says, mincing and prancing at my elbow, "You really must audit my class one of these days. This Wednesday afternoon I start Rimbaud and Verlaine, the first of six lectures on them. Do come around. You'll be on campus Wednesday, won't you?"

Wednesday is the day I must deliver Yahya Lumumba's term paper on the Greek tragedians. I'll be on campus, yes. I'd better be. But how does Guermantes know that? Is he getting into my head somehow? What if he has the gift too? And I'm wide open to him, he knows everything, my poor pathetic secret, my daily increment of loss, and there he stands, patronizing me because I'm failing and he's as sharp as I ever was. Then a quick paranoiac flash: not only does he have the gift but perhaps he's some kind of telepathic leech, draining me, bleeding the power right out of my mind and into his. Perhaps he's been tapping me on the sly ever since '74.

I shake these useless idiocies away. "I expect to be around on Wednesday, yes. Perhaps I will drop in."

There is no chance whatever that I will go to hear Claude Guermantes lecture on Rimbaud or Verlaine. If he's got the power, let him put *that* in his pipe and smoke it!

"I'd love it if you came," he tells me. He leans close to me. His androgynous Mediterranean smoothness permits him casually to breach the established American code of male-to-male distancing customs. I smell hair tonic, shaving lotion, deodorant, and other perfumes. A small blessing: not all my senses are dwindling at once. "Your sister," he murmurs. "Marvelous woman! How I love her! She speaks often of you."

"Does she?"

"With great love. Also with great guilt. It seems you and she were estranged for many years."

"That's over now. We're finally becoming friends."

"How wonderful for you both." He gestures with a flick of his eyes. "That doctor. No good for her. Too old, too static. After fifty most men lose the capacity to grow. He'll bore her to death in six months."

"Maybe boredom is what she needs," I reply. "She's had an exciting life. It hasn't made her happy."

"No one ever needs boredom," Guermantes says, and winks.

"Karl and I would love to have you come for dinner next week, Duv. There's so much we three need to talk about."

"I'll see, Jude. I'm not sure about anything about next week yet. I'll call you."

* * *

Lisa Holstein. John Leibnitz. I think I need another drink.

* * * *

Sunday. Greatly overhung. Hash, rum, wine, pot, God knows what else. And somebody popping amyl nitrite under my nose about two in the morning. That filthy fucking party. I should never have gone. My head, my head, my head. Where's the typewriter? I've got to get some work done. Let's go, then:

We see, thus, the difference in method of approach of these three tragedians to the same story. Aeschylus' primary concern is theological implications of the crime and the inexorable workings of the gods: Orestes is torn between the command of Apollo to slay his mother and his own fear of matricide, and goes mad as a result. Euripides dwells on the characterization, and takes a less allegorical

No damned good. Save it for later.

Silence between my ears. The echoing black void. I have nothing going for me at all today, nothing. I think it may be completely gone. I can't even pick up the clamor of the spics next door. November is the cruelest month, breeding onions out of the dead mind. I'm living an Eliot poem. I'm turning into words on a page. Shall I sit here feeling sorry for myself? No. No. No. No. I'll fight back. Spiritual exercises designed to restore my power. On your knees, Selig. Bow the head. Concentrate. Transform yourself into a fine needle of thought, a slim telepathic laser-beam, stretching from this room to the vicinity of the lovely star Betelgeuse. Got it? Good. That sharp pure mental beam piercing the universe. Hold it. Hold it firm. No spreading at the edges allowed, man. Good. Now ascend. We are climbing Jacob's ladder. This will be an out-of-the-body experience, Duvid. Up, up and away! Rise through the ceiling, through the roof, through the atmosphere, through the ionosphere, through the stratosphere, through the whatsisphere. Outward. Into the vacant interstellar spaces.

O dark dark dark. Cold the sense and lost the motive of action. No, stop that stuff! Only positive thinking is allowed on this trip. Soar! Soar! Toward the little green men of Betelgeuse IX. Reach their minds, Selig. Make contact. Make . . . contact. Soar, you lazy yid-bastard! Why aren't you soaring? *Soar!*

Well?

Nothing. *Nada. Niente.* Nowhere. *Nulla. Nicht.*

Tumbling back to earth. Into the silent funeral. All right, give up, if that's what you want. All right. Rest, for a little while. Rest and then pray, Selig. Pray.

* * *

Monday. The hangover gone. The brain once again receptive. In a glorious burst of creative frenzy I rewrite *The "Electra" Theme in Aeschylus, Sophocles, and Euripides* from gunwale to fetlock, completely recasting it, revoicing it, clarifying and strengthening the ideas while simultaneously catching what I think is just the perfect tone of offhand niggerish hipness. As I hammer out the final words the telephone rings. Nicely timed; I feel sociable now. Who calls? Judith? No. It is Lisa Holstein who calls. "You promised to take me home after the party," she says mournfully, accusingly. "What the hell did you do, sneak away?"

"How did you get my number?"

"From Claude. Professor Guermantes." That sleek devil. He knows everything. "Look, what are you doing right now?"

"Thinking about having a shower. I've been working all morning and I stink like a goat."

"What kind of work do you do?"

"I ghostwrite term papers for Columbia men."

She ponders that a moment. "You sure have a weird head, man. I mean really: what do you do?"

"I just told you."

A long digestive silence. Then: "Okay. I can dig it. You ghostwrite term papers. Look, Dave, go take your

shower. How long is it on the subway from 110th Street
and Broadway to your place?"

"Maybe forty minutes, if you get a train right away."

"Swell. See you in an hour, then." *Click*.

I shrug. A crazy broad. Dave, she calls me. Nobody
calls me Dave. Stripping, I head for the shower, a long
leisurely soaping. Afterward, sprawling out in a rare
interlude of relaxation, Dave Selig re-reads this morning's labors and finds pleasure in what he has wrought.
Let's hope Lumumba does too. Then I pick up the
Updike book. I get to page four and the phone rings
again. Lisa: she's on the train platform at 225th, wants
to know how to get to my apartment. This is more than
a joke, now. Why is she pursuing me so singlemindedly?
But okay. I can play her game. I give her the instructions. Ten minutes later, a knock on the door. Lisa in
thick black sweater, the same sweaty one as Saturday
night, and tight blue jeans. A shy grin, strangely out of
character for her. "Hi," she says. Making herself comfortable. "When I first saw you, I had this intuitive flash
on you: *This guy's got something special. Make it with
him.* If there's one thing I've learned, its that you've got
to trust your intuition. I go with the flow, Dave, I go
with the flow." Her sweater is off by now. Her breasts
are heavy and round, with tiny, almost imperceptible
nipples. A Jewish star nestles in the deep valley between them. She wanders the room, examining my
books, my records, my photographs. "So tell me," she
says. "Now that I'm here. Was I right? *Is* there anything special about you?"

"There once was."

"What?"

"That's for me to know and you to find out," I say,
and gathering my strength, I ram my mind into hers.
It's a brutal frontal assault, a rape, a true mindfuck. Of
course she doesn't feel a thing. I say, "I used to have a
really extraordinary gift. It's mostly worn off by now,
but some of the time I still have it, and as a matter of
fact I'm using it on you right now."

"Far out," she says, and drops her jeans. No under-
pants. She will be fat before she's 30. Her thighs are

thick, her belly protrudes. Her pubic hair is oddly dense and widespread, less a triangle than a sort of diamond, a black diamond reaching past her loins to her hips, almost. Her buttocks are deeply dimpled. While I inspect her flesh I savagely ransack her mind, sparing her no areas of privacy, enjoying my access while it lasts. I don't need to be polite. I owe her nothing: she forced herself on me. I check, first, to see if she had been lying when she said she'd never heard of Kitty. The truth: Kitty is no kin to her. A meaningless coincidence of surnames, is all. "I'm sure you're a poet, Dave," she says as we entwine and drop onto the unmade bed. "That's an intuition flash too. Even if you're doing this term paper thing now, poetry is where you're really at, right?" I run my hands over her breasts and belly. A sharp odor comes from her skin. She hasn't washed in three or four days, I bet. No matter. Her nipples mysteriously emerge, tiny rigid pink nubs. She wriggles. I continue to loot her mind like a Goth plundering the Forum. She is fully open to me; I delight in this unexpected return of vigor. Her autobiography assembles itself for me. Born in Cambridge. Twenty years old. Father a professor. Mother a professor. One younger brother. Tomboy childhood. Measles, chicken pox, scarlet fever. Puberty at eleven, lost her virginity at twelve. Abortion at sixteen. Several Lesbian adventures. Passionate interest in French decadent poets. Acid, mescaline, psilocybin, cocaine, even a sniff of smack. Guermantes gave her that. Guermantes also took her to bed five or six times. Vivid memories of that. Her mind shows me more of Guermantes than I want to see. He's hung very impressively. Lisa comes through with a tough, aggressive self-image, captain of her soul, master of her fate, etc. Underneath that it's just the opposite, of course; she's scared as hell. Not a bad kid. I feel a little guilty about the casual way I slammed into her head, no regard for her privacy at all. But I have my needs. I continue to prowl her, and meanwhile she goes down on me. I can hardly remember the last time anyone did that. I can hardly remember my last lay, it's been so bad lately. She's an expert fellatrice. I'd like to reciprocate but I can't bring myself to do it; sometimes I'm fastidious and she's not the douching type. Oh, well, leave that stuff for the Guermanteses of this world. I lie there picking her brain and accepting the gift of her mouth. I feel virile, bouncy, cocksure, and why not, getting my kicks from two inputs at once, head and crotch? Without withdrawing from her mind I withdraw, at last, from her lips, turn around, part her thighs, slide deep into her tight narrow-mouthed harbor. Selig the stallion. Selig the stud. "Oooh," she says, flexing her knees. "*Oooh*." And we begin to play the beast with two backs. Covertly I feed on feedback, tapping into her pleasure-responses and thereby doubling my own; each thrust brings me a factored and deliciously exponential delight. But then a funny thing happens. Although she is nowhere close to coming—an event that I know will disrupt our mental contact when it occurs—the broadcast from her mind is already becoming erratic and indistinct, more noise than signal. The images break up in a pounding of static. What comes through is garbled and distant; I scramble to maintain my hold on her consciousness, but no use, no use, she slips away, moment by moment receding from me, until there is no communion at all. And in that moment of severance my cock suddenly softens and slips out of her. She is jolted by that, caught by surprise. "What brought you down?" she asks. I find it impossible to tell her. I remember Judith asking me, some weeks back, whether I had ever regarded my loss of mental powers as a kind of metaphor of impotence. Sometimes yes, I told her. And now here, for the first time, metaphor blends with reality; the two failures are integrated. He is impotent here and he is impotent there. Poor David. "I guess I got distracted," I tell her. Well, she has her skills; for half an hour she works me over, fingers, lips, tongue, hair, breasts, not getting a rise out of me with anything, in fact turning me off more than ever by her grim purposefulness. "I don't understand it," she says. "You were doing so well. Was there something about me that brought you down?" I reassure her. You were great, baby. Stuff like this sometimes just happens, no one knows why. I tell her, "Let's just rest and maybe I'll come back to life." We rest. Side by side, stroking her skin in an abstract way, I run a few tentative probing efforts. Not a flicker on the telepathic level. Not a flicker. The silence of the tomb. Is this it, the end, right here and now? Is this where it finally burns out? And I am like all the rest of you now. I am condemned to make do with mere words. "I have an idea," she says. "Let's take a shower together. That sometimes peps a guy up." To this I make no objection; it might just work, and in any case she'll smell better afterward. We head for the bathroom. Torrents of brisk cool water.

Success. The ministrations of her soapy hand revive me.

We spring toward the bed. Still stiff, I top her and take her. Gasp gasp gasp, moan moan moan. I can get nothing on the mental band. Suddenly she goes into a funny little spasm, intense but quick, and my own spurt swiftly follows. So much for sex. We curl up together, cuddly in the afterglow. I try again to probe her. Zero. Zee-ro. Is it gone? I think it's really gone. You have been present today at an historic event, young lady. The perishing of a remarkable extrasensory power. Leaving behind this merely mortal husk of mine. Alas.

"I'd love to read some of your poetry, Dave," she says.

* * *

Monday night, about seven-thirty. Lisa has left, finally. I go out for dinner, to a nearby pizzeria. I am quite calm. The impact of what has befallen me hasn't really registered yet. How strange that I can be so accepting. At any moment, I know, it's bound to come rushing in on me, crushing me, shattering me; I'll weep, I'll scream, I'll bang my head against walls. But for now I'm surprisingly cool. An oddly posthumous feeling, as of having outlived myself. And a feeling of relief: the suspense is over, the process has completed itself, the dying is done, and I've survived it. Of course I don't expect this mood to last. I've lost something central to my being, and now I await the anguish and the grief and the despair that must surely be due to erupt shortly.

But it seems that my mourning must be postponed. What I thought was all over isn't over yet. I walk into the pizzeria and the counterman gives me his flat cold New York smile of welcome, and I get this, unsolicited, from behind his greasy face: *Hey, here's the fag who always wants extra anchovies.*

Reading him clearly. So it's not dead yet! Not quite dead! Only resting a while. Only hiding.

* * *

Tuesday. Bitter cold; one of those terrible late-autumn days when every drop of moisture has been squeezed from the air and the sunlight is like knives. I finish two more term papers for delivery tomorrow. I read Updike. Judith calls after lunch. The usual dinner invitation. My usual oblique reply.

"What did you think of Karl?" she asks.

"A very substantial man."

"He wants me to marry him."

"Well?"

"It's too soon. I don't really know him, Duv. I like him, I admire him tremendously, but I don't know whether I love him."

"Then don't rush into anything with him," I say. Her soap-opera hesitations bore me. I don't understand why anybody old enough to know the score ever gets married, anyway. Why should love require a contract? Why put yourself into the clutches of the state and give it power over you? Why invite lawyers to fuck around with your assets? Marriage is for the immature and the insecure and the ignorant. We who see through such institutions should be content to live together without legal coercion, eh, Toni? Eh? I say, "Besides, if you marry him, he'd probably want you to give up Guermantes. I don't think he could dig it."

"You know about me and Claude?"

"Of course."

"You always know everything."

"This was pretty obvious, Jude."

"I thought your power was waning."

"It is, it is, it's waning faster than ever. But this was still pretty obvious. To the naked eye."

"All right. What did you think of him?"

"He's death. He's a killer."

"You misjudged him, Duv."

"I was in his head. I *saw* him, Jude. He isn't human. People are toys to him."

"If you could hear the sound of your own voice now, Duv. The hostility, the outright jealousy—"

"*Jealousy?* Am I that incestuous?"

"You always were," she says. "But let that pass. I really thought you'd enjoy meeting Claude."

"I did. He's fascinating. I think cobras are fascinating too."

"Oh, fuck you, Duv."

"You want me to pretend I liked him?"

"Don't do me any favors." The old icy Judith.

"What's Karl's reaction to Guermantes?"

She pauses. Finally: "Pretty negative. Karl's very conventional, you know. Just as you are."

"Me?"

"Oh, you're so fucking straight, Duv! You're such a puritan! You've been lecturing me on morality all my goddamned life. The very first time I got laid there you were, wagging your finger at me—"

"Why doesn't Karl like him?"

"I don't know. He thinks Claude's sinister. Exploitive." Her voice is suddenly flat and dull. "Maybe he's just jealous. He knows I'm still sleeping with Claude. Oh, Jesus, Duv, why are we fighting again? Why can't we just *talk?*"

"I'm not the one who's fighting. I'm not the one who raised his voice."

"You're challenging me. That's what you always do. You spy on me and then you challenge me and try to put me down."

"Old habits are hard to break, Jude. Really, though: I'm not angry with you."

"You sound so smug!"

"I'm *not* angry. You are. You got angry when you saw that Karl and I agree about your friend Claude. People always get angry when they're told something they don't want to hear. Listen, Jude, do whatever you want. If Guermantes is your trip, go ahead."

"I don't know. I just don't know." An unexpected concession: "Maybe there *is* something sick about my relationship with him." Her flinty self-assurance vanishes abruptly. That's the wonderful thing about her: you get a different Judith every two minutes. Now, softening, thawing, she sounds uncertain of herself. In a moment she'll turn her concern outward, away from her own troubles, toward me. "Will you come to dinner next week? We very much do want to get together with you."

"I'll try."

"I'm worried about you, Đuv." Yes, here it comes. "You looked so strung out on Saturday night."

"It's been a pretty rough time for me. But I'll manage." I don't feel like talking about myself. I don't want her pity, because after I get hers, I'll start giving myself mine. "Listen, I'll call you soon, okay?"

"Are you still in so much pain, Duv?"

"I'm adapting. I'm accepting the whole thing. I mean, I'll be okay. Keep in touch, Jude. My best to Karl." And Claude, I add, as I put down the receiver.

*   *   *

Wednesday morning. Downtown to deliver my latest batch of masterpieces. It's colder even than yesterday, the air clearer, the sun brighter, more remote. How dry the world seems. The humidity is minus sixteen percent, I think. The sort of weather in which I used to function with overwhelming clarity of perception. But I was picking up hardly anything at all on the subway ride down to Columbia, just muzzy little blurts and squeaks, nothing coherent. I can no longer be certain of having the power on any given day, apparently, and this is one of the days off. Unpredictable. That's what you are, you who live in my head: unpredictable. Thrashing about randomly in your death-throes. I go to the usual place and await my clients. They come, they get from me what they have come for, they cross my palm with greenbacks. David Selig, benefactor of undergraduate mankind. I see Yahya Lumumba like a black sequoia making his way across from Butler Library. Why am I trembling? It's the chill in the air, isn't it, the hint of winter, the death of the year. As the basketball star approaches he waves, nods, grins; everyone knows him, everyone calls out to him. I feel a sense of participation in his glory. When the season starts maybe I'll go watch him play.

"You got the paper, man?"

"Right here." I deal it off the stack. "Aeschylus, Sophocles, Euripides. Six pages. That's $21, minus the five you already gave me is $16 you owe me."

"Wait, man." He sits down beside me on the steps. "I got to read this fucker first, right? How I know you did a righteous job if I don't read it?"

I watch him as he reads. Somehow I expect him to be moving his lips, to be stumbling over the unfamiliar words, but no, his eyes flicker rapidly over the lines. He gnaws his lip. He reads faster and faster, impatiently turning the pages. At length he looks at me and there is death in his eyes.

"This is shit, man," he says. "I mean, this here is just shit. What kind of con you trying to pull?"

"I guarantee you'll get a B+. You don't have to pay me until you get the grade. Anything less than B+ and—"

"No, listen to me. Who talking about grades? I can't turn this fucking thing in *at all*. Look, half this thing is jive-talk, the other half it copied straight out of some book. Crazy shit, that's what. The prof he going to read it, he going to look at me, he going to say, Lumumba, who you think I am? You think I a dummy, Lumumba? You didn't write this crap, he going to say to me. You don't believe Word One of this." Angrily he rises. "Here, I going to read you some of this, man. I show you what you give me." Leafing through the pages, he scowls, spits, shakes his head. "No. Why the hell should I? You know what you up to here, man? You making fun of me, that's what. You playing games with the dumb nigger, man."

"I was trying to make it look plausible that you had written—"

"Crap. You pulling a mindfuck, man. You making up a pile of stinking Jew shit about Europydes and you hoping I get in trouble trying to pass it off as my own stuff."

"That's a lie. I did the best possible job for you, and don't think I didn't sweat plenty. When you hire another man to write a term paper for you, I think you have to be prepared to expect a certain—"

"How long this take you? Fifteen minutes?"

"Eight hours, maybe ten," I say. "You know what I think you're trying to do, Lumumba? You're pulling reverse racism on me. Jew this and Jew that—if you don't like Jews so much, why didn't you get a black to write your paper for you? Why didn't you write it yourself? I did an honest job for you. I don't like hearing it put down as stinking Jew shit. And I tell you that if you turn it in, you'll get a passing grade for sure, you'll probably get a B+ at the very least."

"I gonna get flunked, is what."

"No. No. Maybe you just don't see what I was driving at. Let me try to explain it to you. If you'll give it to me for a minute so I can read you a couple of things—maybe it'll be clearer if I—" Getting to my feet, I extend a hand toward the paper, but he grins and holds it high above my head. I'd need a ladder to reach it. No use jumping. "Come on, damn it, don't play games with me! Let me have it!" I snap, and he flicks his wrist and the six sheets of paper soar into the wind and go sailing eastward along College Walk. Dying, I watch them go. I clench my fists; an astonishing burst of rage explodes in me. I want to smash in his mocking face. "You shouldn't have done that." I say. "You shouldn't have just thrown it away."

"You owe me my five bucks back, man."

"Hold on, now. I did the work you hired me to do, and—"

"You said you don't charge if the paper's no good. Okay, the paper was shit. No charge. Give me the five."

"You aren't playing fair, Lumumba. You're trying to rip me off."

"Who ripping who off? Who set up that money-back deal anyhow? Me? *You*. What I gonna do for a term paper now? I got to take an incomplete and it your fault. Suppose they make me ineligible for the team because of that. Huh? Huh? What then? Look, man, you make me want to puke. Give me the five."

Is he serious about the refund? I can't tell. The idea of paying him back disgusts me, and it isn't just on account of losing the money. I wish I could read him, but I can't get anything out of him on that level; I'm completely blocked now. I'll bluff. I say, "What is this, slavery turned upside down? I did the work. I don't give a damn what kind of crazy irrational reasons you've got for rejecting it. I'm going to keep the five. At least the five."

"Give me the money, man."

"Go to hell."

I start to walk away. He grabs me—his arm, fully outspread toward me, must be as long as one of my legs—and hauls me toward him. He starts to shake me. My teeth are rattling. His grin is broader than ever, but his eyes are demonic. I wave my fists at him, but, held at arm's length, I can't even touch him. I start to yell. A crowd is gathering. Suddenly there are three or four other men in varsity jackets surrounding us, all black, all gigantic, though not as big as he is. His teammates. Laughing, whooping, cavorting. I am a toy to them. "Hey, man, he bothering you?" one of them asks. "You need help, Yahya?" yells another. "What's the mothafuck honkie doing to you, man?" calls a third. They form a ring and Lumumba thrusts me toward the man on his left, who catches me and flings me onward around the circle. I spin; I stumble; I reel; they never let me fall. Around and around and around. An elbow explodes against my lip. I taste blood. Someone slaps me, and my head rockets backward. Fingers jabbing my ribs. I realize that I'm going to get very badly hurt, that in fact

these giants are going to beat me up. A voice I barely
recognize as my own offers Lumumba his refund, but
no one notices. They continue to whirl me from one to
the next. Not slapping now, not jabbing, but punching.
Where are the campus police? Help! Help! Pigs to the
rescue! But no one comes. I can't catch my breath. I'd
like to drop to my knees and huddle against the ground.
They're yelling at me, racial epithets, words I barely
comprehend, soul-brother jargon that must have been
invented last week; I don't know what they're calling
me, but I can feel the hatred in every syllable. Help?
Help? The world spins wildly. I know now how a
basketball would feel, if a basketball could feel. The
steady pounding, the blur of unending motion. Please,
someone, anyone, help me, stop them. Pain in my
chest: a lump of white-hot metal back of my breast-
bone. I can't see. I can only feel. Where are my feet?
I'm falling at last. Look how fast the steps rush toward
me. The cold kiss of the stone bruises my cheek. I may
already have lost consciousness; how can I tell? There's
one comfort, at least. I can't get any further down than
this.

TWENTY-TWO.

He was ready to fall in love when he met Kitty,
overripe and eager for an emotional entanglement.
Perhaps that was the whole trouble; what he felt for her
was not so much love as simply satisfaction at the idea
of being in love. Or perhaps not. He never understood
his feelings for Kitty in any orderly way. They had their
romance in the summer of 1963, which he remembers
as the last summer of hope and good cheer before the
long autumn of entropic chaos and philosophical despair
descended on western society. Jack Kennedy was running
things then, and while things weren't going especially
well for him politically, he still managed to give the
impression that he was going to get it all together, if not

right away then in his inevitable second term. Atmospheric nuclear tests had just been banned. The Washington-to-Moscow hot line was being set up. Secretary of State Rusk announced in August that the South Vietnamese government was rapidly taking control of additional areas of the countryside. The number of Americans killed fighting in Vietnam had not yet reached 100.

Selig, who was 28 years old, had just moved from his Brooklyn Heights apartment to a small place in the West Seventies. He was working as a stockbroker then, of all unlikely things. This was Tom Nyquist's idea. After six years, Nyquist was still his closest and possibly only friend, although the friendship had waned considerably in the last year or two: Nyquist's almost arrogant self-assurance made Selig increasingly more uncomfortable, and he found it desirable to put some distance, psychological and geographical, between himself and the older man. One day Selig had said wistfully that if he could only manage to get a bundle of money together—say, $25,000 or so—he'd go off to a remote island and spend a couple of years writing a novel, a major statement about alienation in contemporary life, something like that. He had never written anything serious and wasn't sure he was sincere about wanting to. He was secretly hoping that Nyquist would simply hand him the money—Nyquist could pick up $25,000 in one afternoon's work, if he felt like it—and say, "Here, chum, go and be creative." But Nyquist didn't do things that way. Instead he said that the easiest way for someone without capital to make a lot of money in a hurry was to take a job as a customer's man with a brokerage firm. The commissions would be decent, enough to live on and something left over, but the real money would come from riding along on all the in-shop maneuvers of the experienced brokers—the short sales, the new-issue purchases, the arbitrage ploys. If you're dedicated enough, Nyquist told him, you can make just about as much as you like. Selig protested that he knew nothing about Wall Street. "I could teach you everything in three days," said Nyquist.

Actually it took less than that. Selig slipped into Nyquist's mind for a quick cram course in financial terminology. Nyquist had all the definitions beautifully arranged: common stocks and preferred, shorts and longs, puts and calls, debentures, convertibles, capital gains, special situations, closed-end versus open-end funds, secondary offerings, specialists and what they do, the over-the-counter market, the Dow-Jones averages, point-and-figure charts, and everything else. Selig memorized all of it. There was a vivid quality about mind-to-mind transferences with Nyquist that made memorizing things easy. The next step was to enroll as a trainee. Every big brokerage firm was looking for beginners—Merrill Lynch, Goodbody, Hayden Stone, Clark Dodge, scads of them. Selig picked one at random and applied. They gave him a stock-market quiz by way of preliminary screening; he knew most of the answers, and those he didn't know he picked up out of the minds of his fellow testees, most of whom had been following the market since childhood. He got a perfect score and was hired. After a brief training period he passed the licensing test, and before long he was a registered representative operating out of a fairly new brokerage office on Broadway near 72nd Street.

He was one of five brokers, all of them fairly young. The clientele was predominantly Jewish and generally geriatric: 75-year-old widows from the huge apartment houses along 72nd Street, and cigar-chomping retired garment manufacturers who lived on West End Avenue and Riverside Drive. Some of them had quite a lot of money, which they invested in the most cautious way possible. Some were practically penniless, but insisted on buying four shares of Con Edison or three shares of Telephone just to have the illusion of prosperity. Since most of the clients were elderly and didn't work, the bulk of dealings at the office were transacted in person rather than by phone; there were always ten or twelve senior citizens schmoozing in front of the stock ticker, and now and then one of them would dodder to the desk of his pet broker and place an order. On Selig's fourth day at work one venerable client suffered a fatal heart attack during a nine-point rally. Nobody seemed surprised or even dismayed, neither the brokers nor the friends of the victim: customers died in the shop about once a month, Selig learned. Kismet. You come to expect your friends to drop dead, once you reach a certain age. He quickly became a favorite, especially among the old ladies; they liked him because he was a nice Jewish boy, and several offered to introduce him to comely granddaughters. These offers he always refused, but politely; he made a point of being courteous and patient with them, of playing grandson. Most of them were ignorant, practically illiterate women, kept in a state of lifelong innocence by their hard-driving, acquisitive, coronary-prone husbands; now, having inherited more money than they could possibly spend, they had no real idea of how to manage it, and were wholly dependent on the nice young broker. Probing their minds, Selig found them almost always to be dim and sadly unformed—how could you live to the age of 75 without ever having had an idea?—but a few of the livelier ladies showed vigorous, passionate peasant rapacity, charming in its way. The men were less agreeable—loaded with dough, yet always on the lookout for more. The vulgarity and ferocity of their ambitions repelled him, and he glanced into their minds no more often than necessary, merely probing to have a better idea of their investment goals so he could serve them as they would be served. A month among such people, he decided, would be sufficient to turn a Rockefeller into a socialist.

Business was steady but unspectacular; once he had acquired his own nucleus of regulars, Selig's commissions ran to about $160 a week, which was more money than he had ever made before, but hardly the kind of income he imagined brokers pulled down. "You're lucky you came here in the spring," one of the other customer's men told him. "In the winter months all the clients go to Florida and we can choke before anybody gives us any business here." As Nyquist had predicted, he was able to turn some pleasant profits by trading for his own account; there were always nice little deals circulating in the office, hot tips with substance behind them. He started with savings of $350 and quickly pyramided his wad to a high four-figure sum, making money on Chrysler and Control Data and RCA and Sunray DX Oil, nimbly trading in and out on rumors of mergers, stock splits, or dynamic earnings gains; but he discovered that Wall Street runs in two directions, and much of his winnings melted away through badly timed trades in Brunswick, Beckman Instruments, and Martin Marietta. He came to see that he was never going to have enough of a stake to go off and write that novel. Possibly just as well: did the world need another amateur novelist? He wondered what he would do next. After three months as a broker he had some money in the bank, but not much, and he was hideously bored.

Luck delivered Kitty to him. She came in one muggy July morning at half past nine. The market hadn't opened yet, most of the customers had fled to the Catskills for the summer, and the only people in the office were Martinson, the manager, Nadel, one of the other customer's men, and Selig. Martinson was going over his totals, Nadel was on the phone to somebody downtown trying to work a complicated finagle in American Photocopy, and Selig, idle, was daydreaming of falling in love with somebody's beautiful granddaughter. Then the door opened and somebody's beautiful granddaughter came in. Not exactly beautiful, maybe, but certainly attractive: a girl in her early twenties, slim and well proportioned, perhaps five feet three or four, with fluffy light-brown hair, blue-green eyes, finely outlined features, a graceful slender figure. She seemed shy, intelligent, somehow innocent, a curious mixture of knowledge and naiveté. She wore a white silk blouse— gold chain lying on the smallish breasts—and an ankle-length brown skirt, offering a hint of excellent legs beneath. No, not a beautiful girl, but certainly pretty. Refreshing to look at. What the hell, Selig wondered, does she want in this temple of Mammon at her age? She's here fifty years too early. Curiosity led him to send a probe drilling into her forehead as she walked toward him. Seeking only surface stuff: name, age, marital status, address, telephone number, purpose of visit—what else?

He got nothing.

That shocked him. It was an incredible experience. Unique. To reach toward a mind and find it absolutely inaccessible, opaque, hidden as if behind an impenetrable wall—he had never had that happen to him before. He got no aura from her at all. She might as well have been a department store's plaster window mannequin, or a mindless robot from another planet. He sat there blinking, trying to account for his failure to make contact. He was so astounded by her total blankness that he forgot to listen to what she was saying to him, and had to ask her to repeat.

"I said, I'd like to open a brokerage account. Are you a broker?"

Sheepish, fumbling, stricken with sudden adolescent clumsiness, he gave her the new-account forms. By this time the other brokers had arrived, but too late: by the rules of the house she was his client. Sitting beside his cluttered desk, she told him of her investment needs while he studied the elegant tapered structure of her high-bridged nose, fought without success against her perplexing and enigmatic mental inaccessibility, and, despite or perhaps because of that inaccessibility, felt himself helplessly falling in love with her.

She was 22, one year out of Radcliffe, came from Long Island, and shared a West End Avenue apartment with two other girls. Unmarried—there had been a long futile love affair ending in a broken engagement not long before, he would discover later. (How strange it was for him not to be discovering everything at once, taking the information as he desired it.) Her background was in mathematics and she worked as a computer programmer, a term which, in 1963, meant very little to him; he wasn't sure whether she designed computers, operated them, or repaired them. Recently she had inherited $6500 from an aunt in Arizona, and her parents, who evidently were stern and formidable advocates of sink-or-swim education, had told her to invest the money on her own, by way of assuming adult responsibilities. So she had gone to her friendly neighborhood brokerage office, a lamb for the shearing, to invest her money. "What do you want?" Selig asked her. "To stash it away in safe blue chips, or to go for a little action, a chance for capital gains?"

"I don't know. I don't know the first thing about the market. I just don't want to do anything silly."

Another broker—Nadel, say—would have given her the Nothing Ventured, Nothing Gained speech, and, advising her to forget about such old and tired concepts as dividends, would have steered her into an action portfolio—Texas Instruments, Collins Radio, Polaroid, stuff like that. Then he would churn her account every few months, switch Polaroid into Xerox, Texas Instruments into Fairchild Camera, Collins into American Motors, American Motors back into Polaroid, running up fancy commissions for himself and, perhaps, making some money for her, or perhaps losing some. Selig had no stomach for such maneuvers. "This is going to sound stodgy," he said, "but let's play it very safe. I'll recommend some decent things that won't ever make you rich but that you won't get hurt on, either. And then you can just put them away and watch them grow, without having to check the market quotations every day to find out if you ought to sell. Because you don't really want to bother worrying about the short-term fluctuations, do you?" This was absolutely not what Martinson had instructed him to tell new clients, but to hell with that. He got her some Jersey Standard, some Telephone, a little IBM, two good electric utilities, and 30 shares of a closed-end fund called Lehman Corporation that a lot of his elderly customers owned. She didn't ask questions, didn't even want to know what a closed-end fund was. "There," he said. "Now you have a portfolio. You're a capitalist." She smiled. It was a shy, half-forced smile, but he thought he detected flirtatiousness in her eyes. It was agony for him not to be able to read her, to be compelled to depend on external signals alone in order to know where he stood with her. But he took the chance. "What are you doing this evening?" he asked. "I get out of here at four o'clock."

She was free, she said. Except that she worked from eleven to six. He arranged to pick her up at her apartment around seven. There was no mistaking the warmth of her smile as she left the office. "You lucky bastard," Nadel said. "What did you do, make a date with her? It violates the SEC rules for customer's men to go around laying the customers."

Selig only laughed. Twenty minutes after the market opened he shorted 200 Molybdenum on the Amex, and covered his sale a point and a half lower at lunchtime. That ought to take care of the cost of dinner, he figured, with some to spare. Nyquist had given him the tip yesterday: Moly's a good short, she's sure to fall out of bed. During the mid-afternoon lull, feeling satisfied with himself, he phoned Nyquist to report on his maneuver. "You covered too soon," Nyquist said immediately. "She'll drop five or six more points this week. The smart money's waiting for that."

"I'm not that greedy. I'll settle for the quick three bills."

"That's no way to get rich."

"I guess I lack the gambling instinct," Selig said. He hesitated. He hadn't really called Nyquist to talk about shorting Molybdenum. I met a girl, he wanted to say, and I have this funny problem with her. I met a girl, I met a girl. Sudden fears held him back. Nyquist's silent passive presence at the other end of the telephone line seemed somehow threatening. He'll laugh at me, Selig thought. He's always laughing at me, quietly, thinking I don't see it. But this is foolishness. He said, "Tom, something strange happened today. A girl came into the office, a very attractive girl. I'm seeing her tonight."

"Congratulations."

"Wait. The thing is, I was entirely unable to read her. I mean, I couldn't even pick up an aura. Blank, absolutely blank. I've never had that with anybody before. Have you?"

"I don't think so."

"A complete blank. I can't understand it. What could account for her having such a strong screen?"

"Maybe you're tired today," Nyquist suggested.

"No. No. I can read everybody else, same as always. Just not her."

"Does that irritate you?"

"Of course it does."

"Why do you say of course?"

It seemed obvious to Selig. He could tell that Nyquist was baiting him: the voice calm, uninflected, neutral. A game. A way of passing time. He wished he hadn't phoned. Something important seemed to be coming across on the ticker, and the other phone was lighting up. Nadel, grabbing it, shot a fierce look at him: *Come on, man, there's work to do!* Brusquely Selig said, "I'm—well, very interested in her. And it bothers me that I have no way of getting through to her real self."

Nyquist said, "You mean you're annoyed that you can't spy on her."

"I don't like that phrase."

"Whose phrase is it? Not mine. That's how you regard what we do, isn't it? As spying. You feel guilty about spying on people, right? But it seems you also feel upset when you can't spy."

"I suppose," Selig admitted sullenly.

"With this girl you find yourself forced back on the same old clumsy guesswork techniques for dealing with people that the rest of the world is condemned to use all the time, and you don't like that. Yes?"

"You make it sound so evil, Tom."

"What do you want me to say?"

"I don't want you to say anything. I'm just telling you that there's this girl I can't read, that I've never been up against this situation before, that I wonder if you have any theories to account for why she's the way she is."

"I don't," Nyquist said. "Not off the top of my head."

"All right, then. I—"

But Nyquist wasn't finished. "You realize that I have no way of telling whether she's opaque to the telepathic process in general or just opaque to you, David." That possibility had occurred to Selig a moment earlier. He found it deeply disturbing. Nyquist went on smoothly, "Suppose you bring her around one of these days and let me take a look at her. Maybe I'll be able to learn something useful about her that way."

"I'll do that," Selig said without enthusiasm. He knew such a meeting was necessary and inevitable, but the idea of exposing Kitty to Nyquist produced agitation in him. He had no clear understanding of why that should be happening. "One of these days soon," he said. "Look, all the phones are lighting up. I'll be in touch, Tom."

"Give her one for me," said Nyquist.

TWENTY-THREE.

David Selig
Selig Studies 101, Prof. Selig
November 10, 1976

Entropy As a Factor in Everyday Life

Entropy is defined in physics as a mathematical expression of the degree to which the energy of a thermodynamic system is so distributed as to be unavailable for conversion into work. In more general metaphorical terms, entropy may be seen as the irreversible tendency of a system, including the universe, toward increasing disorder and inertness. That is to say, things have a way of getting worse and worse all the time, until in the end they get so bad that we lack even the means of knowing how bad they really are.

The great American physicist Josiah Willard Gibbs (1839-1903) was the first to apply the second law of thermodynamics—the law that defines the increasing disorder of energy moving at random within a closed system—to chemistry. It was Gibbs who most firmly enunciated the principle that disorder spontaneously increases as the universe grows older. Among those who extended Gibbs' insights into the realm of philosophy was the brilliant mathematician Norbert Wiener (1894-

1964), who declared, in his book *The Human Use of Human Beings*, "As entropy increases, the universe, and all closed systems in the universe, tend naturally to deteriorate and lose their distinctiveness, to move from the least to the most probable state, from a state of organization and differentiation in which distinctions and forms exist, to a state of chaos and sameness. In Gibbs' universe order is least probable, chaos most probable. But while the universe as a whole, if indeed there is a whole universe, tends to run down, there are local enclaves whose direction seems opposed to that of the universe at large and in which there is a limited and temporary tendency for organization to increase. Life finds its home in some of these enclaves."

Thus Wiener hails living things in general and human beings in particular as heroes in the war against entropy—which he equates in another passage with the war against evil: "This random element, this organic incompleteness [that is, the fundamental element of chance in the texture of the universe], is one which without too violent a figure of speech we may consider evil." Human beings, says Wiener, carry on anti-entropic processes. We have sensory receptors. We communicate with one another. We make use of what we learn from one another. Therefore we are something more than mere passive victims of the spontaneous spread of universal chaos. "We, as human beings, are not isolated systems. We take in food, which generates energy, from the outside, and are, as a result, parts of that larger world which contains those sources of our vitality. But even more important is the fact that we take in information through our sense organs, and we act on information received." There is feedback, in other words. Through communication we learn to control our environment, and, he says, "In control and communication we are always fighting nature's tendency to degrade the organized and to destroy the meaningful; the tendency . . . for entropy to increase." In the very long run entropy must inevitably nail us all; in the short run we can fight back. "We are not yet spectators at the last stages of the world's death."

But what if a human being *turns* himself, inadvertently or by choice, into an isolated system?

A hermit, say. He lives in a dark cave. No information penetrates. He eats mushrooms. They give him just enough energy to keep going, but otherwise he lacks inputs. He's forced back on his own spiritual and mental resources, which he eventually exhausts. Gradually the chaos expands in him, gradually the forces of entropy seize possession of this ganglion, that synapse. He takes in a decreasing amount of sensory data until his surrender to entropy is complete. He ceases to move, to grow, to respire, to function in any way. This condition is known as death.

One doesn't have to hide in a cave. One can make an interior migration, locking oneself away from the life-giving energy sources. Often this is done because it appears that the energy sources are threats to the stability of the self. Indeed, inputs do threaten the self: a push usually will upset equilibrium. However, equilibrium itself is a threat to the self, though this is frequently over-looked. There are married people who strive fiercely to reach equilibrium. They seal themselves off, clinging to one another and shutting out the rest of the universe, making themselves into a two-person closed system from which all vitality is steadily and inexorably expelled by the deadly equilibrium they have established. Two can perish as well as one, if they are sufficiently isolated from everything else. I call this the monogamous fallacy. My sister Judith said she left her husband because she felt herself dying, day by day, while she was living with him. Of course, Judith's a slut.

The sensory shutdown is not always a willed event, naturally. It happens to us whether we like it or not. If we don't climb into the box ourselves, we'll get shoved in anyway. That's what I mean about entropy inevitably nailing us all in the long run. No matter how vital, how vigorous, how world-devouring we are, the inputs dwindle as time goes by. Sight, hearing, touch, smell—everything goes, as good old Will S. said, and we end up sans teeth, sans eyes, sans taste, sans everything. Sans everything. Or, as the same clever man also put it, from hour to hour we ripe and ripe, and then from hour to hour we rot and rot, and thereby hangs a tale.

I offer myself as a case in point. What does this man's sad history reveal? An inexplicable diminution of once-remarkable powers. A shrinkage of the inputs. A small death, endured while he still lives. Am I not a casualty of the entropic wars? Do I not now dwindle into stasis and silence before your very eyes? Is my distress not evident and poignant? Who will I be, when I have ceased to be myself? I am dying the heat death. A spontaneous decay. A random twitch of probability undoes me. And I am made into nothingness. I am becoming cinders and ash. I will wait here for the broom to gather me up.

* * *

That's very eloquent, Selig. Take an A. Your writing is clear and forceful and you show an excellent grasp of the underlying philosophical issues. You may go to the head of the class. Do you feel better now?

TWENTY-FOUR.

It was a crazy idea, Kitty, a dumb fantasy. It could never have worked. I was asking the impossible from you. There was only one conceivable outcome, really: that is, that I would annoy you and bore you and drive you away from me. Well, blame Tom Nyquist. It was his idea. No, blame me. I didn't have to listen to his crazy ideas, did I? Blame me. Blame me.

Axiom: It's a sin against love to try to remake the soul of someone you love, even if you think you'll love her more after you've transformed her into something else.

* * *

Nyquist said, "Maybe she's a mindreader too, and the blockage is a matter of interference, of a clash between your transmissions and hers, canceling out the waves in one direction or in both. So that there's no transmission from her to you and probably none from you to her."

"I doubt that very much," I told him. This was August of 1963, two or three weeks after you and I had met. We weren't living together yet but we had already been to bed a couple of times. "She doesn't have a shred of telepathic ability," I insisted. "She's completely normal. That's the essential thing about her, Tom: she's a completely normal girl."

"Don't be so sure," Nyquist said.

He hadn't met you yet. He wanted to meet you, but I hadn't set anything up. You had never heard his name.

I said, "If there's one thing I know about her, it's that she's a sane, healthy, well-balanced, absolutely normal girl. Therefore she's no mindreader."

"Because mindreaders are insane, unhealthy, and unbalanced. Like you and like me. Q.E.D., eh? Speak for yourself, man."

"The gift tips the spirit," I said. "It darkens the soul."

"Yours, maybe. Not mine."

He was right about that. Telepathy hadn't injured him. Maybe I'd have had the problems I have even if I hadn't been born with the gift. I can't credit all my maladjustments to the presence of one unusual ability; can I? And God knows there are plenty of neurotics around who have never read a mind in their lives.

Syllogism:
Some telepaths are not neurotic.
Some neurotics are not telepaths.
    Therefore telepathy and neurosis aren't necessarily related.
Corollary:
You can seem cherry-pie normal and still have the power.

* * *

I remained skeptical of this. Nyquist agreed, under pressure, that if you did have the power, you would have probably revealed it to me by now through certain unconscious mannerisms that any telepath would readily recognize; I had detected no such mannerisms. He suggested, though, that you might be a latent telepath— that the gift was there, undeveloped, unfunctional, lurking at the core of your mind and serving somehow to screen your mind from my probing. Just a hypothesis, he said. But it tickled me with temptation. "Suppose she's got this latent power," I said. "Could it be awakened, do you think?"

"Why not?" Nyquist asked.

I was willing to believe it. I had this vision of you awakened to full receptive capacity, able to pick up transmissions as easily and as sharply as Nyquist and I. How intense our love would be, then! We would be wholly open to one another, shorn of all the little pretenses and defenses that keep even the closest of lovers from truly achieving a union of souls. I had already tasted a limited form of that sort of closeness with Tom Nyquist, but of course I had no love for him, I didn't even really *like* him, and so it was a waste, a brutal irony, that our minds could have such intimate contact. But you? If I could only awaken you, Kitty! And why not? I asked Nyquist if he thought it might be possible. Try it and find out, he said. Make experiments. Hold hands, sit together in the dark, put some energy into trying to get across to her. It's worth trying, isn't it? Yes, I said, of course it's worth trying.

You seemed latent in so many other ways, Kitty: a potential human being rather than an actual one. An air of adolescence surrounded you. You seemed much younger than you actually were; if I hadn't known you were a college graduate I would have guessed you were 18 or 19. You hadn't read much outside your fields of interest—mathematics, computers, technology—and, since those weren't my fields of interest, I thought of you as not having read anything at all. You hadn't traveled;

your world was limited by the Atlantic and the Mississippi, and the big trip of your life was a summer in
Illinois. You hadn't even had much sexual experience:
three men, wasn't it, in your 22 years, and only one of
those a serious affair? So I saw you as raw material
awaiting the sculptor's hand. I would be your Pyg-
malion.

In September of 1963 you moved in with me. You
were spending so much time at my place anyway that
you agreed it didn't make sense to keep going back and
forth. I felt very married: wet stockings hanging over
the showercurtain rod, an extra toothbrush on the shelf,
long brown hairs in the sink. The warmth of you beside
me in bed every night. My belly against your smooth
cool butt, yang and yin. I gave you books to read:
poetry, novels, essays. How diligently you devoured
them! You read Trilling on the bus going to work and
Conrad in the quiet after-dinner hours and Yeats on a
Sunday morning while I was out hunting for the *Times*.
But nothing really seemed to stick with you; you had no
natural bent for literature; I think you had trouble
distinguishing Lord Jim from Lucky Jim, Malcolm Lowry
from Malcolm Cowley, James Joyce from Joyce Kilmer.
Your fine mind, so easily able to master COBOL and
FORTRAN, could not decipher the language of poetry,
and you would look up from *The Waste Land*, baffled,
to ask some naive high-school-girl question that would
leave me irritated for hours. A hopeless case, I sometimes thought. Although on a day when the stock
market was closed you took me down to the computer
center where you worked and I listened to your expla-
nations of the equipment and your functions as though
you were talking so much Sanskrit to me. Different
worlds, different kinds of mind. Yet I always had hope
of creating a bridge.

At strategically timed moments I spoke elliptically of
my interest in extrasensory phenomena.

I made it out to be a hobby of mine, a cool dispas-
sionate study. I was fascinated, I said, by the possibility
of attaining true mind-to-mind communication between
human beings. I took care not to come on like a fanatic,

not to oversell my case; I kept my desperation out of sight. Because I genuinely couldn't read you, it was easier for me to pretend to a scholarly objectivity than it would have been with anyone else. And I had to pretend. My strategy didn't allow for any true confessions. I didn't want to frighten you, Kitty, I didn't want to turn you off by giving you reason to think I was a freak, or, as I probably would have seemed to you, a lunatic. Just a hobby, then. A hobby.

You couldn't bring yourself to believe in ESP. If it can't be measured with a voltmeter or recorded on an electroencephalograph, you said, it isn't real. Be tolerant, I pleaded. There *are* such things as telepathic powers. I know there are. (Be careful, Duv!) I couldn't cite EEG readings—I've never been near an EEG in my life, have no idea whether my power would register. And I had barred myself from conquering your skepticism by calling in some outsider and doing some party-game mindreading on him. But I could offer other arguments. Look at Rhine's results, look at all these series of correct readings of the Zener cards. How can you explain them, if not by ESP? And the evidence for telekinesis, teleportation, clairvoyance—

You remained skeptical, coolly putting down most of the data I cited. Your reasoning was keen and close; there was nothing fuzzy about your mind when it was on its own home territory, the scientific method. Rhine, you said, fudges his results by testing heterogeneous groups, then selecting for further testing only those subjects who show unusual runs of luck, dropping the others from his surveys. And he publishes only the scores that seem to prove his thesis. It's a statistical anomaly, not an extrasensory one, that turns up all those correct guesses of the Zener cards, you insisted. Besides, the experimenter is prejudiced in favor of belief in ESP, and that surely leads to all sorts of unconscious errors of procedure, tiny accesses of unintentional bias that inevitably skew the outcome. Cautiously I invited you to try some experiments with me, letting you set up the procedures to suit yourself. You said okay, mainly, I think, because it was something we could do together, and—this was early October—we were already searching selfconsciously for areas of closeness, your literary education having become a strain for both of us.

We agreed—how subtly I made it seem like your own idea!—to concentrate on transmitting images or ideas to one another. And right at the outset we had a cruelly deceptive success. We assembled some packets of pictures and tried to relay them mentally. I still have, here in the archives, our notes on those experiments:

Pictures Seen By Me	Your Guess
1. A rowboat	1. Oak Trees
2. Marigolds in a field	2. Bouquet of roses
3. A kangaroo	3. President Kennedy
4. Twin baby girls	4. A statue
5. The Empire State Building	5. The Pentagon
6. A snow-capped mountain	6. ? image unclear
7. Profile of old man's face	7. A pair of scissors
8. Baseball player at bat.	8. A carving knife
9. An elephant	9. A tractor
10. A locomotive	10. An airplane

You had no direct hits. But four out of ten could be considered close associations: marigolds and roses, the Empire State and the Pentagon, elephant and tractor, locomotive and airplane. (Flowers, buildings, heavy-duty equipment, means of transportation.) Enough to give us false hopes of true transmission. Followed by this:

Pictures Seen By You	My Guess
1. A butterfly	1. A railway train
2. An octopus	2. Mountains
3. Tropical beach scene	3. Landscape, bright sunlight
4. Young Negro boy	4. An automobile
5. Map of South America	5. Grapevines
6. George Washington Bridge	6. The Washington Monument

7.	Bowl of apples and bananas	7.	Stock market quotations
8.	El Greco's *Toledo*	8.	A shelf of books
9.	A highway at rush hour	9.	A beehive
10.	An ICBM	10.	Cary Grant

No direct hits for me either. But three close associations, of sorts, out of ten: tropical beach and sunny landscape, George Washington Bridge and Washington Monument, highway at rush hour and beehive, the common denominators being sunlight, George Washington, and intense tight-packed activity. At least we deceived ourselves into seeing them as close associations rather than coincidences. I confess I was stabbing in the dark at all times, guessing rather than receiving, and I had little faith even then in the quality of our responses. Nevertheless those probably random collisions of images aroused your curiosity: there's something in this stuff, maybe, you began to say. And we went onward.

We varied the conditions for thought transmission. We tried doing it in absolute darkness, one room apart. We tried it with the lights on, holding hands. We tried it during sex: I entered you and held you in my arms and thought hard at you, and you thought hard at me. We tried it drunk. We tried it fasting. We tried it under conditions of sleep-deprivation, forcing ourselves to stay up around the clock in the random hope that minds groggy with fatigue might permit mental impulses to slip through the barriers separating us. We would have tried it under the influence of pot or acid, but no one thought much about pot or acid in '63. We sought in a dozen other ways to open the telepathic conduit. Perhaps you recall the details of them even now; embarrassment drives them from my mind. I know we wrestled with our futile project night after night for more than a month, while your involvement with it swelled and peaked and dwindled again, carrying you through a series of phases from skepticism to cool neutral interest to unmistakable fascination and enthusiasm, then to an awareness of inevitable failure, a sense of the impossibility of our goal, leading then to weariness, to bore-

dom, and to irritation. I realized none of this: I thought
you were as dedicated to the work as I was. But it had
ceased to be either an experiment or a game; it was,
you saw, plainly an obsessive quest, and you asked
several times in November if we could quit. All this
mindreading, you said, left you with woeful headaches.
But I couldn't give up, Kitty. I overrode your objections
and insisted we go on. I was hooked, I was impaled, I
browbeat you mercilessly into cooperating, I tyrannized
you in the name of love, seeing always that telepathic
Kitty I would ultimately produce. Every ten days,
maybe, some delusive flicker of seeming contact buoyed
my idiotic optimism. We *would* break through; we
would touch each other's minds. How could I quit now,
when we were so close? But we were never close.

Early in November Nyquist gave one of his occasional dinner parties, catered by a Chinatown restaurant he
favored. His parties were always brilliant events; to
refuse the invitation would have been absurd. So at last
I would have to expose you to him. For more than
three months I had been more or less deliberately
concealing you from him, avoiding the moment of
confrontation, out of a cowardice I didn't fully understand. We came late: you were slow getting ready. The
party was well under way, fifteen or eighteen people,
many of them celebrities, although not to you, for what
did you know of poets, composers, novelists? I introduced you to Nyquist. He smiled and murmured a
sleek compliment and gave you a bland, impersonal
kiss. You seemed shy, almost afraid of him, of his
confidence and smoothness. After a moment of patter
he went spinning away to answer the doorbell. A little
later, as we were handed our first drinks, I planted a
thought for him:

—Well? What do you think of her.

But he was too busy with his other guests to probe
me, and didn't pick up on my question. I had to seek
my own answers in his skull. I inserted myself—he
glanced at me across the room, realizing what I was
doing—and rummaged for information. Layers of hostly
trivia masked his surface levels; he was simultaneously

offering drinks, steering a conversation, signaling for
the eggrolls to be brought from the kitchen, and in-
wardly going over the guest list to see who was yet to
arrive. But I cut swiftly through that stuff and in a
moment found his locus of Kitty-thoughts. At once I
acquired the knowledge I wanted and dreaded. He
could read you. Yes. To him you were as transparent as
anyone else. Only to me were you opaque, for reasons
none of us knew. Nyquist had instantly penetrated you,
had assessed you, had formed his judgment of you,
there for me to examine: he saw you as awkward,
immature, naive, but yet also attractive and charming.
(That's how he really saw you. I'm not trying, for
ulterior reasons of my own, to make him seem more
critical of you than he really was. You were very young,
you were unsophisticated, and he saw that.) The discovery numbed me. Jealousy curdled me. That I should
work so ponderously for so many weeks to reach you,
getting nowhere, and he could knife so easily to your
depths, Kitty! I was instantly suspicious. Nyquist and
his malicious games: was this yet one more? *Could* he
read you? How could I be sure he hadn't planted a
fiction for me? He picked up on that:

—You don't trust me? Of course I'm reading her.
—Maybe yes, maybe no.
—Do you want me to prove it?
—How?
—Watch.

Without interrupting for a moment his role of host,
he entered your mind, while mine remained locked on
his. And so, through him, I had my first and only
glimpse of your inwardness, Kitty, reflected by way of
Tom Nyquist. Oh! It was no glimpse I ever wanted. I
saw myself through your eyes through his mind. Physically I looked, if anything, better than I imagined I
would, my shoulders broader than they really are, my
face leaner, the features more regular. No doubt that
you responded to my body. But the emotional associations! You saw me as stern father, as grim schoolmaster,
as grumbling tyrant. Read this, read that, improve your
mind, girl! Study hard to be worthy of me! Oh! Oh!

And that flaming core of resentment over our ESP experiments: worse than useless to you, a monumental bore, an excursion into insanity, a wearying, grinding drag. Night after night to be bugged by monomaniacal me. Even our screwing invaded by the foolish quest for mind-to-mind contact. How sick you were of me, Kitty! How monstrously dull you thought me!

An instant of such revelation was more than enough. Stung, I retreated, pulling away quickly from Nyquist. You looked at me in a startled way, I recall, as if you knew on some subliminal level that mental energies were flashing around the room, revealing the privacies of your soul. You blinked and your cheeks reddened and you took a hasty diving gulp of your drink. Nyquist shot me a sardonic smile. I couldn't meet his eyes. But even then I resisted what he had showed me. Had I not seen odd refraction effects before in such relays? Should I not mistrust the accuracy of his picture of your image of me? Was he not shading and coloring it? Introducing sly distortions and magnifications? Did I truly bug you all that much, Kitty, or was he not playfully exaggerating mild annoyance into vivid distaste? I chose not to believe I bored you quite so much. We tend to interpret events according to the way we prefer to see them. But I vowed to go easier on you in the future.

Later, after we had eaten, I saw you talking animatedly to Nyquist at the far side of the room. You were flirtatious and giddy, as you had been with me that first day at the brokerage office. I imagined you were discussing me and not being complimentary. I tried to pick up the conversation by way of Nyquist, but at my first tentative probe he glared at me.

—Get out of my head, will you?

I obeyed. I heard your laughter, too loud, rising above the hum of conversation. I drifted off to talk to a lithe little Japanese sculptress whose flat tawny chest sprouted untemptingly from a low-cut black sheath, and found her thinking, in French, that she would like me to ask her to go home with me. But I went home with you, Kitty, sitting sullen and graceless beside you on the empty subway train, and when I asked you what you and Nyquist had been discussing you said, "Oh, we were just kidding around. Just having a little fun."

* * *

About two weeks later, on a clear crisp autumn afternoon, President Kennedy was shot in Dallas. The stock market closed early after a calamitous slide and Martinson shut the office down, turning me out, dazed, into the street. I couldn't easily accept the reality of the progression of events. *Someone shot at the President....* *Someone shot the President.... Someone shot the President in the head.... The President has been critically wounded.... The President has been rushed to Parkland Hospital.... The President has received the last rites.... The President is dead.* I was never a particularly political person, but this rupture of the commonwealth devastated me. Kennedy was the only presidential candidate I ever voted for who won, and they killed him: the story of my life in one compressed bloody parable. And now there would be a President Johnson. Could I adapt? I cling to zones of stability. When I was 10 years old and Roosevelt died, Roosevelt who had been President all my life, I tested the unfamiliar syllables of *President Truman* on my tongue and rejected them at once, telling myself that I would call him President Roosevelt too, for that was what I was accustomed to calling the President.

That November afternoon I picked up emanations of fear on all sides as I walked fearfully home. Paranoia was general everywhere. People sidled warily, one shoulder in front of the other, ready to bolt. Pale female faces peered between parted curtains in the windows of the towering apartment houses, high above the silent streets. The drivers of cars looked in all directions at intersections, as if expecting the tanks of the storm troopers to come rumbling down Broadway. (At this time of day it was generally believed that the assassination was the first blow in a right-wing putsch.) No one lingered in the open; everyone hurried toward shelter. Anything might happen now. Packs of wolves might burst out of

Riverside Drive. Maddened patriots might launch a pogrom. From my apartment—door bolted, windows locked—I tried to phone you at the computer center, thinking you might somehow not have heard the news, or perhaps I just wanted to hear your voice in this traumatic time. The telephone lines were choked. I gave up the attempt after twenty minutes. Then, wandering aimlessly from bedroom to livingroom and back, clutching my transistor, twisting the dial trying to find the one radio station whose newscaster would tell me that he was still alive after all, I detoured into the kitchen and found your note on the table, telling me that you were leaving, that you couldn't stay with me any more. The note was dated 10:30 A.M., before the assassination, in another era. I rushed to the bedroom closet and saw what I had not seen before, that your things were gone. When women leave me, Kitty, they leave suddenly and stealthily, giving no warning.

*   *   *

Toward evening I telephoned Nyquist. This time the lines were open. "Is Kitty there?" I asked. "Yes," he said. "Just a minute." And put you on. You explained that you were going to live with him for a while, until you got yourself sorted out. He had been very helpful. No, you had no hard feelings toward me, no bitterness at all. It was just that I seemed, well, insensitive, whereas he—he had this instinctive, intuitive grasp of your emotional needs—he was able to get onto your trip, Kitty, and I couldn't manage that. So you had gone to him for comfort and love. Goodbye, you said, and thanks for everything, and I muttered a goodbye and put down the phone. During the night the weather changed, and a weekend of black skies and cold rain saw JFK to his grave. I missed everything—the casket in the rotunda, the brave widow and the gallant children, the murder of Oswald, the funeral procession, all that instant history. Saturday and Sunday I slept late, got drunk, read six books without absorbing a word. On Monday, the day of national mourning, I wrote you that

incoherent letter, Kitty, explaining everything, telling
you what I had tried to make out of you and why,
confessing my power to you and describing the effects it
had had on my life, telling you also about Nyquist,
warning you of what he was, that he had the power too,
that he could read you and you would have no secrets
from him, telling you not to mistake him for a real
human being, telling you that he was a machine, self-
programmed for maximum self-realization, telling you
that the power had made him cold and cruelly strong
whereas it had made me weak and jittery, insisting that
essentially he was as sick as I, a manipulative man,
incapable of giving love, capable only of using. I told
you that he would hurt you if you made yourself
vulnerable to him. You didn't answer. I never heard
from you again, never saw you again, never heard from
or saw him again either. Thirteen years. I have no idea
what became of either of you. Probably I'll never know.
But listen. Listen. I loved you, lady, in my clumsy way.
I love you now. And you are lost to me forever.

TWENTY-FIVE.

He wakes, feeling stiff and sore and numb, in a
bleak, dreary hospital ward. Evidently this is St. Luke's,
perhaps the emergency room. His lower lip is swollen,
his left eye opens only reluctantly, and his nose makes
an unfamiliar whistling sound at every intake of air. Did
they bring him here on a stretcher after the basketball
players finished with him? He has spent relatively little
time in hospitals. He wonders if his clothing is stained
with dried blood, but when he succeeds in looking
down—his neck, oddly rigid, does not want to obey
him—he sees only the dingy whiteness of a hospital
gown. Each time he breathes, he imagines he can feel
the ragged edges of broken ribs scraping together;
slipping a hand under the gown, he touches his bare
chest and finds that it has not been taped. He does not

know whether to be relieved or apprehensive about that.

Carefully he sits up. A tumult of impressions strikes him. The room is crowded and noisy, with beds pushed close together. The beds have curtains but no curtains are drawn. Most of his fellow patients are black, and many of them are in serious condition, surrounded by festoons of equipment. Mutilated by knives? Lacerated by windshields? Friends and relatives, clustering around each bed, gesticulate and argue and berate; the normal tone of voice is a yelping shout. Impassive nurses drift through the room, showing much the same distant concern for the patients as museum guards do for mummies in display cases. No one is paying any attention to Selig except Selig, who returns to the examination of himself. His fingertips explore his cheeks. Without a mirror he cannot tell how battered his face is, but there are many tender places. His left clavicle aches as from a light, glancing karate chop. His right knee radiates throbbings and twinges, as though he twisted it in falling. Still, he feels less pain than might have been anticipated; perhaps they have given him some sort of shot.

His mind is foggy. He is receiving some mental input from those about him in the ward, but everything is garbled, nothing is distinct; he picks up auras but no intelligible verbalizations. Trying to get his bearings, he asks passing nurses three times to tell him the time, for his wristwatch is gone; they go by, ignoring him. Finally a bulky, smiling black woman in a frilly pink dress looks over to him and says, "It's quarter to four, love." In the morning? In the afternoon? Probably the afternoon, he decides. Diagonally across from him, two nurses have begun to erect what perhaps is an intravenous feeding system, with a plastic tube snaking into the nostril of a huge unconscious bandage-swathed black. Selig's own stomach sends him no hunger signals. The chemical smell in the hospital air gives him nausea; he can barely salivate. Will they feed him this evening? How long will he be kept here? Who pays? Should he ask that Judith be notified? How badly has he been injured?

An intern enters the ward: a short dark man, concise and fine-boned of body, a Pakistani by the looks of him, moving with bouncy precision. A rumpled and soiled handkerchief jutting from his breast pocket spoils, though, the trig, smart effect of his tight white uniform. Surprisingly, he comes right to Selig. "The X-rays show no breakages," he says without preamble in a firm, unresonant voice. "Therefore your only injuries are minor abrasions, bruises, cuts, and an unimportant concussion. We are ready to authorize your release. Please get up."

"Wait," Selig says feebly. "I just came to. I don't know what's been going on. Who brought me here? How long have I been unconscious? What—"

"I know none of these things. Your discharge has been approved and the hospital has need of this bed. Please. On your feet, now. I have much to do."

"A concussion? Shouldn't I spend the night here, at least, if I had a concussion? Or *did* I spend the night here? What day is today?"

"You were brought in about noon today," says the intern, growing more fretful. "You were treated in the emergency room and given a thorough examination after having been beaten on the steps of Low Library." Once more the command to rise, given wordlessly this time, an imperious glare and a pointing forefinger. Selig probes the intern's mind and finds it accessible, but there is nothing apparent in it except impatience and irritation. Ponderously Selig climbs from the bed. His body seems to be held together with wire. His bones grind and scrape. There is still the sensation of broken rib-ends rubbing in his chest; can the X-ray have been in error? He starts to ask, but too late. The intern, making his rounds, has whirled off to another bed.

They bring him his clothing. He pulls the curtain around his bed and dresses. Yes, bloodstains on his shirt, as he had feared; also on his trousers. A mess. He checks his belongings: everything here, wallet, wristwatch, pocketcomb. What now? Just walk out? Nothing to sign? Selig edges uncertainly toward the door. He actually gets into the corridor unperceived. Then the intern materializes as if from ectoplasm and points to another room across the hall, saying, "You wait in there until the security man comes." Security man? *What* security man?

There are, as he had feared, papers to sign before he is free of the hospital's grasp. Just as he finishes with the red tape, a plump, gray-faced, sixtyish man in the uniform of the campus security force enters the room, puffing slightly, and says, "You Selig?"

He acknowledges that he is.

"The dean wants to see you. You able to walk by yourself or you want me to get you a wheelchair?"

"I'll walk," Selig says.

They go out of the hospital together, up Amsterdam Avenue to the 115th Street campus gate, and into Van Am Quad. The security man stays close beside him, saying nothing. Shortly Selig finds himself waiting outside the office of the Dean of Columbia College. The security man waits with him, arms folded placidly, wrapped in a cocoon of boredom. Selig begins to feel almost as though he is under some sort of arrest. Why is that? An odd thought. What does he have to fear from the dean? He probes the security man's dull mind but can find nothing in it but drifting, wispy masses of fog. He wonders who the dean is, these days. He remembers the deans of his own college era well enough: Lawrence Chamberlain, with the bow ties and the warm smile, was Dean of the College, and Dean McKnight, Nicholas McD. McKnight, a fraternity enthusiast (Sigma Chi?) with a formal, distinctly nineteenth-century manner, was Dean of Students. But that was twenty years ago. Chamberlain and McKnight must have had several successors by now, but he knows nothing about them; he has never been one for reading alumni newsletters.

A voice from within says, "Dean Cushing will see him now."

"Go on in," the security man says.

Cushing? A fine deanly name. Who is he? Selig limps in, awkward from his injuries, bothered by his sore knee. Facing him behind a glistening uncluttered desk

sits a wide-shouldered, smooth-cheeked, youthful-looking
man, junior-executive model, wearing a conservative
dark suit. Selig's first thought is of the mutations worked
by the passage of time: he had always looked upon
deans as lofty symbols of authority, necessarily elderly
or at least of middle years, but here is the Dean of the
College and he seems to be a man of Selig's own age.
Then he realizes that this dean is not merely an anonymous contemporary of his but actually a classmate, Ted
Cushing '56, a campus figure of some repute back then,
class president and football star and A-level scholar,
whom Selig had known at least in a passing way. It
always surprises Selig to be reminded that he is no
longer young, that he has lived into a time when his
generation has control of the mechanisms of power.
"Ted?" he blurts. "Are you dean now, Ted? Christ, I
wouldn't have guessed that. When—"

"Sit down, Dave," Cushing says, politely but with no
great show of friendliness. "Did you get badly hurt?"

"The hospital says nothing's broken. I feel half ruined,
though." As he eases into a chair he indicates the
bloodstains on his clothing, the bruises on his face.
Talking is an effort; his jaws creak at their hinges. "Hey,
Ted, it's been a long time! Must be twenty years since I
last saw you. Did you remember my name, or did they
identify me from my wallet?"

"We've arranged to pay the hospital costs," Cushing
says, not seeming to hear Selig's words. "If there are
any further medical expenses, we'll take care of those
too. You can have that in writing if you'd like."

"The verbal commitment is fine. And in case you're
worrying that I'll press charges, or sue the University,
well, I wouldn't do anything like that. Boys will be
boys, they let their feelings run away with themselves a
little bit, but—"

"We weren't greatly concerned about your pressing
charges, Dave," Cushing says quietly. "The real question is whether we're going to press charges against
you."

"Me? For what? For getting mauled by your basketball players? For damaging their expensive hands with

my face?" He essays a painful grin. Cushing's face remains grave. There is a little moment of silence. Selig struggles to interpret Cushing's joke. Finding no rationale for it, he decides to venture a probe. But he runs into a wall. He is suddenly too timid to push, fearful that he will be inable to break through. "I don't understand what you mean," he says finally. "Press charges for what?"

"For these, Dave." For the first time Selig notices the stack of typewritten pages on the dean's desk. Cushing nudges them forward. "Do you recognize them? Here: take a look."

Selig leafs unhappily through them. They are term papers, all of them of his manufacture. *Odysseus as a Symbol of Society. The Novels of Kafka. Aeschylus and the Aristotelian Tragedy. Resignation and Acceptance in the Philosophy of Montaigne. Virgil as Dante's Mentor.* Some of them bear marks: A−, B+, A−, A and marginal comments, mainly favorable. Some are untouched except by smudges and smears; these are the ones he had been about to deliver when he was set upon by Lumumba. With immense care he tidies the stack, aligning the edges of the sheets precisely, and pushes them back toward Cushing. "All right," he says. "You've got me."

"Did you write those?"

"Yes."

"For a fee?"

"Yes."

"That's sad, Dave. That's awfully sad."

"I needed to earn a living. They don't give scholarships to alumni."

"What were you getting paid for these things?"

"Three or four bucks a typed page."

Cushing shakes his head. "You were good, I'll give you credit for that. There must be eight or ten guys working your racket here, but you're easily the best."

"Thank you."

"But you had one dissatisfied customer, at least. We asked Lumumba why he beat you up. He said he hired you to write a term paper for him and you did a lousy job, you ripped him off, and then you wouldn't refund his money. All right, we're dealing with him in our own way, but we have to deal with you, too. We've been trying to find you for a long time, Dave."

"Have you?"

"We've circulated xeroxes of your work through a dozen departments the last couple of semesters, warning people to be on the lookout for your typewriter and your style. There wasn't a great deal of cooperation. A lot of faculty members didn't seem to care whether the term papers they received were phony or not. But we cared, Dave. We cared very much." Cushing leans forward. His eyes, terribly earnest, seek Selig's. Selig looks away. He cannot abide the searching warmth of those eyes. "We started closing in a few weeks ago," Cushing continues. "We rounded up a couple of your clients and threatened them with expulsion. They gave us your name, but they didn't know where you lived, and we had no way of finding you. So we waited. We knew you'd show up again to deliver and solicit. Then we got this report of a disturbance on the steps of Low, basketball players beating somebody up, and we found you with a pile of undelivered papers clutched in your arm, and that was it. You're out of business, Dave."

"I should ask for a lawyer," Selig says. "I shouldn't admit anything more to you. I should have denied everything when you showed me those papers."

"No need to be so technical about your rights."

"I'll need to be when you take me to court, Ted."

"No," Cushing says. "We aren't going to prosecute, not unless we catch you ghosting more papers. We have no interest in putting you in jail, and in any case I'm not sure that what you've done is a criminal offense. What we really want to do is help you. You're sick, Dave. For a man of your intelligence, of your potential, to have fallen so low, to have ended up faking term papers for college kids—that's sad, Dave, that's awfully sad. We've discussed your case here, Dean Bellini and Dean Tompkins and I, and we've come up with a rehabilitation plan for you. We can find you work on campus, as a research assistant, maybe. There are always doctoral candidates who need assistants, and we have a small fund we could dip into to provide a salary for you, nothing much, but at least as much as you were making on these papers. And we'd admit you to the psychological counseling service here. It wasn't set up for alumni, but I don't see why we need to be inflexible about it, Dave. For myself I have to say that I find it embarrassing that a man of the Class of '56 is in the kind of trouble you're in, and if only out of a spirit of loyalty to our class I want to do everything possible to help you put yourself back together and begin to fulfill the promise that you showed when—"

Cushing rambles on, restating and embellishing his themes, offering pity without censure, promising aid to his suffering classmate. Selig, listening inattentively, discovers that Cushing's mind is beginning to open to him. The wall that earlier had separated their consciousnesses, a product perhaps of Selig's fear and fatigue, has started to dissolve, and Selig is able now to perceive a general image of Cushing's mind, which is energetic, strong, capable, but also conventional and limited, a stolid Republican mind, a prosaic Ivy League mind. Foremost in it is not his concern for Selig but rather his complacent satisfaction with himself: the brightest glow emanates from Cushing's awareness of his happy station in life, ornamented by a suburban split-level, a strapping blonde wife, three handsome children, a shaggy dog, a shining new Lincoln Continental. Pushing a bit deeper, Selig sees that Cushing's show of concern for him is fraudulent. Behind the earnest eyes and the sincere, heartfelt, sympathetic smile lies fierce contempt. Cushing despises him. Cushing thinks he is corrupt, useless, worthless, a disgrace to mankind in general and the Columbia College Class of '56 in particular. Cushing finds him physically as well as morally repugnant, seeing him as unwashed and unclean, possibly syphilitic. Cushing suspects him of being homosexual. Cushing has for him the scorn of the Rotarian for the junkie. It is impossible for Cushing to understand why anyone who has had the benefit of a Columbia education would let himself slide into the degrada-

tions Selig has accepted. Selig shrinks from Cushing's
disgust. Am I so despicable, he wonders, am I such
trash?

His hold on Cushing's mind strengthens and deep-
ens. It ceases to trouble him that Cushing has such
contempt for him. Selig drifts into a mode of abstraction
in which he no longer identifies himself with the miserable churl Cushing sees. What does Cushing know?
Can Cushing penetrate the mind of another? Can Cushing
feel the ecstasy of real contact with a fellow human
being? And there is ecstasy in it. Godlike he rides
passenger in Cushing's mind, sinking past the external
defenses, past the petty prides and snobberies, past the
self-congratulatory smugness, into the realm of absolute
values, into the kingdom of authentic self. Contact!
Ecstasy! That stolid Cushing is the outer husk. Here is
a Cushing that even Cushing does not know: but Selig
does.

Selig has not been so happy in years. Light, golden
and serene, floods his soul. An irresistible gaiety possesses
him. He runs through misty groves at dawn, feeling the
gentle lashing of moist green fern-fronds against his
shins. Sunlight pierces the canopy of high foliage, and
droplets of dew glitter with a cool inner fire. The birds
awaken. Their song is tender and sweet, a distant
cheebling, sleepy and soft. He runs through the forest,
and he is not alone, for a hand grasps his hand; and he
knows that he has never been alone and never will be
alone. The forest floor is damp and spongy beneath his
bare feet. He runs. He runs. An invisible choir strikes a
harmonious note and holds it, holds it, holds it, swell-
ing it in perfect crescendo, until, just as he breaks from
the grove and sprints into a sun-bright meadow, that
swell of tone fills all the cosmos, reverberating in
magical fullness. He throws himself face-forward to the
ground, hugging the earth, writhing against the fragrant
grassy carpet, flattening his hands against the curve of
the planet, and he is aware of the world's inner throbbing. This is ecstasy! This is contact! Other minds
surround his. In whatever direction he moves, he feels
their presence, welcoming him, supporting him, reaching

toward him. Come, they say, join us, join us, be one with us, give up those tattered shreds of self, let go of all that holds you apart from us. Yes, Selig replies. Yes, I affirm the ecstasy of life. I affirm the joy of contact. I give myself to you. They touch him. He touches them. It was for this, he knows, that I received my gift, my blessing, my power. For this moment of affirmation and fulfillment. Join us. Join us. Yes! The birds! The invisible choir! The dew! The meadow! The sun! He laughs; he rises and breaks into an ecstatic dance; he throws back his head to sing, he who has never in his life dared to sing, and the tones that come from him are rich and full, pure, squarely striking the center of the pitch. Yes! Oh, the joining, the touching, the union, the oneness! No longer is he David Selig. He is a part of them, and they are a part of him, and in that joyous blending he experiences loss of self, he gives up all that is tired and worn and sour in him, he gives up his fears and uncertainties, he gives up everything that has separated himself from himself for so many years. He breaks through. He is fully open and the immense signal of the universe rushes freely into him. He receives. He transmits. He absorbs. He radiates. Yes. Yes. Yes. Yes.

He knows this ecstasy will last forever.

But in the moment of that knowledge, he feels it slipping from him. The choir's glad note diminishes. The sun drops toward the horizon. The distant sea, retreating, sucks at the shore. He struggles to hold to the joy, but the more he struggles the more of it he loses. Hold back the tide? How? Delay the fall of night? How? How? The birdsongs are faint now. The air has turned cold. Everything rushes away from him. He stands alone in the gathering darkness, remembering that ecstasy, recapturing it momentarily, reliving it—for it is already gone, and must be summoned back through an act of the will. Gone, yes. It is very quiet, suddenly. He hears one last sound, a stringed instrument in the distance, a cello, perhaps, being plucked, pizzicato, a beautiful melancholy sound. *Twang*. The plangent chord. *Twing*. The breaking string. *Twong*. The lyre untuned. Twang. Twing. Twong. And nothing more. Silence envelops him. A terminal silence, it is, that booms through the caverns of his skull, the silence that follows the shattering of the cello's strings, the silence that comes with the death of music. He can hear nothing. He can feel nothing. He is alone. He is alone.

He is alone.

"So quiet," he murmurs. "So private. It's—so—private—here."

"Selig?" a deep voice asks. "What's the matter with you, Selig?"

"I'm all right," Selig says. He tries to stand, but nothing has any solidity. He is tumbling through Cushing's desk, through the floor of the office, falling through the planet itself, seeking and not finding a stable platform. "So quiet. The silence, Ted, the silence!" Strong arms seize him. He is aware of several figures bustling about him. Someone is calling for a doctor. Selig shakes his head, protesting that nothing is wrong with him, nothing at all, except for the silence in his head, except for the silence, except for the silence.

Except for the silence.

TWENTY-SIX.

Winter is here. Sky and pavement form a seamless, inexorable band of gray. There will be snow soon. For some reason this neighborhood has gone without refuse pickups for three or four days, and bulging plastic sacks of trash are heaped in front of every building, yet there is no odor of garbage in the air. Not even smells can flourish in these temperatures: the cold drains away every stink, every sign of organic reality. Only concrete triumphs here. Silence reigns. Scrawny black and gray cats, motionless, statues of themselves, peer out of alleys. Traffic is light. Walking quickly through the streets from the subway station to Judith's place, I avert my eyes from the faces of the few people I pass. I feel shy and selfconscious among them, like a war veteran who has just been discharged from the rehabilitation center and is still embarrassed about his mutilations. Naturally I'm unable to tell what anybody is thinking; their minds are closed to me now and they go by me wearing shields of impenetrable ice; but, ironically, I have the illusion that they all have access to *me*. They can look right into me and see me for what I've become. There's David Selig, they must be thinking. How careless he was! What a poor custodian of his gift! He messed up and let it all slip away from him, the dope. I feel guilty for causing them this disappointment. Yet I don't feel as guilty as I thought I might. On some ultimate level I just don't give a damn at all. This is what I am, I tell myself. This is what I now shall be. If you don't like it, tough crap. Try to accept me. If you can't do that, just ignore me.

* * *

"As the truest society approaches always nearer to solitude, so the most excellent speech finally falls into silence. Silence is audible to all men, at all times, and in all places." So said Thoreau, in 1849, in *A Week on the Concord and Merrimack Rivers*. Of course, Thoreau was a misfit and an outsider with very serious neurotic problems. When he was a young man just out of college he fell in love with a girl named Ellen Sewall, but she turned him down, and he never married. I wonder if he ever made it with anybody. Probably not. I can't imagine Thoreau actually balling, can you? Oh, maybe he didn't die a virgin, but I bet his sex life was lousy. Perhaps he didn't even masturbate. Can you visualize him sitting next to that pond and whacking off? I can't. Poor Thoreau. Silence is audible, Henry.

* * *

I imagine, as I near Judith's building, that I meet Toni in the street. I seem to see a tall figure walking toward me from Riverside Drive, hatless, bundled up in a bulky orange coat. When we are half a block apart I recognize her. Strangely, I feel neither excitement nor apprehension over this unexpected reunion; I am quite calm, almost unmoved. At another time I might have crossed the street to avoid a possibly disturbing encounter, but not now: coolly I halt in her path, smile, hold up my hands in greeting. "Toni?" I say. "Don't you know me?"

She studies me, frowns, seems puzzled for a moment. But only a moment.

"David. Hello."

Her face looks more lean, the cheekbones higher and sharper. There are some strands of gray in her hair. In the days when I knew her she had one curious gray lock at her temple, very unusual; now the gray is scattered more randomly through the black. Well, of course she's in her middle thirties now. Not exactly a girl. As old now, in fact, as I was when I first met her. But in fact I know she has hardly changed at all, only matured a little. She seems as beautiful as ever. Yet desire is absent from me. All passion spent, Selig. All passion spent. And she too is mysteriously free of turbulence. I remember our last meeting, the look of pain on her face, her obsessive heap of cigarette butts. Now her expression is amiable and casual. We both have passed through the realm of storms.

"You're looking good," I say. "What is it, eight years, nine?"

I know the answer to that. I'm merely testing her. And she passes the test, saying, "The summer of '68." I'm relieved to see that she hasn't forgotten. I'm still a chapter of her autobiography, then. "How have you been, David?"

"Not bad." The conversational inanities. "What are you doing these days?"

"I'm with Random House now. And you?"

"Freelancing," I say. "Here and there." Is she married? Her gloved hands offer no data. I don't dare ask. I'm incapable of probing. I force a smile and shift my weight from foot to foot. The silence that has come between us suddenly seems unbridgeable. Have we exhausted all feasible topics so soon? Are there no areas of contact left except those too pain-filled to reopen?

She says, "You've changed."

"I'm older. Tireder. Balder."

"It isn't that. You've changed somewhere inside."

"I suppose I have."

"You used to make me feel uncomfortable. I'd get a sort of queasy feeling. I don't any more."

"You mean, after the trip?"

"Before and after both," she says.

"You were always uncomfortable with me?"

"Always. I never knew why. Even when we were really close, I felt—I don't know, on guard, off balance, ill at ease, when I was with you. And that's gone now. It's entirely gone. I wonder why."

"Time heals all wounds," I say. Oracular wisdom.

"I suppose you're right. God, it's cold! Do you think it'll snow?"

"It's bound to, before long."

"I hate the cold weather." She huddles into her coat. I never knew her in cold weather. Spring and summer, then goodbye, get out, goodbye, goodbye. Odd how little I feel for her now. If she invited me up to her apartment I'd probably say, No, thank you, I'm on my way to visit my sister. Of course she's imaginary; that may have something to do with it. But also I'm not getting an aura from her. She's not broadcasting, or rather I'm not receiving. She's only a statue of herself, like the cats in the alleys. Will I be incapable of feeling, now that I'm incapable of receiving? She says, "It's been good to see you, David. Let's get together some time, shall we?"

"By all means. We'll have a drink and talk about old times."

"I'd like that."

"So would I. Very much."

"Take care of yourself, David."

"You too, Toni."

We smile. I give her a little mock-salute of farewell. We move apart; I continue walking west, she hurries up the windy street toward Broadway. I feel a little warmer for having met her. Everything cool, friendly, unemotional between us. Everything dead, in fact. All passion spent. It's been good to see you, David. Let's get together some time, shall we? When I reach the corner I realize I have forgotten to ask for her phone number. Toni? Toni? But she is out of sight. As though she never was there at all.

* * *

It is the little rift within the lute,
That by and by will make the music mute,
And ever widening slowly silence all.

That's Tennyson: *Merlin and Vivien*. You've heard that line about the rift within the lute before, haven't you? But you never knew it was Tennyson. Neither did I. My lute is riven. Twang. Twing. Twong.
Here's another little literary gem:

Every sound shall end in silence, but the silence never dies.

Samuel Miller Hageman wrote that, in 1876, in a poem called *Silence*. Have you ever heard of Samuel Miller Hageman before? I haven't. You were a wise old cat, Sam, whoever you were.

* * *

One summer when I was eight or nine—it was before they adopted Judith, anyway—I went with my parents to a resort in the Catskills for a few weeks. There was a daycamp for the kiddies, in which we received instruction in swimming, tennis, softball, arts & crafts, and other activities, thus leaving the older folks free for gin rummy and creative drinking. One afternoon the daycamp staged some boxing matches. I had never worn boxing gloves, and in the free-for-alls of boyhood I had found myself to be an incompetent fighter, so I was unenthusiastic. I watched the first five matches in much dismay. All that hitting! All those bloody noses!

Then it was my turn. My opponent was a boy named Jimmy, a few months younger than I but taller and heavier and much more athletic. I think the counselors matched us deliberately, hoping Jimmy would kill me: I was not their favorite child. I started to shake even before they put the gloves on me. "Round One!" called a counselor, and we approached each other. I distinctly heard Jimmy thinking about hitting me on the chin, and as his glove came toward my face I ducked and hit him in the belly. That made him furious. He proposed now to clobber me on the back of the head, but I saw that coming too and stepped aside and hit him on the neck close to his adam's-apple. He gagged and turned away, half in tears. After a moment he returned to the attack, but I continued to anticipate his moves and he never touched me. For the first time in my life I felt tough, competent, aggressive. As I battered him I looked past the improvised ring and saw my father flushed with pride, and Jimmy's father next to him looking angry and perplexed. End of round one. I was sweating, bouncy, grinning.

Round two: Jimmy came forth determined to knock me to pieces. Swinging wildly, frantically, still going for my head. I kept my head where he couldn't reach it and danced around to his side and hit him in the belly again, very hard, and when he folded up I hit him on the nose and he fell down, crying. The counselor in charge very quickly counted to ten and raised my hand. "Hey, Joe Louis!" my father yelled. "Hey, Willie Pep!" The counselor suggested I go over to Jimmy and help him up and shake his hand. As he got to his feet I very clearly detected him deciding to butt me in the teeth with his head, and I pretended to be paying no attention, except when he charged I stepped coolly to one side and banged my fists down on his lowered back. That shattered him. "David cheats!" he moaned. "David cheats!"

How they all hated me for my cleverness! What they interpreted as my cleverness, that is. My sly knack of always guessing what was going to happen. Well, that wouldn't be a problem now. They'd all love me. Loving me, they'd beat me to a pulp.

* * *

Judith answers the door. She wears an old gray sweater and blue slacks with a hole in the knee. She holds her arms out to me and I embrace her warmly, pulling her tight against my body for perhaps half a minute. I hear music from within: the *Siegfried Idyll*, I think. Sweet, loving, accepting music.

"Is it snowing yet?" she asks.

"Not yet. Gray and cold, that's all."

"I'll get you a drink. Go into the livingroom."

I stand by the window. A few snowflakes blow by. My nephew appears and studies me at a distance of thirty feet. To my amazement he smiles. He says warmly, "Hi, Uncle David!"

Judith must have put him up to it. Be nice to Uncle David, she must have said. He isn't feeling well, he's had a lot of trouble lately. So there the kid stands, being nice to Uncle David. I don't think he's ever smiled at me before. He didn't even gurgle and coo at me out of his cradle. Hi, Uncle David. All right, kid. I can dig it.

"Hello, Pauly. How have you been?"

"Fine," he says. With that his social graces are exhausted; he does not inquire in return about the state of my health, but picks up one of his toys and absorbs himself in its intricacies. Yet his large dark glossy eyes continue to examine me every few moments, and there does not seem to be any hostility in his glance.

Wagner ends. I prowl through the record racks, select one, put it on the turntable. Schoenberg. *Verklaerte Nacht*. Music of tempestuous anguish followed by calmness and resignation. The theme of acceptance again. Fine. Fine. The swirling strings enfold me. Rich, lush chords. Judith appears, bringing me a glass of rum. She has something mild for herself, sherry or vermouth. She looks a little peaked but very friendly, very open.

"Cheers," she says.

"Cheers."

"That's good music you put on. A lot of people won't believe Schoenberg could be sensuous and tender. Of course, it's very early Schoenberg."

"Yes," I say. "The romantic juices tend to dry up as you get older, eh? What have you been up to lately, Jude?"

"Nothing much. A lot of the same old."

"How's Karl?"

"I don't see Karl any more."

"Oh."

"Didn't I tell you that?"

"No," I say. "It's the first I've heard of it."

"I'm not accustomed to needing to *tell* you things, Duv."

"You'd better get accustomed to it. You and Karl—"

"He became very insistent about marrying me. I told him it was too soon, that I didn't know him well enough, that I was afraid of structuring my life again when it might possibly be the wrong structure for me. He was hurt. He began lecturing me about retreats from involvement and commitment, about self-destructiveness, a lot of stuff like that. I looked right at him in the middle of it and I flashed on him as a kind of father-figure; you know, big and pompous and stern, not a lover but a mentor, a professor, and I didn't want that. And I started thinking about what he'd be like in another ten or twelve years. He'd be in his sixties and I'd still be young. And I realized there was no future for us together. I told him that as gently as I could. He hasn't called in ten days or so. I suppose he won't."

"I'm sorry."

"No need to be, Duv. I did the smart thing. I'm sure of it. Karl was good for me, but it couldn't have been permanent. My Karl phase. A very healthy phase. The thing is not to let a phase go on too long after you know it's really over."

"Yes," I say. "Certainly."

"Would you like some more rum?"

"In a little while."

"What about you?" she asks. "Tell me about yourself.
How you're making out, now that—now that—"

"Now that my superman phase is over?"

"Yes," she says. "It's really gone, eh?"

"Really. All gone. No doubt."

"And so, Duv? How has it been for you since it
happened?"

* * *

Justice. You hear a lot about justice, God's justice.
He looketh after the righteous. He doeth dirt to the
ungodly. Justice? Where's justice? Where's God, for
that matter? Is He really dead, or merely on vacation,
or only absent-minded? Look at His justice. He sends a
flood to Pakistan. Zap, a million people dead, the
adulterer and the virgin both. Justice? Maybe. Maybe
the supposedly innocent victims weren't so innocent
after all. Zap, the dedicated nun at the leprosarium gets
leprosy and her lips fall off overnight. Justice. Zap, the
cathedral that the congregation has been building for
the past two hundred years is reduced to rubble by an
earthquake the day before Easter. Zap. Zap. God laughs
in our faces. This is justice? Where? How? I mean,
consider my case. I'm not trying to wring some pity
from you now; I'm being purely objective. Listen, I
didn't *ask* to be a superman. It was handed to me at the
moment of my conception. God's incomprehensible
whim. A whim that defined me, shaped me, malformed
me, dislocated me, and it was unearned, unasked for,
entirely undesired, unless you want to think of my
genetic heritage in terms of somebody else's bad karma,
and crap on that. It was a random twitch. God said, Let
this kid be a superman, and Lo! young Selig was a
superman, in one limited sense of the word. For a time,
anyhow. God set me up for everything that happened:
the isolation, the suffering, the loneliness, even the
self-pity. Justice? Where? The Lord giveth, who the
hell knoweth why, and the Lord taketh away. Which He
has now done. The power's gone. I'm just plain folks,
even as you and you and you. Don't misunderstand: I

accept my fate, I'm completely reconciled to it, I am NOT asking you to feel sorry for me. I simply want to make a little sense out of this. Now that the power's gone, who am I? How do I define myself now? I've lost my special thing, my power, my wound, my reason for apartness. All I have left now is the memory of having been different. The scars of it. What am I supposed to do now? How do I relate to mankind, now that the difference is gone and I'm still here? *It* died. I live on. What a strange thing you did to me, God. I'm not protesting, you understand. I'm just asking things, in a quiet, reasonable tone of voice. I'm inquiring into the nature of divine justice. I think Goethe's old harpist had the right slant on you, God. You lead us forth into life, you let the poor man fall into guilt, and then you leave him to his misery. For all guilt is revenged on earth. That's a reasonable complaint. You have ultimate power, God, but you refuse to take ultimate responsibility. Is that fair? I think I have a reasonable complaint too. If there's justice, why does so much of life seem unjust? If you're really on our side, God, why do you hand us a life of pain? Where's justice for the baby born without eyes? The baby born with two heads? The baby born with a power men weren't meant to have? Just asking, God. I accept your decree, believe me, I bow to your will, because I might as well—what choice do I have, after all?—but I'm still entitled to ask. Right?

Hey, God? God? Are you listening, God?

I don't think you are. I don't think you give a crap. God, I think you've been fucking me.

                    *   *   *

Dee-dah-de-doo-dah-dee-da. The music is ending. Celestial harmonies filling the room. Everything merging into oneness. Snowflakes swirling beyond the windowpane. Right on, Schoenberg. You understood, at least when you were young. You caught truth and put it on paper. I hear what you're saying, man. Don't ask questions, you say. Accept. Only accept, that's the motto. Accept. Accept. Whatever comes to you, accept.

* * *

Judith says, "Claude Guermantes has invited me to go skiing with him in Switzerland over Christmas. I can leave the baby with a friend in Connecticut. But I won't go if you need me, Duv. Are you okay? Can you manage?"

"Sure I can. I'm not paralyzed, Jude. I haven't lost my sight. Go to Switzerland, if that's what you want."

"I'll only be gone eight days."

"I'll survive."

"When I come back, I hope you'll move out of that housing project. You ought to live down here close to me. We should see more of each other."

"Maybe."

"I might even introduce you to some girlfriends of mine. If you're interested."

"Wonderful, Jude."

"You don't sound enthusiastic about it."

"Go easy with me," I tell her. "Don't rush me with a million things. I need time to sort things out."

"All right. It's like a new life, isn't it, Duv?"

"A new life. Yes. A new life, that's what it is, Jude."

* * *

The storm is intense, now. Cars are vanishing under the first layers of whiteness. At dinner time the radio weather forecaster talked of an accumulation of eight to ten inches before morning. Judith has invited me to spend the night here, in the maid's room. Well, why not? Now of all times, why should I spurn her? I'll stay. In the morning we'll take Pauly out to the park, with his sled, into the new snow. It's really coming down, now. The snow is so beautiful. Covering everything, cleansing everything, briefly purifying this tired eroded city and its tired eroded people. I can't take my eyes from it. My face is close to the window. I hold a brandy snifter in one hand, but I don't remember to drink from it, because the snow has caught me in its hypnotic spell.

"*Boo!*" someone cries behind me.

I jump so violently that the cognac leaps from the snifter and splashes the window. In terror I whirl, crouching, ready to defend myself; then the instinctive fear subsides and I laugh. Judith laughs too.

"That's the first time I've ever surprised you," she says. "In 31 years, the first time!"

"You gave me one hell of a jolt."

"I've been standing here for three or four minutes *thinking* things at you. Trying to get a rise out of you, but no, no, you didn't react, you just went on staring at the snow. So I sneaked up and yelled in your ear. You were really startled, Duv. You weren't faking at all."

"Did you think I was lying to you about what had happened to me?"

"No, of course not."

"Then why'd you think I'd be faking?"

"I don't know. I guess I doubted you just a little. I don't any more. Oh, Duv, Duv, I feel so sad for you!"

"Don't," I say. "Please, Jude."

She is crying softly. How strange that is, to watch Judith cry. For love of me, no less. For love of me.

* * *

It's very quiet now.

The world is white outside and gray within. I accept that. I think life will be more peaceful. Silence will become my mother tongue. There will be discoveries and revelations, but no upheavals. Perhaps some color will come back into the world for me, later on. Perhaps.

Living, we fret. Dying, we live. I'll keep that in mind. I'll be of good cheer. Twang. Twing. Twong. Until I die again, hello, hello, hello, hello.

ABOUT THE AUTHOR

ROBERT SILVERBERG was born in New York and makes his home in the San Francisco area. He has written several hundred science fiction stories and over seventy science fiction novels. He has won two Hugo awards and four Nebula awards. He is a past president of the Science Fiction Writers of America. Silverberg's other Bantam titles include LORD VALENTINE'S CASTLE, MAJIPOOR CHRONICLES, THE BOOK OF SKULLS, THE WORLD INSIDE, THORNS, THE MASKS OF TIME, DOWNWARD TO EARTH, and THE TOWER OF GLASS.

Read the powerful novels of award-winning author

ROBERT SILVERBERG

One of the most brilliant and beloved science fiction authors of our time, Robert Silverberg has been honored with two Hugo awards and four Nebula awards. His stirring combination of vivid imagery, evocative prose, and rousing storytelling promise his audience a reading experience like no other.

- ☐ DYING INSIDE (24018 • $2.50)
- ☐ LORD VALENTINE'S CASTLE (23063 • $3.50)
- ☐ MAJIPOOR CHRONICLES (22928 • $3.50)
- ☐ THE BOOK OF SKULLS (23057 • $2.95)
- ☐ THE WORLD INSIDE (23279 • $2.50)
- ☐ DOWNWARD TO THE EARTH (24043 • $2.50)
- ☐ MASKS OF TIME (23494 • $2.95)
- ☐ THORNS (23573 • $2.75)

Prices and availability subject to change without notice.

Read these fine works by Robert Silverberg, on sale now wherever Bantam paperbacks are sold or use the handy coupon below for ordering.
